"Filled [...] powerful as the first, an[...] [...]ore."

—*Darque Reviews*

"An insidious plot is coming to fruition in the second book of Banks's electrifying werewolf saga, Crimson Moon. Part special-ops thriller, part supernatural adventure, it has swift action and intense danger. Utilizing her storytelling flair, Banks imbues her characters with both nobility and kick-ass attitude. It doesn't get much better than this!"

—*Romantic Times BOOKreviews*

BAD BLOOD

"Super-talented Banks launches the complex and darkly thrilling new Crimson Moon series, which bursts with treachery and supernatural chills. The plot intricacies are carefully woven throughout, but Banks piles on the danger, making this one exciting thrill ride!" —*Romantic Times BOOKreviews*

"An action-packed thrill ride! L. A. Banks tells a mean tale of love, redemption, and horror. Her books kick major werewolf ass." —Sherrilyn Kenyon, *New York Times* bestselling author

The Vampire Huntress Legend™ series

THE SHADOWS

"Watch out for paper cuts—you'll be turning the pages at a rapid pace to see who will win. This is just like every book in this amazing series—powerful, intense, and compelling. There's just one more book in this series, so pick a side—light or dark."

—*Romantic Times BOOKreviews*

"L. A. Banks's latest entry in her Huntress Legend saga is an exciting and evocative thriller filled with the trademark supernatural battles, romance, and plenty of suspense."

—Harriet Klausner

THE DARKNESS

"Banks has her fingers on the pulse of vampire paranormal writing."
—*The RAWSISTAZ Reviewers*

"Starts with a bang, continues at a spine-tingling pace, and is just as thrilling and rousing as all the other series offerings. Banks's talent is amazing." —*Romantic Times BOOKreviews*

THE CURSED

"This 'end of days' scenario is a wild amalgam of Christianity, vampire lore, world myth, functional morality, street philosophy, and hot sex." —*Publishers Weekly*

"A splendid tale that brings together action, suspense, mystery, mind-blowing battle scenes, and love scenes."
—*Urban Reviews*

THE WICKED

"Banks's sizzling eighth Vampire Huntress Legend (after *The Forsaken*) explodes . . . In her inimitable combination of street and baroque language, Banks offers more dramatic sex, action-packed good vs. evil adventure, and multicultural mythology to reinforce ethical lessons." —*Publishers Weekly*

"The action is nonstop in this tale and totally engrossing . . . Absolutely fabulous and highly, highly recommended!"
—*Love Romances and More*

"Touching and heartbreaking. As with the other novels in this series, putting this one down—even for a meal—will prove challenging. Banks outdoes herself with her prose and her imagination. Her storytelling is amazing and captivating."
—*Romantic Times BOOKreviews*

THE DAMNED

"All hell breaks loose—literally—in the complex sixth installment . . . stunning." —*Publishers Weekly*

"Fans of this series will love *The Damned* and, no doubt, will eagerly await the next book."
—*Romantic Times BOOKreviews*

St. Martin's Paperbacks Titles by

L. A. BANKS

Undead on Arrival

A Crimson Moon Novel

L. A. BANKS

St. Martin's Paperbacks

This is a work of fiction. All of the characters, organizations, and events portrayed in this novel are either products of the author's imagination or are used fictitiously.

UNDEAD ON ARRIVAL

Copyright © 2009 by L. A. Banks.

Cover photo © Barry David Marcus

For information address St. Martin's Press, 175 Fifth Avenue, New York, NY 10010.

ISBN: 0-312-94913-8
EAN: 978-0-312-94913-6

Printed in the United States of America

St. Martin's Paperbacks edition / April 2009

St. Martin's Paperbacks are published by St. Martin's Press, 175 Fifth Avenue, New York, NY 10010.

10 9 8 7 6 5 4 3 2 1

There are times in one's life that you just have to say thank you to the Creator with resounding joy in your heart, counting your blessings in earnest as you realize how many you've been given.

That's how I view my friends, as a rainbow of blessings . . . just wonderful, loving, positive people who I've been blessed to be surrounded by. They each know who they are and know how special they are to me . . . got a whole family of them in the Street Team and on the forums and blogs. I also have a whole bunch that go way, way back to childhood here in Philly and NY and ATL and Chicago and NC and DC and out West, yep. But I have to give an extra thanks to my "ride or die" sista, Tina, plus her husband, Andre, and two beautiful children—my "niece and nephew," Cheyenne and Cody . . . I knew them before they were born, smile (in belly). Then I've got a whole posse of crazy "blood family," too. Most of all, I have a fabulous daughter, Helena . . . who makes me know my blessings are pressed down and overflowing. That's who I do this for—all of you. Thank you, everybody. Much love!

ACKNOWLEDGMENTS

What can I say—Manie and me, LOL, we cook up the best kind of trouble together . . . and of course, Ms. Mo . . . the three of us shouldn't be allowed to get too quiet for too long—like bad little children, the world oughta know something is brewing! I'd also like to thank the St. Martin's staff, for always so graciously going along with all the wild ideas we cook up—thank you for the hard work and dedication!

Undead on Arrival

CHAPTER 1

New Orleans ... four weeks after the UCE Conference

Sasha cringed, the large bed and breakfast suite suddenly making her feel claustrophobic. Watching her lover shoot up with demon-Werewolf anti-toxin made Sasha's insides churn. As the squad leader for the US military's Paranormal Containment Unit, she couldn't passively watch this and make it all right, personal relationship notwithstanding. During the past three weeks she'd told herself so many lies, which was easy to do when she didn't actually see Hunter take the meds. But throughout this final week of her official leave the truth had gut-punched her. Everything about Hunter's deteriorating condition not only was antithetical to her job—ensuring that no humans were at risk—but pure and simple broke her heart.

Right now she had to finally admit that her lover was a six-foot-five, 220-pound potential explosive in a civilian environment. Max Hunter had been severely infected. Max Hunter could go through a hard transition on any given full moon, and could possibly wreak unspeakable havoc. Max Hunter was therefore a bio-hazmat. Denial was no longer acceptable. The fact that he hadn't totally Turned yet was probably moot.

"Why don't you go get something to eat, since I know you hate watching me do this." Hunter didn't even look at her as he spoke.

She didn't look at him, either.

"I'd better stay . . . in case there's a Reaction."

He laughed a low, hollow laugh and shook his head. "All the more reason I need you to take your sweet ass anywhere but here. I'm practically DOA—or maybe undead on arrival. What the hell."

This time she looked at him. Hard. "All the more reason I should stay—in case I need to shoot *your ass*."

Sasha paced across the room, hating that he needed to take stabilizing meds. She couldn't watch it. Didn't want to hear the sounds of him working with the syringe, tying off his arm to make the vein bulge. She swallowed hard and forced her gaze out the window while forcing her mind to flee past the panes the way she wished her body could. It was like watching someone slowly inject death.

Sasha closed her eyes for a moment, trying to wrestle Captain Sasha Trudeau, the woman she'd been, to the forefront of her mind. It felt like the walls of Dugan's Bed & Breakfast were closing in on her. How was she supposed to stay here or explain to the barrel-chested Elf who owned the place that he, his patrons, and his entire staff were at risk?

Hunter was *not* supposed to be this!

All demon-infected Werewolves had been sent back behind the demon doors or exterminated in the region. As far as anyone knew, every infected Shadow Wolf on North American soil had also been exterminated. People and supernaturals felt safe walking the streets again. She and Hunter were United Council of Entities icons of a supposed new era in supernatural diplomacy and law enforcement.

There were supposed to be clear categories of their kind—Shadow Wolves, those of the phyla who were honorable and sworn to protect humans; Werewolves—perhaps not so honorable but they didn't ravage humans unless provoked . . . then there was the demon-infected version of their species. Those were the Werewolves that got the deadly contagion and couldn't shake it because they didn't possess the life-saving Shadow Wolf immunity. That was how it had been for eons. That was the way it was supposed to be. Clear-cut and black and white, with no shades of gray.

How had her man fallen between the clearly demarked lines of safety? Hunter was never supposed to fall between the cracks. Was never supposed to be what he sullenly joked about—something undead on arrival!

The normally timid believed in them and had banded together to find uncommon courage in the name of justice. The Fae Parliament had come together in an unusual display of solidarity with the Were Clans and the Shadow Clans to vote out the devious Vampire Cartel, which had masterminded the entire black-market, demon-wolf toxin scheme. Even the Mythics and Phantoms gave up their fierce feudal independence for once to join forces and oust those who supported the illicit demon-toxin trade. Uninfected Werewolf Clans had a fragile peace with the clean Shadow Clans, voting as huge blocs, which left a vendetta on the table with the Vampires. They had to watch their backs; everyone who'd gone against the Vampire Cartel had to stay sharp.

And now her man was fighting a very private, seemingly losing battle against the thing he'd championed at the conference—honor among wolves.

Defeat made each inhale ache as Sasha drew in shallow breaths. There were local business-supernaturals and pub owners to worry about, too, like Ethan McGregor and his gentle, healing wife, Margaret, who also worked at Tulane posing as a human ER trauma unit nurse when not helping out at her husband's tavern. The couple were just now getting their lives back on track, trying to keep unsuspecting human patrons obliviously coexisting with their steady supernatural clientele at their lively Fae alehouse around the corner. She'd half expected The Fair Lady to be firebombed after Ethan and Margaret had testified against the Vamps, effectively putting their lives on the line and exposing themselves and their young children to possible retaliation.

Hunter, therefore, had to hold the line for more than himself; the community looked up to him . . . them. Even her military brass had given her and her squad a much-needed month's leave following the glowing, albeit somewhat doctored, reports—courtesy Xavier Holland—for a mission well accomplished. Bless Doc for his golden pen. Disaster had been averted. After the tragic loss of five-star General Donald Wilkerson, no one questioned her methods as long as they worked and the public was none the wiser. She knew a part of them was scared shitless and didn't really want to know. As far as the brass was concerned, her squad had averted a potential civilian catastrophe—and perhaps they had.

But the fact that one *could have* occurred meant that the pressure was on from the schizophrenic human military forces, which wanted to learn more about all things preternatural. Brass wanted to know, but didn't want to know. People needed deniability, but also needed to be able to sleep at night. Fear factors had to be addressed. That was real.

That meant sooner or later questions would be asked, there'd be a demand for cogent intel, and anything the least bit suspect would make every high-ranking official up the food chain extremely nervous.

For now, they viewed her and her team as the best operatives to mine sensitive data. However, they didn't know jack about Hunter or the various Wolf Clans she'd kept on the down-low. Yet in the supernatural community, she and Hunter were supposed to be the law, diplomats from the North American Shadow Wolf Clan—protectors of the weaker supernaturals and humans. They'd even won a rare seat for Shadows and Werewolves to co-represent at the UCE Elder's Bench.

Now this . . . *horrible* secret, the kind of thing she'd always sworn she'd never be a party to. Easier said than done. If the Shadow Clans learned of Hunter's struggle, after all they'd been through, they might exterminate him on sight. His own enforcer, Bear Shadow, would be sent. That was the way of the wolf. Clean. Nonnegotiable. Efficient. Then the local pack of his ancestry would grieve in long, mournful howls. His grandfather, Silver Hawk, would be given his remains, and then it would become pack and clan history told orally for generations to follow.

But she also had the other part of her life to worry about, the human side. If her military brass learned she was harboring a potential virus carrier, and had slept with him, they'd have them both targeted. Best case, they'd shoot him and court-martial her for treason, then hang her. At this point, she wasn't really sure that she cared. Her insides were dying very slowly as she watched the man she loved and had once admired slowly become lost to himself. A silver bullet to the center of her forehead would've been more merciful than this.

Sasha gazed out the window from where she sat amid mussed bed linens. Her squad was nearby; she could feel Fisher's presence, along with Woods's. The signature of her wolf familiars was strong enough to raise the hair on her arms, and where those guys were no doubt the rest of her squad would be, too. Clarissa, Winters, and Bradley hung with Woods and Fisher like family, which was a good thing. Couldn't hurt to have two good soldiers with solid wolf senses in a loose formation with a seer, a kinetics guy, and someone versed in the dark arts all watching one another's backs in Voodoo town.

The sadder point, though, was that they'd all bonded like family . . . they loved Hunter like a brother, the same way Doc had taken him into his heart like a son. Confusion ate at her mind as she wrestled with the question of who to go to first—Doc, or Hunter's grandfather Silver Hawk? Or maybe she'd quietly speak to the team's biochemist and resident seer, Clarissa, before alerting the elders.

Sasha kept her gaze trained on the window, trying her best to ignore the sight that haunted her peripheral vision—of Hunter prepping a vein. She then mentally shunted aside the sounds in the room until she could only hear the revelry going on at Finnegan's Wake bar across the street . . . a fitting name for the merry Fae community that frequented the establishment, but the happiness had long been bled out of their room.

For more than three weeks after the blue-moon-coordinated United Council of Entities Conference, Hunter had hidden his worsening condition from her like a junkie. The only reason he'd been able to shape-shift so quickly at the conference was because Doc had slipped him some meds. If she'd only known then, maybe she could have convinced him to go in for a full eval before it got this far. Hundreds of thoughts battled for dominance in her brain. There had to be something that could be done! Why had he hidden it for so long?

But little by little his condition had grown impossible to conceal from the person who'd shared his body and bed. Now his need eclipsed the shame and he'd simply stopped trying to pretend anymore. It was what it was.

She'd seen the tracks; knew what they were from having taken those same meds at Doc's insistence. After a while, shooting up in less obvious places just didn't cut it; you needed a vein, a mainline artery. Denial had claimed her—making her pray they were spider bites, when she knew better. Now he was needle-dependent . . . even though he'd ironically been the one to free her from the purgatory of life on metabolic drugs. There was no justice in the world. Each injection worked more slowly, was more painful. That's how she'd found out—the night he'd shot up in the bathroom and had fallen, convulsing.

The look of humiliation in his eyes remained burned into her mind. For all Hunter's strength there was a pleading quality that begged her not to flee, not to leave him, but also not to come help him up as his canines ripped through his gums. She'd been paralyzed in the doorway, just as she was paralyzed now sitting on the side of the bed sipping shallow breaths while he pumped a fist with his belt in his teeth and tightly pulled against his bicep.

Where was his inner wolf . . . that pristine, free being who disbelieved in Western medicine? The drugs would make his wolf senses dull. He would no longer be able to hear at peak efficiency, or move like lightning, or see in the shadows . . . or become one with the shadows. He wouldn't see auras or sense approaching danger—all the things he'd given her a glimpse off when she came off the meds were now de-

nied him because of a cruel blow of fate. Because an
honorable man had tried to do the right thing, he'd
been handicapped by the very scourge he'd hunted.
He'd battled evil, and it had bitten him, polluting his
system so severely that his Shadow Wolf immunity
was not kicking in to stop it. The injustice of it stabbed
her spirit. There had to be a way to get Max back to
normal, back to his glorious Shadow Wolf self. And
that was the part that made her so angry that she
snarled at him; his inner wolf wasn't fighting back.

Tasting tears as she swallowed hard, she refused
to let them fall. "Tap the oxygen out of it," she said
quietly, knowing that he was so eager for a second hit
of his meds, he was about to make a deadly mistake.

A first-quarter moon washed a blue-white haze
across Hunter's handsome, ebony face, and she
watched him struggle to stop to take a few seconds
to tap the hypodermic. It wasn't even a full moon
yet and already he was in agony. She wondered what
would happen when the luminous disk in the sky
became a waxing gibbous then went full. His disheveled hair spilled in an onyx wash across his
broad shoulders. It had lost the eagle feather and
leather thong, along with some of its natural luster.
That made her sadder as she stared at him wondering if this time would be the tipping point, the point
of no return for his Shadow Wolf.

"I waited too long," he said with a wince. "Let it
get too near dark and let the moon come up on me.
Every time I keep hoping this will be the last, but it
isn't."

Sasha stood and quickly walked toward him, drawing on all her military training to remain calm despite the weight on her heart and soul. "Let me prep your needle before you kill yourself," she said in a quiet but firm tone.

"If it's gotten this far where I can't even wait to prep a damned needle," he said with a bitter chuckle, "then it doesn't much matter, does it?"

She held his sinew-thick forearm. "Yeah. It matters to me. Kill yourself on your own watch, but not in front of my face." She snatched the needle from him, held it up to the moonlight, and gave it a few quick taps before expressing some of the serum. "After you take this, we need to talk." She stabbed into a bulging vein without mercy, tears that she'd refused to let fall slightly blurring her vision. "That's a double dose . . . more than enough to hold back a hard transition." She yanked the needle out and stared at him as he shuddered and his lids lowered. "Enough to get you high. When did you start double-dosing, Max?"

Hunter nodded and allowed his head to slowly loll back. "Yeah . . . enough to get me high."

Sasha hurled the needle across the room and went in search of her jeans, T-shirt, and sneakers. She had to get out before she shot him. Yet at the same time, in her soul she knew it would be the same as murdering the victim.

"You okay?" he asked calmly, finally lifting his head with a lazy smile and appraising her in her French-cut gray cotton briefs and midriff cotton camisole.

"No! I'm *not* okay," she shouted, whirling around to snatch her nine-millimeter off the dresser and to slip on her shoulder holster over her T-shirt.

"Why not, beyond the obvious?" he said, rubbing his palms down his face and sitting forward in his boxers.

"Why not? Why not! Because *you're* not okay, Hunter!" Her fingers felt like they'd become fat sausages as she tried to work her weapon into place and zip up her jeans. Her mind was scrambled, her words unclear, her vision blurry. She couldn't breathe.

"So what else is new?" he said drily. "Is this the part where you tell me we're breaking up, or what?" He stood, no longer looking at her, and began searching for his jeans.

"We have to get you to Doc. You have to stop overdosing on the meds. The amount you're taking is—"

"Killing the fucking pain, Sasha," he said in a low, rumbling murmur that came out near a growl. "So if you've leaving me, then do it in one swift, decisive move—like a razor cut. Don't stab me over and over again with the goddamned threat." He yanked on his pants and stripped the belt from his arm as an afterthought. "I've gotta go eat; this bullshit makes me nauseous on an empty stomach. I would ask you to join me, but on nights like this, it's gotta be raw."

For a moment she just stared at him. Then slowly, very slowly, she turned away without a word, opened the door, and walked down the hall toward fresh air.

CHAPTER 2

Purpose filled each of Sasha's long strides as she walked down the hall and then jogged down the curved staircase. Giving the genteel house staff a quick greeting, she then pushed past the ornate, antebellum-furnished space, through the French doors, and out into the humid night. Freedom.

The contrast between the air-conditioned, upscale interior she'd just left and the bawdy tourist district, compounded by thick, warm air, made her seek balance in the tavern across the street. Finnegan's Wake had a Corona with her name on it. She was now a woman on a mission.

But as that instant-reflex thought crossed her mind, it also gave her a moment of pause. What was different about her going on a beer bender and what Hunter was doing? Pain was pain, painkiller was painkiller, and self-medication was exactly that, either way.

Sasha quickly thrust through the tavern doors and let the air-conditioned coolness and hard thrum of music flow over her senses. Thinking too hard about it all would make her upgrade from a beer to Wild Turkey or tequila, maybe even kamikaze shots with the fellas.

The local supernatural citizenry smiled at her or gave a respectful nod as though the sheriff had just walked into a Wild West saloon. If only the human tourists and kids escaping school on break knew.

There were only a few Fae peacekeeping forces left in the area since most of the conference diplomats had pulled out. Sasha had to smile as a couple of very handsome archers discreetly lifted an ale in her direction with a question in their eyes after they'd quickly scouted the premises for signs of the big wolf who normally escorted her. That was a factor she hadn't expected: how things would look if she suddenly started showing up places in the supernatural community alone. She hated that it now made a difference, when all her life she'd gone wherever she'd wanted as her own woman—not *somebody's* woman. The entire concept was not only alien but Neanderthal-thinking as far as she was concerned. However, she'd also been a diplomat long enough to know these things mattered. Every species had a protocol.

Sasha let out a quiet sigh and looked harder through the crowd for her team. Country music and its sad-story lyrics chafed her nerves. Why couldn't it have been all-things-Irish night? Sasha glanced at the Fae soldiers again as she elbowed her way toward the tables in the rear. At least it wasn't R&B or the blues.

Two pairs of dark, intense eyes stared back at her from beneath a heavy fringe of dark lashes. One of the archers wore a chocolate leather jacket, pants, and boots so finely tooled that she shoved her hands in her pockets to stem her longing to touch them.

On first glance she might have thought he was a Vampire, because the pure sensuality that oozed off him was completely hypnotic. Yet his multihued aura and the warmth that emanated from him told her he was anything but dead. His smile also told her that he'd appreciated her thorough assessment of him and that she'd given herself away.

Still, it was hard not to stare at him or his patrol partner. They were both stunning. The first one in brown leather had a wash of silky milk-chocolate tresses that shone like glass spread over his broad shoulders, and his lush mouth was set so perfectly in the flawless café-au-lait frame of his face, complete with deep dimples, that he was mesmerizing. A thin darkening shadow of new beard covered his jaw like velvet. Yet for all his Fae beauty, she was a wolf down deep and preferred her males a bit more rugged. Maybe a cut over the eye, an imperfect nose from a brawl . . . it was sick but what could she say? The fact that any of this had entered her mind was disturbing, though.

The first archer's partner leaned forward, his midnight-blue irises filled with wonder, and his face no less handsome in its stark contrast with the spill of blue-black hair that draped his black-leather-clad shoulders. What he lacked in dimples, he made up for in a regal aquiline nose, chin cleft, and dashing smile. Tall, sinewy like ballet dancers, with long graceful hands, they were absolutely breathtaking as a pair.

They lifted a brow at the same time, brought their

ales up to their mouths slowly, and then set them down in unison with exact precision. It was like watching a synchronized dance. However, the very serious proposition was in the subtle eyebrow gesture and the way they glanced at each other for a moment before taking a very purposeful sip from their steins.

Ménage à trois . . . ? *Noooo*. Sasha chuckled quietly and kept walking.

They seemed disappointed as she tilted her head, bowed slightly, closed her eyes for a beat longer than a normal blink required, and thus declined without a word. Yet that would be enough to keep the more bashful of the species at bay. It was clear that if she'd said no to the tall, lithe archers, who were positively gorgeous, then the Gnomes and other less aesthetically gifted members of the Fae society could assume she wasn't about to cross the line. Cool.

But she was also well aware that this wouldn't mean jack to any Werewolf males present. Any Shadow Wolf males would be respectful of the so-called mate bond that had been displayed at the UCE Conference, but Werewolves . . . it was all about continual presence and show of force. New awareness of just how precarious this situation had become stoked defiance within her. Screw it. She wanted a beer.

Thick-bodied males from The Order of the Dragon smiled at her as she shoved past them to get to the bar where she could better scout for her squad. They seemed to take her subtle refusal of the Fae as an invitation that only meant she didn't do that species . . . and since her big Shadow Wolf was AWOL, hey. She cast them a glare with a low, warning snarl, which they cheerfully accepted as she passed them. Damn, why did it have to be all of this? She was just glad that the Vampires had been so completely offended by the events of the conference, they'd retreated to their own private blood clubs for now. Tonight she wouldn't have the personal wherewithal to remain politically correct if a member of the undead propositioned her.

Sasha ruffled her hair up off her neck in frustration. Where were her guys, and when had entering a bar gotten so complicated? It was bad enough navigating all this bull as a human female; now she had to deal with the supernatural crap, too—all because of a change in rank in relationship to Hunter? Geez!

"Finally by yourself, I see," a deep voice said in a low, sensual growl behind her.

This particular voice didn't make her spin on it with anger. Instead it made her stomach do flip-flops.

"Just came in for a cold one and to catch up with my squad before we move out," she said as calmly as possible, straightening her spine and turning slowly.

For a moment, neither of them spoke. Both took their time openly assessing each other.

"You look good," Shogun said in a low rumble, not hiding his admiration.

"You do, too," she replied quietly, wishing she'd put more cavalier confidence in her tone. "Thanks for the support back at the UCE Conference. We needed your voting bloc—as well as the show of force. We also deeply appreciated your willingness to go down swinging with us in a firefight."

An intense stare met hers. A graceful mouth slowly lifted into a lopsided smile. Dazzling white upper and lower canines caught the tavern's overhead lights before receding into a perfect human dental line. A ruggedly handsome, copper-hued face slowly grew serious as they said nothing. Almond-shaped eyes appraised the shape of her mouth, and she watched an Adam's apple bounce in a throat that seemed momentarily at a loss for words.

He'd tied his dark hair back into a ponytail—a new image; he once was bald. Through his light cotton, collared polo shirt and jeans, she was well aware that his wolf wanted out. It seemed as though every tense, sculpted muscle in his toned biceps, abs, and chest was trying to hold it back. It was the kind of thing that could start a civil war.

"I notice you're using the terms *we* and *us* but I only see you here tonight. Am I reading too much into things, or is there an opportunity present because you've finally made some hard personal decisions?"

Now it was her turn to swallow hard. Of all the individuals who could have approached her, why would it have to be this one?

"Nothing's changed," she said with false bravado. "I just came in for a beer and to hang out."

"Alone?"

"Yeah," she scoffed. "This is *America,* last I checked. Women are allowed to go to a bar alone for the sole purpose of having a drink."

His smile widened. "True," he said, stepping closer. "In the human world. It's just that, this close to a full moon, when one has openly declared a mate . . . it could send mixed signals in *our* world." He gave a swift nod in the direction of the disappointed Fae archers. "That's why they tried a bedazzling spell."

Sasha blinked twice and refused to comment. The last thing she wanted was to seem ignorant of yet another supernatural cultural fine point. Damn, she should have known that!

"There's a lot your Shadow might not have exposed you to as a permanent mate," Shogun said with a confident chuckle, ignoring how her gaze narrowed on him. "Who knows . . . maybe I could fill in the gaps as a temporary but regular lover?"

"Excuse me," she said calmly, beginning to leave. "But thanks for the support."

"Wait . . . I'm sorry," he said, staying her leave with a tentative caress against her forearm. "That was out of order. Blame it on the moon."

She let her breath out hard but kept her tone easy. Although she didn't understand why, she didn't want to hurt his feelings. "Look . . . I know there's been chemistry since that first time we bumped into each other in North Korea, but . . ."

"I'm just satisfied that you've finally admitted that," he said quietly, staring at her with an unblinking gaze. "There was chemistry when I saw you fight in the mountains . . . I just wish it would have been with me, rather than him. We fought well together in that Vamp house to free your pack brother. It was like a dance, Sasha. I haven't forgotten it, or you."

She looked away for a moment, but was drawn back to his magnetic stare. "To even comment on any of that is way too volatile given the issues at hand," she said in a very private reply. "Now it's gone beyond just a matter of right and wrong—there's détente between huge clans that haven't had peace in eons. Right now this new alliance and new peace is very fragile . . . the last thing I want to do is tip the balance. There's a lot to consider, like *mega* Federations on your side and mine, all right?"

He swallowed hard and nodded. "The fact that you've processed all that . . . have turned each component around and around in your mind like the colored squares on a Rubik's Cube, trying to see if there was any way for the colors to line up . . ."

"No. That's not what I was doing," she said, scanning the crowd, now not so much looking for her team as she was monitoring the crowd for signs of Hunter.

"Then why is the hair standing up on your arms and the nape of your neck like you're on guard just from talking about it, much less thinking it? You never even mentioned his name or the fact that the way you felt about him was the primary reason you wouldn't consider—"

"I have to go."

"He's not himself, is he?"

Again she stopped and couldn't move.

"Why would you ask me something like that?" she said in a near whisper, panic making her heart slam against rib bones.

"It's in your eyes," Shogun said in a soft rumble, blocking her retreat with a quick sidestep.

Sasha looked away and moved around his body, careful not to brush against him as she did so. "I need to catch up with my team. Hunter is fine."

Shogun's grasp melted into her bicep. "You're staying at a B and B across the street," he said with a quick nod in the direction of the establishment. "For a week now leading up to a full moon, *while it's waxing,* you've eaten alone every morning. You walk the streets looking in shop windows by yourself. And this close to a full moon, with a woman like you, the man should be howling the paint off the walls. Your room has been dead silent. That's unnatural. Something is wrong."

She snatched herself away from Shogun's grasp.

"And," he said in a low, gravelly murmur, "I can't smell him on you, and I should . . . A month together, Sasha, is too soon for it to be like this. Maybe if you and I became one, it wouldn't spell war, but would be a first—a strong she-Shadow alpha and a strong Werewolf alpha. Perhaps we could make the new alliance permanent like humans did in times of old . . . sealing it with a strategic relationship that both participants could also thoroughly enjoy? Consider it. The offer stands."

She lurched away from him, parting bodies in the sea of humans and supernaturals around her as though she were being chased. Almost stumbling into a clearing by the back of the tavern, she saw her squad seated in a small private room to the left of the main hall, eating crawfish and mastering shots.

Face flushed, blinking back hot moisture in her eyes, she prayed that the handsome Werewolf who'd hunted her had gone. Woods and Fisher saw her first and raised shot glasses in an unsteady wave.

"Yo, Trudeau, what's cooking!" Fisher said, his movements reminding her of a huge, gangly Labrador.

Woods threw back his shot, shuddered, and then slammed his glass on the table before giving her a wobbly salute. His brunette hair was a disheveled mess on top of his head. Her guys were pickled.

"I keep tellin' 'em, Captain, it's lime, tequila, then salt," Woods argued good-naturedly.

Good God, her familiars were drunk as skunks.

"No, dude," Winters slurred, his relatively thin, computer-tech arm and small fist going up against Woods's military-conditioned bulk. "It's salt, tequila, lime," he continued with a quick succession of actions and then shuddered hard. "Ooooohhhh, that's Coyote Ugly!"

"I don't understand the purpose of this ritual," Bradley said, studying the dark amber liquid in his rocks glass. "Not when a perfectly fine Irish whiskey is available."

"They're totaled," Clarissa said with an unsteady wobble while raising a glass of white wine. "This team needs balance. I told them if anyone knew the order of things, it would be Trudeau." Then suddenly Clarissa's gaze seemed to sober. She lowered her glass slowly, her smile now frozen in place. "I've gotta pee, and I could use an escort. C'mon, Trudeau. March."

Sasha never had a chance to enter the small private dining room but waited for Clarissa to join her in the doorway. It was the smoothest recovery she'd ever witnessed, and the guys at the table were completely oblivious.

"See, McGill," Winters said, laughing, "what I don't understand is why women have to pee in pairs.

That's because you can't hold your liquor—who does white wine on their last night of leave? It's un-American."

"We'll argue politics when I get back, Winters," Clarissa said, mussing his thicket of dark brown hair as she passed him.

"Hey, be careful," he complained with a wide grin. "I might get lucky tonight if you don't mess up my mojo. This is New Orleans, the Big Easy."

"In your dreams, kid," Bradley said. "The Runes say don't count on it."

Sasha turned away from the revelry, ignoring the drunken conversation as Clarissa looped her arm through Sasha's elbow.

"Hold me up so I don't trip and make a fool of myself, okay?"

Sasha simply nodded, walking like a Zombie as she navigated Clarissa through the throng.

"Single stall," Sasha said, opening the bathroom door to shove Clarissa through.

"Good. Then we can talk," Clarissa said, yanking her through the door and then locking it behind them.

Before Sasha could respond, Clarissa spun on her.

"What's the matter?" Clarissa whispered, her eyes frantic. She kept wiggling as she spoke, and the fumes off her breath were enough to make Sasha's eyes water.

"If you've gotta pee, then—"

"Yeah, I do, but don't leave." Clarissa hustled over to the toilet while Sasha quickly turned her back.

"Aw, man, this is really TMI . . ."

"Oh, relax and talk to me."

"How am I supposed to do that over the echo?" Sasha said, suddenly laughing. It was so absurd.

Clarissa fell quiet for a moment as she finished and then burst out laughing. "Okay, it takes some getting used to—but I could tell something was wrong the second you walked up. This is the only private place. I know something's up, though, so spill it."

"That's because you're the team's resident psychic and always think something's wrong." Sasha rested her forehead on the door as the toilet behind her flushed and the sink water went on.

"I'm done. Satisfied? Now can you cut the diplomatic crap and tell me where the big guy is?"

"I don't know," Sasha whispered.

"Whaddya mean, you don't know?" Clarissa said too loudly.

Sasha spun, and the expression on her face made Clarissa step closer.

"Oh, shit . . . what's happened?"

"I need a favor," Sasha said in a low murmur. "He's taking too many meds. Should have been weaned from them by now and his Shadow Wolf system should have normalized. He should have fought the infection he got from bites and scratches when we were at war with Dexter, and then built up immunity."

"He's still fluxing?" Clarissa whispered, looking horrified.

"Yeah," Sasha said and then glanced away. This was the first time she'd admitted as much out loud, and it terrified her. "You've got his blood samples in the lab at Tulane from Doc's anti-toxin development efforts, mine from the transfusion I gave and had at the ready for his grandfather . . . you've got his grandfather's, even have pure Shadow blood from a pack brother closer to his age, Crow Shadow—from the injuries everybody sustained during the battles leading up to the UCE Conference, right?"

"Yeah, we've got that in the lab. But Doc needs—"

"I don't want to go to Doc with this yet," Sasha said, cutting her off. "If . . . if it's too late, it'll break his heart, and I'll tell him after I do what I have to do. But right now I need you to look at Hunter's blood. See if there's anything in his DNA spiral that's different from the others like him, maybe even look at Doc's, because they are both male, have the same ethnicity foundation—see if you can isolate what's different from his human markers and the Shadow Wolf markers . . ." Sasha raked her fingers through her hair. "I'm grasping at straws to try to understand what's making Hunter not build up the immunity again like he did before." Her furtive gaze sought Clarissa's. "What's wrong with him, Rissa? I've gotta know what it is before I have to put a bullet in his skull."

Clarissa grabbed Sasha by her upper arms. "Okay, listen to me carefully. We're not giving up on Hunter, all right? People inherit one set of genes from their mother, one from their father, but some of those genes are switched off at birth. Take the gene that fights cancer. In some people, both parents' cancer-fighting genes are switched on. In some people, only one is, and if that lone gene gets disabled, there's no redundancy. There's no backup. That person is more susceptible to cancer than someone with a dual operating set of cancer fighters. Understand?"

"But we don't have time for lengthy genetic research," Sasha shot back through her teeth.

"The lengthy research is already under way. Doc has been at it for years, as have others," Clarissa said, employing her tone and her tender expression to try to calm Sasha. "The Duke University study that was laid out in *Genome Research* is all about silenced genes, and they're looking at how stress, food, pollution, all kinds of environmental factors could cause that phenomenon. Hunter had a foreign agent hit his system. He's been stressed to the nines. So I'm gonna try my best, as quickly as I can, to find out if or why a set of imprinted genes is knocking out his backup set—the set that's supposed to fight off demon-Werewolf infection."

"I don't understand it," Sasha said, shrugging away from Clarissa so she could pace within the tight space. "He was born from two Shadow Wolves, should have had a dual set of anti-viral genes coded to take out whatever hit his system—even if he did sustain a toxic Werewolf infection as an infant. If one gene set failed, the other should have stepped up."

"Under normal circumstances," Clarissa said carefully. "But genetic imprinting knocks out that backup. Molecular signals tell or imprint the backup copy to be silent." She dropped her voice to a near whisper again. "When we looked at Werewolf blood in the lab back at NORAD before, they have the imprinted gene weakness—and I haven't seen that in the dual Shadow Wolf gene sets. That seems to be one of the fine differences between the cousin species. Normal Werewolves who haven't been infected don't have the redundancy that Shadow Wolf genetics provide."

"You looked at Rod's blood before he went full-blown," Sasha said quietly, horrified, as she turned away. Her old mentor and friend had been used as a lab rat, and then once the disease the military had given him erupted, she'd had to blow him away at point-blank range. The memory and images were enough to make her hurl. Rather than do that, Sasha simply closed her eyes and swallowed hard.

"I'm sorry," Clarissa said, coming to her. "But what we learned from Rod might well save Hunter's life. The problem is, nobody can get to the NORAD stash except Doc—not since a five-star general had his face ripped off in his own house from a supernatural. I need pure Werewolf strain, not the demon-infected variety anyway, to compare what's in that DNA spiral versus what seems to be mutating in Hunter's."

"I'll get it."

Clarissa rounded on her. "Not at the risk of you getting *your* face ripped off."

"I said I'll get it," Sasha repeated firmly as she stared at Clarissa.

"How?" Clarissa folded her meaty arms over her breasts in protest.

"In the spirit of détente, I've got a contact," Sasha said quietly on a hard exhale, and then exited the bathroom.

CHAPTER 3

Hunter lowered his nose and briefly closed his eyes, allowing the tantalizing scent of meat and blood to wash over him. He could literally taste the air, the flavors hanging on it before covering his tongue, building saliva in his mouth. Heat wafted up to meet his face . . . There was simply nothing like a good steak.

"Is everything to your liking, sir?" the waiter asked, coming up behind him.

Hunter spun in his chair so quickly and growled so severely that the poor man backed up and lost his tray. Several supernatural patrons glared at the waiter in reproach, while human guests of The Fair Lady looked on in confusion and Fae wait staff came over to help clean up the mess. Clearly disgusted, the proprietor waved off the human server and pointed toward the kitchen.

"My apologies," Ethan said quickly, his ruddy Elf cheeks thoroughly flushed. He leaned in toward Hunter from a vantage point where Hunter could see him head-on, and kept his voice low. "Humans . . . I shouldn't have hired a young college student, as they aren't familiar with certain protocols—like never coming up behind our wolf clientele unannounced while they're dining. Normally, I have Phoenixes in to supplement our Fae servers, but my Phoenixes were all burning this evening, sir."

"No problem," Hunter said, but his angry stare and the tone of his voice said otherwise. The kid had startled him and bristled the hair on his neck. He should have felt him coming, and didn't—that was the bitch of it.

"Let us courtesy your meal, sir, for the affront," Ethan said nervously.

"Not necessary," Hunter muttered, and then concentrated hard to retract the canines that had ripped his gums. Ethan was good people, a fixture in the supernatural community down here. No sense in upsetting an ally.

"You'll let me know, personally, then . . . if you need anything?" Ethan said, still seeming unsure. "Because we value your patronage—yours and Captain Trudeau's, sir, to the utmost."

"Thank you, I'm fine," Hunter said, the mention of Sasha grating his nerves. He cut into the twenty-eight-ounce steak before him and watched it bleed onto the plate. Stabbing at the huge hunk he'd cut off, he brought it into his mouth with an angry shove as Ethan slipped away from his table.

This time nothing would catch him off guard. Hunter kept his gaze level with the bodies in the establishment while he ate. He saw the female flash him a little canine before she stood and sauntered over to his table. True, he was mated, but he wasn't blind, either.

Until recently, she-Shadows had shunned him based on his clan legacy. Werewolf females had always done the same, given the long-running feud between the Federations. But this Were-female looked anything but put off by his presence. Hunter glanced up as she stood in front of his table in a provocative pose.

"Mind if I join you?"

Now, what was a man supposed to say to that?

Hunter looked over her tall, voluptuous frame and the way the black lace from her bra peeked over the edge of her red blouse, exposing a fantastic rack. The little black leather skirt she wore was killer against her long legs, too. Creole women would be the death of him.

"Or will your woman object?"

He'd obviously taken a beat longer than she'd expected him to answer her. She tossed thick auburn hair over her shoulder and waited, seeming almost indignant. Her hazel eyes had begun to glow amber. Pure testosterone made his boot connect with the chair leg in front of him and shove it away from the table toward her in a surly invitation. What the hell was he doing?

She yanked the chair back with a satisfied smile and sat sideways, seductively crossing her shapely legs. "Thank you." She eyed his steak and licked her bottom lip.

Reflex made him cut a piece of it off for her.

Without consulting his brain, he handed her the knife that he'd stabbed the steak with. A smooth female hand caressed his knuckles as she accepted the knife from him and then slowly bit into the steak. He watched a drip of hot steak juice land on her left breast and run down her cleavage. She dabbed it with a finger. Her eyes met his as she put the forefinger in her mouth then slowly extracted it. This time he was the one to lick his bottom lip.

"So . . . you want to?"

What kind of question was that? Hell yeah he wanted to, but there were considerations. On the other hand . . . Sasha had been acting really pissy for the last week and was treating him like he was some sort of invalid—just wanted to cuddle, wanted to talk. Okay, he needed to cut the crap and stop rationalizing the irrational.

"Well?" the gorgeous female before him said, leaning forward as she took another bite of steak. "Do Shadows always make you ask them twice?" Her smile was warm and engaging, no malice in her tone.

She had a really nice voice . . .

"No . . . you don't have to ask me twice," Hunter said with a low chuckle. "Not a woman as beautiful as you. I'm just trying to decide if dying under a gibbous moon is what I'd want on my tombstone."

She laughed and leaned closer, allowing him a full view of her spectacular cleavage. "I heard your mate is a true warrior."

"She is," Hunter said, sitting back and collecting his knife to cut another piece of steak.

"But then, so are you," she murmured, dipping her

finger into the steak juices on his plate and tasting them again. "And I don't see her here tonight."

The offer definitely had merit, and there was certainly no denying the erection this new female had given him. Torn, he opted to shove another thick piece of steak in his mouth. "You want a drink?"

"Dewar's . . . neat," she said, her canines cresting as she breathed out the request.

The timbre of her voice almost made him set down his knife and fork. Instead he hailed the new waiter. "Give this lady *anything* she wants," he rumbled deeper than intended.

"Right now, that'd be a Dewar's neat," she told the waiter, and then turned to slide her legs under the table to caress Hunter's. "Wow," she said as her knee gently slid against his inner thigh. "Anything the lady wants?"

He cut her another piece of steak and gave her his fork without a word. She didn't accept it, but rather bit the offering off the fork as she kept her eyes on him.

"That's not the piece of meat I wanted."

This new woman was making him figure things out with limited blood supply going to his brain. Sasha would slaughter him . . . then again, maybe she wouldn't. Maybe she didn't even fucking care. Maybe they'd already broken up—it sure seemed that way when she left their room. Or maybe he was about to do something really stupid.

"Tell me how it works in the Shadow world," the woman at his table murmured. "Do I have to alpha-challenge her, or are you a free agent?"

"Uh . . ."

"Because, darling, the way I'm feeling right now, I don't think she could take me."

A pair of glowing amber eyes locked his gaze in place as a vise-like grip of supple female thighs tensed around his leg, rhythmically squeezing his hard-on in the process. Hunter swallowed past the lump in his throat.

"Listen . . . there's more to it than just what I want to do right now. Our clans have been at war for decades, Federations diametrically opposed . . . and . . ." Her hand under the table stopped his words for a moment. "Damn . . . who's your mate?" he murmured against his will.

"Does it matter?"

"It could," he said with effort.

"I saw your wolf emerge at the UCE Conference," she said huskily. "Absolutely majestic. I've been waiting for you to ditch your she-Shadow and get a little space of your own. Anybody I might have been with, baby, I know you could take . . . so how about if we go get naked under the moon?"

The thought of banging this chick on all fours had his mind in a temporary chokehold. Somehow he'd managed to signal for the check, and seeing him do that had made her begin to slightly pant. It was a chain reaction that happened quickly—too quickly. The moment she'd begun to pant, all he could think about was the singular goal of mounting her.

"You're gonna make me kill a man tonight," Hunter said, pushing back from the table, but hesitating to stand.

"I'd be honored," she said in a hard rasp, standing, her nipples now erect peaks beneath the sheer fabric of her blouse. He could smell the liquid heat that smoldered between her thighs.

Celebrity clearly had its privileges and perils. Hunter stood slowly, unfolding his six-foot-five frame out of the restaurant chair. There weren't enough meds in the world to preempt this. Right versus wrong had nothing to do with it; this was purely primal.

A low warning growl from behind made him grab the female's wrist in complete ownership—that is, until he saw who owned the growl.

"Bear?" Hunter said, letting go of the female beside him.

She folded her arms and rounded on him. "He's a beta!"

Hunter stared at his pack enforcer. "He's also my friend." He watched Bear Shadow's shoulders begin to relax. "In Shadow culture, we honor territories."

Bear nodded at Hunter. "And *mates*," he said, signifying Sasha without directly mentioning her.

"Is this your . . . friend?" Hunter asked, fighting to retract his canines.

"While in New Orleans," Bear grumbled.

"Not anymore," the female said angrily, folding her arms and still looking at Hunter with longing. "Can we get out of here?"

"No. I honor my pack brother's territory—"

"But you can beat—"

A sharp growl from Hunter cut off her argument, and in his peripheral vision he noticed relief wash over Ethan. It wasn't hard to guess why; a male wolf brawl wasn't about to erupt in his establishment. Yet at the same time, Fae archers and bouncers from The Order of the Dragon seemed prepared for any eventuality. The only ones who seemed disappointed were the few Werewolves who had been watching the entire spectacle.

Bear Shadow's gaze met Hunter's with appreciation. No words were necessary as the miffed female angrily yanked away from the table to go find an alpha male from the Werewolf Clans.

"Thank you," Hunter said after a moment, trying to soothe his pack brother's battered ego. But it was hard not to stare of the female's retreating form. She had a positively lovely ass.

"It was nothing," Bear grumbled, shifting his stocky three-hundred-pound frame to stare at the lost female, too.

"Might keep me from getting shot by Sasha tonight," Hunter said with a lopsided grin.

"Yeah, maybe," Bear said, with no amusement in his tone, and then inclined his head toward the bar.

Sasha's steely gray stare met Hunter's. She didn't say a word, just slid into a shadow and was gone.

"Oh, shit . . ." Hunter rounded the table and headed out the front door. But out on the street, everything created a shadow in the darkness.

"C'mon, Sasha," he said, jogging as he looked five ways at once. He was glad that people walking the streets assumed he had a Bluetooth in his ear and didn't think he was talking to himself.

Dead silence met him. The fact that he couldn't

accurately feel her disturbed him. Under normal circumstances, as a mated pair, he should have been able to feel her presence moving in and out of the shadows around them. Tonight he couldn't. Hadn't for the last few weeks. Couldn't even shadow-dance with her. His shadow moved with him, not as its own living, breathing entity. His could no longer reach out and caress hers to frenzy across the room without ever touching her in the flesh—didn't she understand what this was doing to him? Hers could still do that . . . hers blew him away. Hers wasn't crippled by a virus he didn't understand.

He stopped jogging and then dipped into an alley entrance, sure that he'd felt her there. Hoped that he had. They needed to talk. Every shadow coming off the building and Dumpsters loomed long and lean. The chase and quick hunt made his wolf claw at his insides. Doubling over in pain, he stopped running for a moment, then released a mournful howl.

Echoing howls met him from the distance. The call of the wolf lit up the night air, renewing his erection, renewing the need to go feral, yet the shadows were no longer gateways to him. They were no more to him than they were to Werewolves or humans. A hard tap on his shoulder spun him around just as Sasha's punch dropped him.

Hunter sprang up from the asphalt, spoiling for a fight, holding his jaw. She'd actually used the brick building's shadow to level him—knowing he couldn't shadow-hop? A snarl was his answer before something insane snapped within and he rushed her.

She spun into a shadow and out again, no weapon in her hand but pure rage burning in her eyes. "Even money says you didn't even get that bitch's name!"

Hunter stopped dead in his tracks and rubbed his jaw again. "It's not what it looked like."

Sasha's normally gray eyes began to flicker amber as her upper and lower canines filled her lovely mouth. "Are you out of your damned mind?" she shouted. "You put alliances on the line for a piece of tail?"

"I've been the fucking North American Clan alpha for the last decade, Sasha! The last thing I would do is create a political—"

"Just stop!" she said, storming up to him. "This isn't about me or you or what we want personally or whatever's going wrong between us. It's bigger than that and you're out of control, Hunter!"

He yanked her to him by the front of her T-shirt and kissed her hard. "I know."

She snatched herself away and stared at him, furious.

"I'm out of control," he admitted, circling her.

She matched his movements, wary, her eyes glittering with rage.

"Don't go into the shadows," he breathed out in a rush. "I can't follow you there and it's eating me up."

"You would have fucked her," Sasha growled.

"I thought you said this wasn't about us," he said in a low rumble, trying to keep her from a shadowy section of alley where she could disappear.

"It's not. It's about détente!"

Lightning-fast he snagged her shirt again, able to

propel her forward and off balance. They both knew she had enough military skills to have stopped him—if she'd wanted to. Her abdomen collided with his, almost knocking the wind out of him.

"Then in the spirit of diplomacy," he said, thrusting his fingers into her hair and drawing in the glorious scent of it, "let's keep our alliance strong. All right?"

Her body was rigid, but there were any number of self-defense moves she could have made to hurt him—and she hadn't. He'd left himself wide open to let her decide this dance.

"What's happening to us?" he said, breathing the words into her hair. Her familiar warmth coated him and soaked into his bones. "I miss this—us."

"So you'd get that from wherever?" she said, her voice still tight like her body.

His mind was on fire; his mouth sought hers nonetheless, unable to argue with her. His hands found the dip in her spine, the high, tight rise of her backside, felt the tautness of her thighs . . . damn it all on the almost full moon. Her arms had finally encircled him and the tension in her body was slowly draining away.

"No," he finally said, tearing his mouth away from hers. "I'll admit to being flattered, but—"

Sasha wound his ponytail around her fist and yanked it hard to stare at him. "Hunter . . . you're lying." It was a flat statement of fact, now strangely containing no anger. "I've never seen you lie. Shadow Wolves can't, not very easily. You won me that first time telling me you were no liar." She dropped her hand away as tears filled her eyes. "That was the one thing I most admired about you."

Seeing her this way, her body struggling to pull away from his, her soul shredding as it disconnected from him, made him panic. He let her go, the humid night air no match for her warmth, the separation knifing his groin.

"Sasha . . . I don't know what to say to you to get you to understand any of this . . . any of what I'm going through." He let his breath out hard. "We shouldn't be having this conversation in a god-damned alley."

"Oh, what would be better—a bar?"

"Right now, yeah. Buy you a round."

She stared at him and lifted her chin. "A six-pack in the room and you're on."

He nodded but didn't move for a moment. "When I shoot up with the meds . . . it's like my wolf is on fire . . . needs to come out, but can't. Everything is intense, almost like what I guess a Were's full-moon transition would be—but because I'm not one of them, I don't change. It hurts like hell, is all I can say."

Sasha stared at him, assessing his statement. This time he was telling the truth. She sniffed the air and walked in closer. "You're also trailing male Werewolf pheromone," she admitted. "You'd better stay out of the bars or you might piss them off and get jumped."

As diesel as Hunter was, with the rep he owned in the clans, oh, yeah . . . she could see why the alpha Werewolf female had made a move to work her way up his pack ranks to try to get to him. Made sense. Yet another part of her was suspicious. It was too contrived, too happenstance for her liking . . . Not that even the average human female wouldn't want to jump his bones—still, it was the timing. Timing that seemed designed to create irreparable damage between them. Split the leadership, you could advance an agenda. The question was: Who?

"On this subject," Hunter said quietly, misreading her long silence. "I swear I am no liar." He looked away. "And . . . if I'm trailing pheromone like you say, then trust me when I tell you that the hormone flux that goes with it is a true bitch."

Again she stared at him, watching his stone-cut chest expand and contract with deep breaths that he took in through his mouth. His damp T-shirt was practically welded to him, and the eight-pack in his abs trembled ever so slightly with each inhalation. The erection he owned was ridiculous and—given the shift in conversation—shouldn't have been.

"Hunter, listen . . . maybe I'm not fully understanding everything about this. The meds, before we realized we didn't need them, were like downers for me and the squad when we used to take them . . ."

"It starts out like that," Hunter said, stretching out his arms to flat-palm the brick wall before him. He dropped his head, closing his eyes as he spoke. "First hit chills me out, brings me down, keeps the wolf at bay . . . then it can't get out—I can't transition," he said through his teeth. "I'm half afraid of what will . . . but it hurts like hell. Second shot eases the pain, but drives me fucking nuts when the moon is waxing." He looked at her, eyes now amber-rimmed in the dark.

"But before . . . you took one shot and then would nod off."

"The moon was waning," he said. "After the full moon of the conference, I was myself. Didn't have to take the meds daily—and when I began to have to, that first time when you found me . . ."

"The convulsions—"

"Yeah, the convulsions!" he shouted, punching the wall and making a section of the brick crumble. "Remember how I was when I got up off the floor?"

Sasha looked away into the dark, dark night. How could she forget?

"That was a double shot on the night, midpoint, when the moon went from waning to waxing." He pushed away from the wall and circled her. "So I tried to make it all week with one shot, nodding off in your arms, trying not to take a double hit until I thought I'd puke up my guts—and every night it's gotten worse while you've treated me like an invalid! Shit! Tonight I need you to be my lover, not my fucking nurse!"

He pointed at her hard, breathing hard. "On that I am no liar, Sasha! But what I've just said probably isn't politically correct enough for you, or hasn't been analyzed enough for you. If you wanna bed a Were-wolf, then goddamn it, bed me! You don't think I can smell Shogun on you? He must have been standing close enough to you at Finnegan's to leech his scent into your clothes. Tell me I'm a liar."

She turned on her heel. "Let's go."

"So that's it? Just like that, you're pissed off and don't want to hear any more, right?"

"Wrong," she said quietly. "I just understand the condition."

He jogged to catch up with her. "What the hell is that supposed to mean?"

She grabbed the front of his shirt and kissed him hard. "Shut up. Go back to the room. I promise not to be your nurse, unless that's a pending fantasy, all right?"

A pair of shrewd, gleaming eyes opened within the depth of the alley. A low, satisfied chuckle whispered on the night and then, just as quickly, was gone.

CHAPTER 4

The breath literally was knocked out of Sasha on her way through the double French doors of the B&B. Her back took the brunt of the impact and almost shattered priceless stained glass. There wasn't enough time to be thoroughly humiliated by the very wide smiles of the establishment staff and a few wandering guests that greeted them. All of that would have to be sorted out later.

Hand-to-hand combat was a must to get Hunter to bypass body-slamming her against the parlor furnishings once they'd cleared the doors, and she'd had to make a break for the stairs to salvage any dignity or privacy she once owned. That had required flip-rolling him hard on the floor and a mad dash, then bolting up three steps at a time to the third floor and down the long hallway. The evasive tactic didn't dissuade him in the least; instead, it thoroughly turned him on.

A few seconds of distance was her friend as she fumbled to get the key in the door to avoid having to explain to Dugan why his best B&B suite door was off its hinges.

Hunter hit the third-floor landing only moments behind her as though his wolf had finally broken free. Skidding into the wall, he stopped partially stunned, shook his head for a moment to study his quarry, eyes glowing amber, canines in full. Oh, shit, this was gonna be bad . . .

The only speed advantage she had was that her wolf was just under her surface and still accessible to her human form. But what Hunter currently lacked in speed he made up for in mass. His six five versus her five seven: It didn't take a rocket scientist to do the math.

Once in the room, Sasha stood to the side of the door hidden in a shadow as he barreled through. Then she slammed it behind him. Hunter's sheer momentum took out the coffee table and a lamp. She quickly removed her weapon and tossed it across the room, lest she be tempted to use it. In his condition, if he tried to yank off her leather holster, he'd probably dislocate her shoulder.

Gone was her patient, careful Shadow Wolf lover. Gone was the man who would drive her insane with lengthy foreplay and shadow caresses. Max Hunter had gone straight animal.

Disarming in front of him clearly had the same effect as a pole dance. She saw that as Hunter got up from the floor slowly, his gaze following her every move. But there was also something extremely exciting, in a twisted sort of way, about seeing him like that. It pulled at the primal side of her being, calling her wolf, hers taunting his to make it more ferocious.

He instantly stripped his T-shirt over his head. Her gaze raked the dark mahogany surface of the skin he'd exposed, appreciating every single chiseled brick. Immediately she took off her sneakers and shimmied out of her jeans. For a few seconds he closed his eyes as though she'd punched him. He quickly bent to unlace his boots but winced and had to back off for a moment to stop, panting from the pain. She came forward to help, stripping off her shirt as she walked toward him. By the time she got to him naked his hands were shaking.

She said nothing, just laid her cheek and palms again his hot chest for a moment then kissed his stomach as she slid down his body. The man was burning up; the contact practically seared her cheek and lips. Hunter's breath audibly hitched the moment she'd grazed him. His skin was on fire, at that transition heat where his wolf should have leapt through his human form.

Pain from his repressed wolf coated her insides as she hugged him, laying her cheek against his stomach for a moment, trying to calm that tormented creature within him. To no avail.

Even as a shadow healer, her hands only seemed to add to his agony. An intricate network of thick abdominal muscles contracted against her face as a deep moan erupted from his throat. The sound of his suffering made her hands work more quickly to get him out of his boots and jeans. She tried to remove the cumbersome denim fabric, tried to slide it down

and over his slim hips without inadvertently hurting
him, but apparently she wasn't moving fast enough.

Tearing at the fabric blindly once his boots were
off, he shed his jeans like a second skin. She looked
up at him for a moment; he looked down at her, his
hands slowly balling into fists. When she quickly
sheathed him with her mouth, his voice rent the air
and his knees buckled. Another quick glance up explained everything. His head was tipped back, mouth
open, eyes tightly shut, tears streaming from their
corners as he slowly shook his head. She understood;
he was too far gone to play at this thing. He needed
her pronto. Required total body heat and friction . . .
in the way of the wolf.

Sasha backed up. Hunter dropped to his knees
where he'd been standing. An agonized amber stare
trapped her. She turned around and nestled into the
cave he'd made for her body to fit against on all fours.
He mounted her with a wail, coaxing one from her,
too—hot skin sliding against hot skin, sweat and female essence providing heat-slathered sound.

On every power thrust she could feel his wolf
begging to come out, dying to come out, filling his
lungs with deep rumbling thunder that reverberated
through her bones.

Wide male hands braced against the floor to soon
score an area rug, pulling up nap and damaging hardwood. Frustration and pleasure sank him deeper into
her each time, making her throw her head back and
cry out. Primal, driving pleasure lifted her hips and
dip-swayed her back, bringing her breasts to sweep

the floor, until a hard arm welded itself to her waist for more leverage.

His body was hot stone, burning up. Every return to her body released a guttural moan from his depths. She could barely get his name out, much less her next breath, but the moment she cried out again both his arms gripped her waist and his sweat-damped face scorched her back.

A sudden, blinding climax left her convulsing hard enough to nearly swallow her tongue. Needing an anchor, she dug her nails into Hunter's muscle-corded thighs as he pulled her back against him, still thrusting.

Sensations ricocheted from his body into hers then back, the shadows in the room holding a life echo all their own. She could feel that blend in with their sweat-saturated skins, compounding ecstasy into every touch. It was all too much at once . . . all too insane and frantic. She was on the verge of passing out; he was breathing erratically. From the way his body dry-heaved against hers and the way his thrusts had devolved to inconsistent jabs, she knew he was in a place where pure agony resided.

A pair of rough hands aggressively covered her breasts, then swept down her torso to hold her hips as she fell forward again, palms pressed to the floor. Sweat from his burning face splattered her spine. His deep-timbred moans now had a mournful, pleading quality that sent shivers down her spine.

Hot breath pelted her shoulders in steaming bursts. Her man was trapped between heaven and hell, between his wolf and his human, between release and torture, and no matter how hard she worked, he was stuck there at midpoint.

Peering backward she saw how pain had contorted his expression, furrowing his brows above tightly shut eyes. His dark, handsome face glistened in the moonlight from pure sweat effort. His hair was a wild mane of dark velvet across his shoulders. Five o'clock shadow was thickening on his square jaw, the muscle in it pulsing to his thrusts. His need had become so great that she could intermittently hear him whimper between ragged gulps of air. Every now and again he bit his bottom lip and then suddenly stopped breathing altogether, bracing for the release that didn't come before letting the anticipated sensation go with a hard shudder on a low, agonized groan.

"Sasha . . . baby . . . shit . . ." Hunter lowered his burning forehead against her shoulder blades for a moment and sucked in several huge inhales, slowing down.

A charley horse cramp was kicking his ass. Words wouldn't form; his body hurt to the point of trembling. His balls ached so badly that it made his kidneys throb. Then she moved and cold air stabbed his groin; for a split second he didn't know whether to cry or puke. *Oh . . . God . . .* All he could do was slowly pound the floor with his fist until the wicked sensation abated. Never in his life had his wolf trapped him like this. It was a merciless betrayal that sent his pulse into arrhythmia.

But mercy found him before he could give in to the heart attack that sought him. Relief came as a pair of satin-smooth female legs that found his waist . . . a hot slide into paradise as firm breasts pressed against his chest and graceful hands swept up his back. He fell into Sasha's arms in a cold sweat, stuttering.

"I need to . . . but I can't, I dunno what's the matter," he said in a gravelly rush, holding her against him so tightly he could barely breathe himself.

"If your wolf won't come out, then let the man run hard," she murmured into his ear on a husky moan. "Give in to him, Hunter," she demanded, taking his mouth and fisting his hair. She arched hard, causing his eyes to cross beneath his lids. "Track me."

His nose instantly sought her hair, and he pulled her into his senses on a sharp, wincing inhale. Thick sex with Sasha-scent coated his insides. *Oh, yeah* . . . She-Shadow rippled under her skin, driving him insane. His hands couldn't touch enough of her at once. Her body was fluid, liquid shadows filled with she-heat. Tears stung his eyes. He could feel her wolf just beneath her satiny skin, could taste it in every wanton kiss . . . could hear it in her moan.

"Sasha!"

"Track me," she commanded, thrusting harder as her hands slid down his back to grasp the lobes of his ass.

She bit his shoulder, making him see stars. "Don't lose me. You with me, Hunter? Keeping pace . . . ," she asked in a sensual timbre that almost made him break stride with his hard shudder.

"Yeah," he breathed out, each inhale now ragged. She'd said his name like it was a verb, like something of action, something she wanted, on that breathy, deep whisper of hers that shot right through him. Hell no, he wouldn't lose her. *Never.* His wolf was on her and everything male within him paced her.

Sasha's sudden moan and a hard rake of her nails up his back fused with her arch. It made his breaths sync up to his muscles, wound everything tighter around his skeleton as his heart slammed against his rib cage. Hell yes he was with her. The moment she lost it again, so would he.

Tight contractions sucked at his shaft, breaking his thrusts down into erratic, long lunges. The shit felt so good he couldn't even howl.

"I'm so close, Hunter," she said between her teeth. "You still tracking me, baby?"

"I swear I'm with you, baby," he panted, and then dropped his head forward, near the breaking point.

"No you're not," she said in a hard rush into his ear and then bit his earlobe as she began to slow.

Pressure built, his mind snapped, his hands were in her hair, his mouth punishing hers as he lifted her beneath him in a hard arch. "Don't stop, Sasha—don't . . ."

Words tumbled into a howling wail as she scored his sides and he came so hard he couldn't breathe. Granite thrusts crippled his mind and stole his breath. Insane pleasure jags felt like they were pulling his spinal cord through every disk in his back as tears and sweat ran down his face. Sasha's hard climax twisted his stomach in pleasure knots. Her hot, pulsing sheath was going to make him drool on himself; his body was already twitching like he'd been lightning-struck. Then slowly, but surely, it was all over. He could breathe . . . he just couldn't move. He couldn't even lift his own body to give hers a break.

"You okay?" she asked softly, struggling under his deadweight.

He slowly rolled over with her anchored by his right arm. There was nothing to do but simply nod. When he felt her try to move, though, he shook his head. "Please . . . not yet." That was all he could get out.

Okay, so he'd begged her. His mouth wasn't cooperating with his brain. But how could he make her understand the pleasure that was still radiating up his shaft, practically leaving him blind? It had been intense between them before, but nothing like this. He was just thankful that she lay against him peacefully and allowed him to stay deeply embedded within her for now.

She wasn't sure how long they lay there in the middle of the floor, but she could tell by the change in the pitch of the moon it had been a while. Each time she tried to gently slip out of Hunter's dozing hold, he tightened it. Finally she gave up trying not to wake him and simply kissed him.

"I'm going to at least get us a blanket."

A pair of hot hands caressed her back, and a kiss brushed the crown of her head.

"How about we go to bed?" he murmured with his eyes closed. "I just couldn't move for a little while."

"How're you feeling?" she asked quietly.

"Way better than I did before we came back to the room."

She could hear the smile in his voice and was glad of it. She also hoped he would simply let her run-in with Shogun pass, chalk it up to aroused male wolves squaring off over body turf—as primitive as that concept was. But when she lifted her head to begin the tough process of getting up off the floor, she met a pair of sad wolf eyes in the dark.

"I'm sorry," Hunter said in a quiet, faraway tone.

She cradled the side of his face with her palm. "Baby . . ."

He closed his eyes. "You're not going to be able to go on like this forever. I can't expect that." He sat up slowly, gathering her into his arms as their bodies shifted and parted.

"What do you mean?' She stood as he stood, blocking his escape to the bed.

He closed his eyes and leaned his forehead against hers. "The way . . . Things aren't right, in Shadow terms."

She knew he was talking about the way they now made love. He couldn't shadow-dance, couldn't shift on a run. Her hand rested in the center of his chest for a moment, feeling his heart.

"By your next heat, this has to be fixed or you'll have to shoot me."

"Why would you say something like that?" Horror filled her as she stepped away from him and began collecting clothes.

"Because now you know what it's like to make love to a Werewolf," he said flatly, finding his discarded clothes and kicking the coffee table out of the way.

"What?" Sasha stood in the middle of the floor

holding jeans and a T-shirt, stunned. Was he accusing her? Shoot him—he couldn't be preparing to dominance-battle Shogun over a moot point ... noooo ...

Hunter stared at her for a moment. "Now you know."

"Whoa, whoa, whoa, things have *not* gone that far and ..." Her voice trailed off as his expression became perplexed. Damn.

"Sasha, what are *you* talking about?"

Hunter raked his fingers through his hair and then folded his arms over his chest. In the dark with moonlight bathing his dark symmetry and eyes glowing amber, he was awesome. The problem was, she'd inadvertently put her foot in her mouth. There was no defensible comeback as he waited. Not one that wouldn't irreparably damage an already very wounded male ego.

"Before you go asking *me* what *I* meant—since you're the one who's speaking in vast metaphors, Hunter, why don't *you* clarify what *you're* talking about?" she said, trying to sound casual and righteous. "I'm not sure that I like your tone, either. Why can't we just go to bed and ... maybe do what we just did all over again? I have to leave in the morning and I don't want ... Oh, c'mon, baby, seriously. What's up?"

She stared at him, waiting, hoping that female double talk might work while standing in front of a male wolf in the nude. At least it was worth a try. Sasha raked her hair; this man was making her crazy. Worse, he was making her sort out things about another man

that she didn't even want to think about while standing in the middle of a bedroom stark naked!

"I meant," Hunter said between his teeth, "that
now that you've seen how very unrefined the male
Werewolf style is, I'd have to get this virus out of my
system and the situation rectified before your next
calendar heat—or you'd have to shoot me for being
all over you day and night . . . like this. Why don't
you tell me what *you* were referring to?"

"Nothing, Hunter. Let's just get some shut-eye—"

He pointed toward the window in a hard snap, indi-
cating the tavern that they could see across the street.
"But maybe curiosity about the Were Clan Federation
has left a void. Was that what you thought I meant?
That I was referring to Shogun? Or when I said you'd
have to shoot me, I was talking about a dominance
battle?" Hunter dragged his fingers through his hair
and began to walk in a circle. "Reference to a Werewolf immediately conjures the image of him in your
mind, not me . . . the one who just made love to you
like one because of a—"

"You are not being fair," she said, heaving her
clothes onto the sofa in a jumble and then pointing at
his chest. "We both got approached tonight, so what?
We both maybe took a look at expanded possibilities
after we'd had a fight. But nobody acted on anything.
You and I ended up here practically devouring each
other. What's the big deal? I'm here, you're here—
and as best I can tell, it was a wild and crazy night. I
hope you had fun, because I sure did."

"Is that what happened?" he said quietly, his tone
distant and hurt. "We just had fun. Okay."

Oh, for Pete's sake!

"What happened over at The Fair Lady, then?" Sasha folded her arms over her breasts.

He looked away.

"Uh-huh, I thought so." She gave him a hard glare before righting the coffee table and the broken lamp.

"I had virus competing with meds in my system." Hunter strolled over to the bed and sat down on it hard. He picked up the room-service menu, staring at it in the dark.

"I had a flight from a testosterone rush and good old-fashioned anger competing in mine, so?"

"Are you hungry?" he said, changing the subject.

"Hell yeah," she said, angry but not sure why.

"Burgers and fries are all they've got that looks good on the twenty-four-hour menu."

"That'll work," she said, coming to flop down beside him. "The usual—rare."

He gave her a sidelong glance, leaning his weight on his forearms and thighs. "Look, Sasha, if at any time you want out of this, you let me know, okay? I'd rather it be decided privately between us than humiliate myself in the streets in a dominance battle for a woman who's lost interest. At least allow me to save face in public and in front of my pack . . . in front of the North American Shadow Clan. That's all I ask. We're both at a level politically where there's more at stake here than our own personal bull . . . you were right about that."

Their eyes met in a sad stalemate.

"I'm not going anywhere, Hunter," she said in a slightly annoyed tone. "Except to report in to the base

tomorrow. I haven't lost interest. If you couldn't tell
that from what just happened in here, then I'm at a
loss for what to say to you."

Hunter let his breath out hard. "The Werewolves
dominance-battle all the time over selected, but temporary, mates. They have a very different worldview
than Shadows. In our culture, we go there once in a
lifetime. I've already been there."

"I know," she said, more softly now, not sure what
else she could tell him as he moved a stray wisp of
hair off her cheek. He hadn't completely read the
Shogun conflict within her wrong. That fact at the
moment was killing her.

Lei sidled up to her brother at the bar in Finnegan's
Wake and slid onto a stool beside him.

"Why do you persist in torturing yourself like this,
Shogun? It isn't becoming for a Were-royal to be
scouring the dank alleys of New Orleans looking for
a stray she-Shadow like he's some forlorn hunting
dog. Nor would I *ever* allow *anyone* to see me practically baying at the windows of the back of a bed-and-
breakfast establishment. The Elves are probably all
gossiping; you know the Fae." She smiled smugly and
inclined her head toward the B&B across the street.
"It's quiet now . . . good thing the human community
doesn't hear like we do, nor do the Fae or Mythics,
but I bet—"

"Enough," Shogun snarled, and then tossed back
a Jack Daniel's shot, standing. "Get what you want
and put it on my tab."

Lei held his arm. "Sit. We have much to discuss."

"We have nothing to discuss." Shogun snatched his arm from his sister's hold.

"It's about her."

Shogun hesitated. Lei smiled.

"While I am sure that after listening to her get naked with the big Shadow, you need to quickly go find an available, unaccompanied she-alpha tonight— rare at this hour since all the pretty ones are taken— you do need to discuss how she could possibly factor into your complete rule of both Federations. A coup, if ever I saw one on the horizon."

"Why are you always so quick to deceive a friend and to cut the throat of an ally, Lei?" Shogun said close to her ear in a warning growl.

"If you could have Hunter's woman, tell me you wouldn't cut his throat. Didn't you try without success to do that tonight? Be honest. We're family. I know how much you want her."

"If you weren't my blood sibling, I would shun you," Shogun whispered, straightening. Rage made him clasp his hands behind his back to keep them from finding their way around Lei's neck.

"But you need me, as you have always needed me. You try to run this clan and all its packs with an Old World sense of honor and chivalry that nearly eclipsed our parents. What I am offering you is an opportunity."

"Do not ever speak ill of our parents' honor," Shogun growled. "Before they made irreparable decisions, they ruled with integrity, and that is the part of their legacy that I will restore!"

Lei's eyes narrowed as her voice dipped to a

threatening murmur. "Do *not* lecture me on the history of the Eighteenth Dynasty of the Xi-Ho Clan. I have not forgotten what it took to unite the Werewolf Clans of China, Japan, Korea, Thailand, Mongolia, the Philippines, and Malaysia—all of it. The entire region under one rule—now yours. I know how much blood was shed, how many sacrifices, how many secret deals and strategies it required, dear brother. Do you?"

When he looked away, she grabbed his arm. "I also know that its current alpha leader is a direct descendant of those mighty clans that crossed into the vast wilderness of Siberia, battling the fearsome Russian Wolf Clans to cross the Bering Strait. It is our seed that entered North America to become the foundation of the North American Clans. So yes, Shogun, I am well versed in the history of honor and duty."

Without apology in her tone or gaze, Lei lifted her chin, releasing Shogun's arm. "I am asking that you honor your ancestry by not attempting to sully the Xi-Ho name by consorting with Shadows as a second pick, as though you were a mere beta male, and by refusing to share your rightful rulership of the combined Federations with their alpha male long-term. The Shadow Wolves are imposters! Mutants that adapted from our gene pool, not the other way around. Our birthright supersedes theirs, was the foundation of theirs, so it is no wonder that our parents made the ultimate sacrifice to accept the demon virus to strengthen themselves as well as their warrior ranks against invaders. I am not ashamed of our complete history. Unlike you, I am not conflicted and haven't chosen to pick and choose from the rubble of past lives. Thus, who is more honorable—one who hides half of his history in shame, or the one who lifts her chin with complete dignity and says, *Yes, there were hard choices that had to be made for the preservation of the future?*"

"I am leaving," Shogun said between his teeth. "Don't follow me."

"She will only come to you once he is either dead or disgraced. Take your pick." A devious smile widened on Lei's gorgeous, exotic face when Shogun stopped walking but didn't turn around. "It is the way of a woman of honor, yes?"

Her brother didn't move and didn't turn. That's when she knew she had his ear.

Sliding off the stool she came to him to speak more privately. "Hunter is struggling with battle contagion. They are dosing him with external medicines, something no Shadow has ever had to do that we know of. If he doesn't shake the contagion . . . they will put him to his death within their ranks or banish him. You know the circumstances of his birth."

Shogun lifted his chin. "He was clawed from his mother's womb and somehow survived."

"His grandfather put a silver shell in your father's skull," Lei hissed between her teeth. "*This* has all come full circle through the generations."

Shogun grabbed her arm hard. "The Shadow Clans do not know whose parents had willingly sided with the demon-Were Clans for strength—and the North American Shadow Wolf contingent need not *ever* know such an abomination came from our clan, especially not during this fragile new alliance. If it spills from your lips, and if this peace gets broken by your treacherous hand, I swear I will banish you from our family. You will be dead to me!"

Lei touched her brother's face, her graceful hand sliding over his jaw. "Dear brother, I respect your role as family alpha, even though I am your elder. I am only making you aware of multiple political opportunities. If his health condition worsens, which is of no fault of yours—it was an accident that happened during battle, one you fought admirably with him to win—then he must step down. Perhaps he will be martyred. Regardless, his current mate will not be able to go into exile with him. She is also a part of the human military Paranormal Containment Unit within the US territory of North America. This means she is bound by duty to distance herself from him should he be diagnosed with contagion . . . it is also a part of her job as both a clan leader and a human military captain to kill him if he offers a clear and present danger. There would be no blood on your hands."

Shogun rubbed his palms down his face, feeling a slight rush of perspiration cover his body. His sister was sick, twisted, but had brilliantly composed a fail-safe scenario for events that even he didn't want to admit had kept him up nights.

"But there will be a void in her life, Shogun, as well as at the helm of the already resource-diminished North American Shadow Clan," Lei pressed on carefully, her voice low and seductive. "In the interest of keeping the wolf Federations united as a whole, and keeping the Vampire Cartel voting bloc from again reigning supreme . . . I could see how an alliance between you two could have groundbreaking merit. This is all that I am asking you to consider, brother. If the opportunity presents itself, take it. As has been said within the Chinese tradition—better to be prepared for the opportunity that does not come than unprepared for the one that does."

"I have to go," Shogun said quietly, his voice thick with emotion.

Lei looked him up and down until shame made his face burn. "You want her so badly you are practically trembling. We need an heir. If you act with strategic focus, maybe you can sire one."

"That's enough—this discussion is over. It is also the last time we shall have it."

"All right, as you wish," Lei said with a slight bow.

"As I *command*," Shogun said in a low rumble.

"Then as an apology for any affront to your sensibilities, let me offer you an alternative, at least for now. In the spirit of peace between siblings." With a sly grin, Lei motioned toward a Werewolf female at a far table. "Seems she'd been propositioned by Hunter's beta enforcer, but declined the Shadow in search of a real male . . . nothing locally suited her fancy, although she'd been interested in you since the conference, never sure you'd look her way. She's a high-bred North American Were alpha from a very influential family. I personally tested her when she inquired about your availability. In life, there are always alternatives to what we truly desire . . . sometimes it is best that we settle for them, rather than torture ourselves over that which is beyond our reach."

His sister's words sliced at his pride and sent a jolt

of defiance through him. "I never settle," Shogun said.

"Of course not, darling. It is not the way of the Werewolf—or the Xi-Ho Clan."

As much as he hated his sister's meddling, it was hard to turn away from the auburn beauty with the hourglass figure and long legs situated at a provocative angle adjacent the bar. Her bored, sophisticated pout was poised at the rim of a short tumbler of scotch served straight. The red blouse she wore left little to the imagination, much like the formfitting black leather skirt that kissed the tops of her thighs. Red stilettos gave her shapely legs the appearance of being even longer, and her coppery hue added a finish to her vastly exposed skin that temporarily made his mouth go dry. A pair of hazel eyes suddenly looked up and captured his gaze, hunting it. He told himself he wasn't settling . . . just choosing.

But pride made him square his shoulders more solidly to resist the temptation across the room, determined not to allow Lei to witness how significantly his need for Sasha, and hearing her in the throes of passion, had broken him down . . . that is, until a bold Fae archer stood and left the bar, headed in the lovely socialite's direction. A low rumble filled Shogun's throat. Poachers.

"Her name is Dana," his sister murmured with a soft chuckle, melting into the thinning crowd. "Go on over and make yourself known to her. She won't bite—unless you ask her very nicely."

CHAPTER 5

Sasha rolled over and cold, empty space chilled her body. She sat up quickly and listened, but only the distant sounds of the B&B beginning to wake to its daily routine greeted her ears. Hunter was gone.

"Damn!" Her feet hit the floor as she flung off the tangled covers. This was not in the plan. In fact, it was dangerous for him to be AWOL this close to a full moon. She hated male ego bullshit! Time was running out, he had a medical condition that could go haywire at any moment, and he was missing on the very day she had to go in to meet the brass and concoct a story about why she and her team needed more time in New Orleans.

Pacing to the bathroom, she squeezed toothpaste onto her toothbrush and then shoved it in her mouth while scavenging in her jacket pocket for the cell phone she rarely used. Doc's number was on speed dial. She pressed the button hard while going back to the bathroom to spit.

"Doc, listen," she said breathlessly, not even waiting for a hello the moment the call connected. "I'm gonna meet you at the helipad on top of Tulane Hospital at oh-nine-hundred as planned so we can get that lift to base. But there's been an incident that, uhmmm . . . I need more time here in New Orleans with my squad to investigate. I don't mind going in to do the dog-and-pony show, but I need more time on the ground here to secure the perimeter, make sure everything checks out." She was babbling as mild hysteria thrummed through her. Sasha closed her eyes and counted to ten.

"Understood," Doc said crisply. "Given the circumstances this morning."

His tone made her open her eyes and slowly pull the toothbrush out of her cheek. She could almost see his gaunt brown face contorted with worry and his silvery brows knit in deep concern; it was all in his voice.

Tension crackled on the line between them as she tried to think of something reasonable to say. It was only a few seconds, but it felt like ten minutes. She needed to ask him what had happened, but she'd already implied that she knew. Why she'd fed a line of bullshit to the man who was more than a project leader, but had been her surrogate father all these years, she wasn't quite sure. Perhaps it had to do with not wanting him to know how deeply she'd blurred the lines between her personal and professional lives—to the point of potentially jeopardizing missions. Beyond opting for evasive tactics, she threw out the simple truth of her not knowing as her stomach did flip-flops.

"What do you know about the situation so far, sir?" she asked in her best military-authority voice.

"That the boy was nineteen . . . a college student. Had only begun working at The Fair Lady as a waiter about a week ago. The way they found him in the Dumpster behind the establishment has been called a mauling. It has been attributed to area pit bull rings and drug gangs—a possible revenge assassination for unpaid drug money, retaliation for a love triangle of some sort, or just a sick homicide at ringside for big bets to see how long a human could last in the ring with a couple of pit bulls. That's the current gamut of police speculation thus far. But I swabbed the body and examined it with the forensics team. That boy wasn't mauled—he was half eaten. You and I both know the predator that leaves that kind of signature. I'll see you on top of Tulane, Captain."

The call disconnected in her ear. Doc Holland gave as good as he got. Sketchy intel. Cold sweat made Sasha wrap her arms around herself as she folded the phone in her palm.

When the hell did Hunter leave their room, and why?

He woke up in his wolf form bloody, his wolf coat wet and matted . . . his hunger thoroughly sated.

Hunter rolled over and jumped up, his paws making a gentle padding sound on the carpet of new grass beneath his feet. How had he gotten through the shadow passageways without his amulet? He didn't remember the pain of transition. Had it been so bad he'd blacked out?

Thoughts crowded into Hunter's groggy mind as he glanced around at the pristine Uncompahgre wilderness. *Home.* He threw his head back and howled, bristling the hair on his neck and back as the sound came up from the depths of his soul.

He was finally home, hundreds of miles away from the godforsaken swamps of Louisiana. The pathways had brought him to a place of comfort. Home—where his DNA danced and his people had flourished since time immemorial. This was where he'd needed to come to heal. Only the scent of his natural wilderness, with its indescribable mountain ranges and crystal-clear streams and lakes, could coax his Shadow Wolf out of hiding. The blackouts be damned, he was where cellular memory could guide him. Sasha didn't understand; this was where he could be what he truly was . . . all wolf. *Shadow Wolf.*

Taking off in a flat-out dash, he ran free, feeling the wind on his face, cutting through his blood-damp coat. The scent of blood made every aching muscle in his shoulders and back defy the burn of exertion. He was wolf. Never again would he allow himself to be trapped in his man skin when his wolf raged for release under the moon.

Ecstasy made him high. He'd beaten the beast—his wolf had come to him under the glorious sun! He wasn't trapped by moon phases like his Werewolf brethren. He could change! Shape-shift! Dance amid the shadows and disappear. He could graze the ground like a swirl of fallen leaves simply by melding into their shadows, or soar with returning Canada geese as their thick bodies moved across the sky but left shadows for him to leap into on the ground. He was free, thank the Great Spirit, he was free!

Ice-cold mountain water shocked his system as he thundered through it, washing his coat, and then tore off for the opposite streambank to shake himself out before running again. Damp, fertile earth and new foliage stung his nose, making him leap for joy in a circle for a moment and then tear off again across a clearing. All he needed to do was find his pack.

Wait till Sasha saw him like this!

Sasha entered Tulane Hospital freshly showered and wearing her military dress blues. Security guards and hospital staff gave her nods of recognition as she passed them stone-faced. Who could forget the female soldier who'd strolled into Tulane with a huge black wolf dog at her side just a month prior?

Her eyes straight ahead, Sasha pushed the elevator button and waited, seeing nothing, feeling everything. The lab was her destination before she went to the helipad. She needed to give her squad last-minute instructions; the timetable had shifted. Clarissa needed to know that, too.

Instead of friendly hellos as she entered the room, her squad stood and slowly saluted her as though witnessing a funeral procession. Doc Holland pushed away from a microscope, his gaze meeting Sasha's as she ended her own salute to the team. He wasn't supposed to be here. He was supposed to be waiting for her up on the roof. Acid roiled in her stomach. The look on his face made her want to weep. If she weren't a soldier, she might have given in to the urge to go to him to hug him and just let it all out.

She hated her job; hated her life. Doctor Xavier Holland, friend, mentor, geneticist, genius, seemed like today he hated his, too.

"You're early, Captain," he said, putting professional distance in their relationship, normally much like a father and daughter.

"Circumstances dictated I should be, sir."

They stared at each other, the question of Hunter's whereabouts a silent partner in the room. Unable to stand it, Sasha turned her gaze to her team.

"Woods, Fisher, as I'm sure you've been briefed, we have a critical situation on our hands. Need you to guard the lab. Dr. Holland and I will be meeting with the general this morning at the naval air station, but it is imperative that none of our hazmats get out of this lab. Understood?"

"Roger that," Woods said, his tone military but his expression pained.

Grief had crippled the team, but the only indicator was in their eyes.

"Bradley," Sasha said, her voice strained as she addressed the team's dark arts expert. "I want you on human-supernatural intel. Find me Voodoo priests, psychics in the area, parlor madams, every- and anybody who interfaces with the supernatural community from the human side of that equation who might have heard an underground buzz about that kid's death."

"On it," Bradley said, his voice tough but eyes holding a silent apology.

She turned away from him to Winters; she had to if she hoped to keep her mask intact. "I want you on every GPS satellite and radar system we've got, Winters. I want to know what opened that kid up and I want it found." Before he could respond, she sent a steely glare toward Clarissa. "How much anti-toxin do we have left in cold storage? I need shells loaded with it so—"

"None," Clarissa said quietly.

"What do you mean, *none*," Sasha said more curtly than she'd intended, practically barking the question. She pointed at the men across the room. "Once Winters and Bradley locate the target, we'll need that to load in Woods's and Fisher's shells. I want whatever we're hunting to transition back to human form so we know which target was terminated. That's vital intel to stem a potential civil war in the supernatural community."

"The vials in the lab are gone, Sasha," Doc Holland said carefully. "It takes time and very specific reagents to develop more. We have the luxury of neither. So you will have to build your case the old-fashioned way for the United Council of Entities and present findings from human forensic technology."

Sasha didn't even look at Doc as he spoke. Her eyes were on Clarissa, pleading. Clarissa's expression acknowledged the plea and forgave the outburst.

"Then load 'em up with silver shells," she said to Woods and Fisher. "Anything comes in here or tries to attack a member of the team, forget détente."

"Roger that," Fisher said quietly, his eyes searching her face with open suffering.

"Captain," Doc said, his tone gentle. "We're going to be late."

Silver Hawk placed another log on the fire and watched the shadows dance on the rough-hewn cave wall. Thick plumes of smoke rose from incense pots and his pipe as his eyelids fluttered. His precious grandson . . . the child who had beaten the odds and fulfilled more than the prophecy but had filled his heart and closed the void. He tasted tears and let them fall. How could he deny his grandson's increasing requests for more medicine that would keep the demon disease at bay? Every night he'd taken a few vials more; every night Hunter required more still. But he'd give his life for his beloved grandson, if the exchange would be accepted by the skies.

Hunter was more than a grandson, he was a son that he'd raised . . . he was a piece of his soul. The Great Spirit had to have mercy on him, and perhaps on one very lonely old man who'd seen the death of his mate, his daughter, pack brothers . . . too many to count. Not this.

The elderly shaman threw his head back and howled a long, mournful wail, shedding his human form to become Silver Shadow on his spirit walk. Maybe his long-dead daughter would guide him. Hunter's mother would know what to do.

He was the clan elder, but she was the man's *mother*. There was nothing stronger than a mother spirit. Only a mother spirit could quell his heart and guide him to the truth. Only a mother spirit would know how to heal her sick child when the white man's medicine didn't work.

Strength and new resolve entered Silver Shadow's wolf body, made virile by the transformation. In the shadow lands the mist played tricks with his eyes, but his nose could never be fooled. She was near. He closed his eyes and howled, sending the echoing call forth into the nothingness. *Daughter. Come to me.*

She stepped through the mist in silence, her spirit radiant in its human form. His wolf eyes looked up and again he tasted tears. But rather than run to him to hug his neck as she'd always done, a thick tide of tears filled her beautiful brown eyes and then spilled over her dark lashes in a river that washed her face. She covered her mouth with one graceful hand; the other was clenched in a fist at the pit of her stomach as though she'd been stabbed. She then turned away, shame the last expression she allowed him to glimpse. He turned away, needing to run but only able to lope to the edges of the shadows before collapsing as a broken man in sobs.

A retinue of burly MPs met their chopper as it landed at the New Orleans NAS. There'd been no way to talk over the helicopter din, and she certainly didn't want to express anything private to Doc in front of the unknown pilot. She and Doc hadn't said two words to each other during the entire flight, but then again, what was there to say?

Sasha climbed into the jeep with Doc at her side and held on until the vehicle came to a halt at the base's administration building. She knew the drill, had been through enough come-to-Jesus meetings with the brass to know how to defuse a potentially volatile situation . . . she just wished she knew how to defuse her heart so she could start breathing again.

On automatic pilot her body moved through the military courtesies and sign-in procedures that would allow her an audience with the newly installed general. What a day to have to meet a new commander.

As she and Doc stepped into the Situation Room, a tall, burly blond in his midfifties greeted them formally. His blue eyes looked haunted.

"General Westford, Xavier Holland, Paranormal Containment Unit's geneticist."

"Sir. Captain Sasha Trudeau," she said, announcing herself after Doc had made his own introduction and everyone had shaken hands.

"Thank you both for what you do," the general said, walking away from them and returning to the long, polished mahogany table, which held several files. He didn't sit, just picked up the files and then flung them down the table away from him in clear disgust.

"I don't mind telling you folks that this whole supernatural business is keeping me up at night. I mean, what's the world coming to? Spooks jumping up from graves and we've gotta be politically correct and call 'em demons, Vampires, and Zombies. Mad dogs killing good folk—and we've gotta make a species distinction between Werewolves, proper, and the demon-infected variety? If you ask me, I wanna just call the boys in from the Joint Readiness Center at Fort Polk, along with the fly boys from Barksdale AFB's Second Bomb Wing and their Mighty Eighth, and just leave a smokin' black hole in every cemetery here to Texas."

"Unadvisable, sir," Sasha said calmly, but completely understanding where the beleaguered man was coming from. "That could set off a chain reaction of retaliation against humans."

"You mean I might get my face ripped off, like Donald Wilkerson did . . . I read the reports," General Westford said, his eyes as hard as his voice.

"Affirmative, sir," Sasha said, needing this new cowboy to quickly understand what he was dealing with.

"Your suggestion, then? Before we open up the teleconference to the Joint Chiefs, I need to get this off my chest." The general dragged his fingers through his stubbly crew cut. "What are we gonna tell that boy's mama and daddy who've gotta close his casket to put him in the ground? You know? This ain't natural. I don't care that the spin doctors are working with local authorities and the media has been poised to keep down panic. I've got personal questions keeping me up at night, Captain. For me, it's a question of, how does the US military allow a predator to *eat* a goddamned student in America and call ourselves on point? What if this is the first of many? I want this contained, Captain! Whatever this thing is, I want it hunted down and wiped off the map. Do you know how hard it was to do public awareness damage control after the war that broke out in the streets of New

Orleans? How in God's name are we gonna keep the lid on this whole thing if creatures are now eating civilians alive?"

The general's questions and impassioned rant carved at her conscience. She knew the man didn't want a real answer any more than she was prepared to give one right now. He had to vent; she wished she could, too, but her rank didn't allow her that option in front of a five-star.

A kid had lost his life on her watch, and possibly by a predator that she didn't put down when she'd had a chance. A silver slug should have gone in the target's skull. Instead she'd willingly disarmed before him . . . had thrown her gun on the sofa and had gotten down on her hands and knees for him. She wanted to close her eyes and disappear right where she was standing.

The room grew suddenly too small as the general continued to rant and she kept her eyes straight ahead. She couldn't even risk a glimpse at Doc right now. Guilt lacerated her, ripped at the medals she wore, and cut away at her epaulets. How could she have been so blind . . . so stupid?

"I can't help but think—all right, serial killers, that's the province of local cops, the FBI, whoever," the general said, barely having taken a breath. He then began to pace and talk with his hands, his emotions getting the better of him. "Drug dealers and international politics, the CIA, Washington who's who, FBI, and Interpol can have at it. Defending our borders, that's *our job*. Putting things aright if it's a threat to the American way of life—I'm honored to be in uniform. We *are* Homeland Security, no matter what anybody else says, or whatever layers of cockamamie bureaucracy they throw at us. We're the ones with our faces in the mud and our asses in the foxholes, not the suits. But this supernatural crap . . . In all my born days . . ." He shook his head and allowed his words to trail off as he stared at Sasha and Doc for answers.

"Sir," Sasha said without hesitation. "This is a new day, a new beast, a new threat. The US military, especially Delta Force, always rises to the occasion."

CHAPTER 6

He didn't understand. As he stood on the edge of his Shadow pack's territory, low, resonant growls met him. Hunter sniffed the air, scenting for any additional danger as well as allowing his own wolf signature to coat his palate. He bore the scent of a true Shadow Wolf. There was no demon contagion in it. He'd shown himself fully in the center of a pool of sunlight. Yet his border guards had not followed the howling command to stand down and greet him as a returning member from the hunt.

Confusion blistered his mind as he watched Bear Shadow step out of a stand of trees bearing attack canines, practically foaming at the mouth. The huge amber wolf was crouched low, stalking forward in a threatening stance, and then stopped to begin barking. His longtime friend Crow Shadow was at Bear Shadow's side, two huge wolves clearly ready for mortal combat if he so much as flinched. Hunter could also feel the presence of snarling wolves behind him. He remained stock-still and then shape-shifted into his more vulnerable human form, hoping that would demonstrate his intent for peace.

Rapid angry barks were his pack's initial response before they finally settled down enough to take their man forms.

"Bear, Crow . . . brothers . . . what—"

"There's been a human death!" Bear Shadow said, cutting Hunter off, his voice trembling with rage and disappointment.

"Where?" Hunter shouted back across the clearing, not liking the tone of the statement, which had the unmistakable ring of accusation.

"In New Orleans," Crow Shadow said, swallowing hard. "A boy. A student. Eaten and left for the flies in a Dumpster behind the Elf's tavern."

"They say you argued with him, brother," Bear Shadow said, his voice quavering with emotion. He lifted his chin as a shotgun whirred toward him from behind a stand of trees. He caught it with one hand.

Hunter didn't move. He understood immediately and remained very, very still. Horror threaded through him: The blackouts. The blood. Sasha!

Several clicks of pump shotguns engaging and the definitive scent of silver filled the air as pack brothers slowly stepped out of the shadows armed and extremely dangerous. A UCE tribunal would be called, evidence presented. Things had to follow protocol to avoid an all-out wolf hunt, as long as he went willingly and quietly. They had to ensure he was taken into custody, and he would allow them to do that to save the countless Shadows and innocent Werewolves who would be slaughtered if the Vampires could call for an open season on his kind once again. But more importantly, if he'd hurt Sasha, it would all be moot. He'd put a silver shell in his own temple.

Grim expressions stared back at Hunter as his gaze tore around the group for any sign that he hadn't committed his worst nightmare.

"Where's Sasha?" he finally shouted, unable to hold his panic in check any longer.

"As the North American Shadow Wolf Clan chief enforcer," Bear Shadow said in an authoritative tone now devoid of all emotion, "it is hereby my prime directive to take you into custody, dead or alive, until further notice. So says the ruling body of the United Counsel of Entities."

Pandemonium had broken out among the PCU team members the moment Sasha and Doc left the lab. Woods kicked over two chairs and then stormed off, bereft; Fisher was out the door behind him, headed to get heavy artillery from the safe-house stash. Winters was still sitting in the same spot staring at his monitors in disbelief. Bradley was already gone, headed who knew where—probably just needing fresh air before the team actually saw him break down and cry.

Although heartbreak claimed her, Clarissa kept moving. Getting a blood sample from Doc now would be tricky, but there were several ways to gather DNA evidence.

Clarissa moved to the microscope Doc had been using and casually collected his coffee cup. She then went to the sink as though washing it out and gathered up his white lab coat. The collar might offer up a strand or two of hair.

They sat side by side in silence on the way back to Tulane. Hurt radiated off Doc's skin in painful waves so acutely that she could almost see them form in the air. What could she possibly tell this man to make it all right? What the hell could she tell herself, for that matter? But she knew the discussion was inevitable, and as soon as they left the helipad and returned to the building, they'd have it out in Doc's new temporary office away from the prying ears of the team. Oh, yes, they would argue, but in secretive, whispering bursts of emotion to keep anyone else from overhearing, especially the few top staff members who had been panicked, then deputized into preternatural service during the supernatural crisis last month.

Sasha watched her mentor take long, weary strides before her. His posture was rigid and tall with pride and righteous indignation. Yet sheer disappointment slowed his normally swift stride. Xavier Holland walked like a man going to his own execution after spending years waiting to hear the final verdict. The man looked tired, spent; deep creases in his ebony face replaced the character etchings time had dutifully left. His camel and charcoal tweed jacket now seemed too large for his thin frame, just as his charcoal pants seemed to hang from him in a way she'd never noticed before.

Doc never turned around to face her as they entered his office. He just allowed the door to bang against the stop and began to loosen his university rep tie. She watched him blot perspiration from his brow with the back of his forearm before he removed his jacket and carefully hung it up, and then opened the top button on his button-down white oxford shirt.

"I'm sorry," she said quietly once she'd clicked the door shut behind her. She knew it wasn't nearly enough, but it was the truth.

Doc looked up at her as he sat down heavily on the edge of his desk and closed his eyes. "Why, Sasha? Why didn't you tell me he was getting worse?"

"I thought you could tell from his increased dosages."

Doc opened his eyes, the anguish in them halting her breath.

"I never increased his dosages. I would have told you if I had. Someone very skillfully came in here and replaced our unspent vials with sugar water. I didn't notice there were any missing until I'd received a call this morning about the boy and went into the locked refrigerators to remove several vials to take with me on location. That's when I saw that the serum had been tampered with . . . it was too thin, not viscous enough. I was looking at it under a scope when you arrived, trying to figure out who . . . but you just confirmed my worst fear. If he had extra doses, there was only one way for him to obtain that, and it would be to steal it from this facility."

Sasha closed her eyes and hugged herself.

"I'm sorry, sweet pea," Doc said in a gravelly voice.

His term of endearment from when she was a child and he'd cared for her wet her lashes. "So am I," she whispered.

"This goes beyond my technical ability . . . I tried for years to break the code and I failed. Damn!" Doc hurled a thick medical text off his desk across the room and stood, smoothing a palm over his thinning hair. "I don't know where I went wrong, what other factors I could have overlooked—the anti-toxin is supposed to work like snakebite antivenin . . . using a little of the toxic substance to allow the victim to build an immunity against it. Why isn't his body fighting it, Sasha? Why?" Doc shouted, opening his arms toward her as though she had the critical scientific answer.

But the plea in his voice drew her as if she did. Sasha crossed the room and hugged him, needing Doc to do what he always did—to make it all right because he was hers. Wide old hands rubbed her back as she held in a sob.

"If I cure him, it doesn't change what he's probably done . . . why save him to be executed? Let him go out as a wolf—let his pack take him down while he's running free. I don't know what else to do, honey. We can't cage him in the penal system."

"Oh, God . . ." Her voice broke and she bit her lip. "I just want to know for sure, even though . . ."

"The evidence is damning. The meds were gone and he had them. What else is there to know? Even if there's more than one beast left over from the last outbreak, I don't know if I can cure Hunter this time,

Sasha," Doc said into her hair, his breath damp with unspent tears.

"I know . . . neither can I."

Shogun sat at the long table in the private dining area of The Fair Lady, listening to the chaotic comments zinging among alarmed Fae citizenry, his Werewolf Clan captains, and disgruntled Mythics. Dana's possessive hold on his arm—as though she were a queen being presented at court—made him snarl and stand. Lei, as expected, was on his flank in a flash.

"You must make a decision quickly," Lei urged.

"We must do a thorough investigation," Shogun said loud enough to quiet the caucus before him. "Our peace with the Shadow Clans is tenuous. To accuse one of theirs of murdering and cannibalizing a human without fair evidence would always leave a stain of doubt, and where there are doubts, there is mistrust—which leads to war."

"We have evidence," the Elf Dugan said, slamming a spent hypodermic needle on the table in front of Shogun with a meaty hand. His normally ruddy face was now a deeper shade of crimson, and agitation had puffed his barrel chest up so much that he looked like he might explode. "He's been shooting up with the stuff! Could be the same thing that the Vamps were tradin' and the rogue Shadows that had followed Dexter were taking. My Pixie cleaning crews found it in their room. That bad business all came out of his local pack . . . who's to say he wasn't caught up in it. Has 'appened to more genteel types than the likes of him."

"I saw him charge his mate—was ballistic when he came through the doors of the B and B," a Brownie shouted from the back of the room. "Was crazed."

"That doesn't make a man guilty of murder," said a deep Werewolf voice from the crowd. "Just makes him all wolf—especially if you saw the babe he was with."

Werewolf laughter rang out. Shogun growled to again quiet the rowdy group and then rounded on the table, not wanting to be reminded of the incident.

"Max Hunter did argue with that poor boy," a fire-eyed Phoenix server said, the edges of her long red hair beginning to smolder.

"Yessss," a sensual Dragon dancer said with a hiss. She swayed as she talked, placing her delicate hands on her hips, mesmerizing the crowd with her jewel-green eyes. "The young waiter triggered his mood, then Max Hunter became very upset that his pack brother interrupted a hunt." She gave Dana a purposeful glance. "His own beta enforcer challenged him for a female and the big Shadow gave in . . . but stalked off, clearly unhappy about it. That's when his mate cornered him and they left together after a fight. They went into the alley . . . into the shadows. Who knows what could have transsssspired there if they were on drugs?"

"But we can't jump to conclusions," Ethan said, trying to play peacemaker as the establishment's owner. He inserted his short, round frame between the verbal combatants and smoothed down the spikes of brown hair on his head, which rimmed a large bald spot. "People, if we disintegrate as allies here, the

Vampire Cartel will come back, and come back with a vengeance. As soon as it gets dark, they'll send their own investigators . . . after their disgrace at the UCE they'll be calling for an all-out wolf hunt!"

The Fae in the room fell silent along with the Werewolves.

"If they call for an open wolf hunt," Ethan said, glancing around as he pressed his point, "then anyone who voted against the Vampires at the UCE Conference will no longer be protected. The Werewolf Clans will have to defend themselves and watch their backs against the Vampires, as will the Shadow Wolves . . . and the old bad blood between the Wolf Clans could erupt again if there are any accidental deaths. What will happen to us?" Ethan shook his head. "I have children . . . a wife. I say we wait and allow the Shadow Wolves due process and we assist, in a positive manner only, in the investigation."

"Maybe old Ethan is right," Dugan piped up, quickly swaying the Fae vote.

"Word on the air from the Woodland Fairies is the Shadows have sent a hunting party after him using their best trackers," a Fae archer said, materializing a silver-tipped arrow in his grip. "We can send our archers through the network of trees in his home region. We can bring him down a mile off without incident. If we have a body, that should appease the Vamps."

"What about his missing mate?" Dugan said, glancing around. "Who's seen her, what if she's got the contagion, too?"

"I don't think we should jump to conclusions about

'er," a thick, buxom Gnome said. "She checked out, like regulations require at the B and B—paid 'er bill and left. Go over your records, Dugan. Plus, Ethan's Margaret said they saw her at Tulane with her humans early this morn. Not like she's running and hiding in the shadows with him . . . I think he left her, if you ask me."

"By right and by honor," Shogun said, commandeering the group by physically walking through the center of it as he spoke, "the Shadow Clans should quarantine their own man until the full moon two nights from now." His message was clear in the very term he used, *man*—Sasha wasn't part of this wolf hunt. When no one raised an objection, he continued. "Vampires do not sway this vote, since they have allegedly been behind every offense against our kind in the past. Each Wolf Clan reserves the right to martial law within its ranks—this time should be no different. It is the way we've functioned as wolves since time immemorial. The moon will bring all things to light. If Max Hunter is infected, he will Turn . . . they will see it, and they will put him to death—his blood will thus be on their hands, just as his escape or release will be, should they choose not to do the right thing. Only then do we act, not before."

"It is true; the moon brings things to light," Lei said in a falsely submissive voice, bowing to her brother. "But let us also not forget that it was the Shadow Wolves' breach of this tradition to allow us to hunt our own infected members that began the civil war."

"Which is why," Shogun said with a snarl, "we do not want to repeat history. Those who do not know their history and learn from it are destined to repeat it." He eyed her with an angry glare. "No pre-emptive strikes."

The room had gone dead-still at the tense exchange between siblings. Lei smiled and bowed again, but her eyes burned with mischief. Sauntering over toward the door, she inclined her head and placed a long, graceful finger to her lips for a moment before speaking.

"You are patient and wise, my dear brother. And the opportunity I spoke of earlier to ensure everlasting harmony has just presented itself." Lei straightened with a smile and stepped away from the entrance to allow Sasha to come into the room. "Welcome. We were just talking about you."

No one moved. No one spoke. All eyes were on her. Sasha surveyed the semi-hostile faces as she entered the room, the hair standing up on the back of her neck. It seemed everyone—except maybe Shogun and, strangely, Lei—had made up their minds already. The auburn bitch who had tried Hunter was standing, her movements a slow stalk.

Sasha kept her peripheral vision on Dana as she gazed around the room. The questions set deeply in each pair of supernatural irises were the same: Did Hunter do it? Was she involved? Where was he? While she couldn't blame them, it still killed her that he was being tried in the court of public opinion without evidence . . . she had hard evidence, they didn't. But it made all the difference in the world that the other wolf Federation leader seemed open.

"I came here directly, after doing damage control

among the human ranks, because I knew you'd have questions." Sasha let her breath out hard and spoke monotone, military facts. "At approximately oh-seven-hundred, Max Hunter, aka Wolf Shadow, was located and within the hour quarantined by his local Shadow pack. The North American Shadow Clan elder—his grandfather, Silver Hawk, aka Silver Shadow—was informed by pack enforcer Bear Shadow of his capture."

She paused, deciding not to tell them that Silver Hawk had informed Doc on his private cell phone, rather than speaking directly to her. To expose their old friendship and her snub as Hunter's mate was just too raw a scab to pick at right now. Murmurs slowly began to fill in the silence, however, and she knew she had to keep going, press forward with information to quell any brewing dissent for the moment.

"A full investigation is now under way. He has been silver-caged under heavy guard—and will remain that way to allow the moon to tell the rest of the story. Anyone with valid, pertinent information can let us know. If it's on the record, your testimony will also be a part of the tribunal proceedings that will convene the second night of the full moon."

When no one responded, she sought Shogun with her eyes. Sasha held his gaze, hoping he could see the urgency in her unspoken request. What she had to say didn't need a public forum—she needed a political favor, his help to be sure this wasn't another Vampire-inspired ruse. She also needed a deeply personal favor . . . a sample of his blood.

"As Federation leader for the Werewolf Clans, may I ask you for a moment to discuss this matter in private . . . as co-regent of the Shadow Wolf Federation that has sadly just lost its leader?"

"Unadvisable. Right now he has deniability, and the Were Clans want to keep it that way," the auburn female said, rounding the table and bristling. "For Shogun to have a private meeting with you now could compromise his—"

"I didn't ask you," Sasha said between her teeth in a tone that cleared the floor. "The last time I checked, Lei was Shogun's female enforcer and political adviser." Sasha turned to Lei, snubbing the troublemaker. Her nerves were way too raw for this. "I am asking for diplomatic courtesy."

"Dana, be nice," Lei said with a sly smile. "Sasha just wants to tell Shogun her side of the story, I'm sure."

"And I said no to that bitch," Dana snarled, staring Sasha down. "I know what she's trying to do. There's no amnesty to be had here. When the moon comes up and Hunter flips out, he's dead. You think you can sashay into Werewolf territory with a contagious Shadow male, hump him then dump him, and then go after an alpha clan leader of *ours*—telling him lies and sad stories to save your sorry half-human hide?"

Sasha transformed in a blink, shedding military blues to release her silver wolf majesty. Her paws found the center of Dana's chest and they both hit the floor in a hard *thud*. Saliva-slick fangs bore down close to the auburn female's face in a warning snarl. Then Sasha released several quick angry barks that finally made Dana close her eyes and cringe.

"Archers, archers!" Dugan cried out, edging his way to the door. "No more bloodshed!"

A Fae archer smiled. "No, laddie, let her wolf have her run. The transition back into all woman is simply awesome. This is pure she-Shadow. They can transition at will, don't have to wait for the moon."

High-fives rippled through the crowd and a burly Werewolf pounded a fist overhead.

"Oh, yeah—the way of the wolf," he said, laughing hard, making his brothers in the room join in a howl.

The sound broke Sasha's attack trance. Her nerves were so taut and emotions so keen that she'd flipped. In an instant she was back in her human form, albeit completely nude. A low, resonant whistle of appreciation sounded behind her, making her face burn as she backed off the downed Were-female troublemaker. Sasha swept up her clothes, glad that Shogun hadn't smiled or leered as he turned his back to her, shielding her from the small gathering.

"Diplomatic courtesy granted," he said in a low rumble. "Just tell me where."

CHAPTER 7

Sasha walked in front of Shogun, head held high, jacket on askew, buttoning her shirt. Her underwear was clutched in one fist as she hurriedly jammed her feet into her shoes and swept her hat off the floor as though what had just occurred was the most common thing in the world.

Mortified did not begin to describe it.

Yes, she had transitioned in full UCE court at the conference—but so had her entire pack, as did Hunter . . . as did Shogun. That was a unified show of force. That had not been a solo act to leave her naked and flashing too-eager Fae and Werewolf males. *This* was a travesty, the result of her nerves being wound too tight and losing her cool.

Sasha cringed as she shoved her unmentionables into her jacket pocket. Jeans and a T-shirt were calling her name. All eyes in the private dining area were on her as she marched out of the rear exit of the establishment. This looked *so* tacky: coming out of the back of a saloon in a dress military uniform, half undressed.

It was no way to begin a thorough investigation. She needed a change of clothes, a place to literally hang her hat now that she'd checked out of Dugan's B&B. The only problem was that her clothes, like her weapon, were packed in her luggage, as were Hunter's personal effects that she'd gathered up, and all of it was in the employee locker Doc had given her to temporarily use back at the lab. That was the last place in the world she wanted to go right now: back to the lab, where her team could see her discombobulation and the wild look in the eye. Maybe she really was too close to this situation, had lost perspective.

"You never said where you wanted to have this private conversation?"

Shogun's voice behind her made her turn quickly to address his question; she'd almost forgotten he was there.

She didn't answer for a few seconds, but her bewildered expression was something he'd never expected to see in a woman like Sasha.

"I understand that it's hard to know where to go in New Orleans . . . where the walls don't have ears," he offered, trying to let her save face. He knew the wolf attack had been spurred by Dana's bitchiness, and that Sasha's shape-shift back into her nude human form in front of strangers had humiliated her beyond comprehension.

When Sasha didn't immediately respond, he tried

again, giving her more physical space as he casually walked off a bit. "There's a tea salon not far from here. It has private booths where we could discuss your private, diplomatic matter."

Sasha nodded, let her breath out hard, and dusted off her hat, still fidgeting with her clothes for a moment before looking up at him. He knew it had cost her dearly to meet his gaze head-on. He wished he could tell her that she'd looked absolutely stunning as she'd stepped through the entrance of The Fair Lady in uniform ... wished he could tell her how mesmerizing her authority was ... or could say that her transformation had been majestic, awe-inspiring, her fearlessness legendary, her eyes liquid fire, her nude human form ... devastating. There was nothing shameful about what had happened. What she'd done before him was living art.

But he said none of that. When his vocal cords could work again, he rumbled out a change of subject that was no less fluid than her shape-shift.

"Let's go to the tea salon, Sasha. It's a short walk. They have a gift shop on the premises with T-shirts and souvenirs so you can get out of the military duds and not feel stared at. We can sit in a screened booth, or walk in the small, but very beautiful, Japanese gardens."

Again, she didn't speak; just looked at him. He waited, not sure whether she'd changed her mind about wanting to talk to him alone—praying she hadn't. Then she nodded, allowing him to breathe

again. It was a curt, military nod before she released
one word.

"Okay."

How did he know? How did he sense it all, even
down to her desire to change into civvy gear to better
blend in so she didn't stick out like a sore thumb? He
was wearing khakis and a white, collared golf shirt
with a pair of casual leather slip-ons; it made her
look completely ridiculous and very obvious in her
dress blues.

His innate understanding of her was both endear-
ing and alarming. Their eyes met briefly, and then
he slowly turned away and began walking. It was a
sensual wolf gesture of follow-the-leader that reminded her of the way they'd met in South Korea.

She tracked Shogun through a maze of narrow
back streets and alleys to a semi-residential district
before they finally stopped at what seemed like a
large corner property, fenced in with an odd combination of open New Orleans wrought iron and a
blind of bamboo saplings. Quiet patience seemed to
live here, even down to the carefully laid stone path-
way. Cobbled beauty in sandstone and multihued
granite led from the concrete street, up a small flight
of wide slate steps, to a broad, hardwood porch
that gave way to the front entrance. There elegantly
carved, shellacked wood doors met patrons.

An oval pond covered by a small zigzag footbridge
and filled with irises, carp, and smooth green paddle
stones graced the front lawn. Sections of that space
had efficiently been devoted to Japanese wisteria and

trained black and white pines planted in granite chips or nestled among small Himalayan boulders. Sheared dwarf azaleas in outrageous splashes of color winked amid strategically placed, tiny stone walls that gave the entire landscape a layered look, as though it were cut into the side of a mountain.

A small, hand-painted oval just above the door read CHAYA, followed by what Sasha could only assume was the same name written in Japanese calligraphy. Discreet peace reigned here off the beaten path, and she wondered at the effort that must have gone into restoring such simple beauty in the aftermath of Hurricane Katrina.

Sasha's gaze swept the gorgeous terrain. A weeping cherry spilled pink blossoms onto the green carpet of lawn and dusted the slate steps. Graceful roses bowed, offering delicate white blossoms as a generous welcome. Small artificial ridges in the lawn held slate and carefully selected stones to bookend lilies, wildflowers, elephant grasses, and small bonsais, while granite Yukimi lanterns dotted the front garden. She tried not to gape, but then gave in. This enchanted garden seemed to have been transported from the places she'd visited while on assignments abroad, but had never expected to see in New Orleans.

She glimpsed Shogun, about to ask him how he'd found such an oasis, and then thought better of it. Instead she trained her attention on the carefully manicured yew trees set in huge Japanese ceramic pots as though waiting patiently for visitors on the porch. It was all so pretty that it made her pleasantly suspicious that Fairies had been at work. A few ducks lazily strolled across the small area of green, capturing her attention before she really noticed Shogun's hopeful expression in her peripheral vision. She stared at the carp disturbing the water lilies in their relentless search of water fleas instead.

"This is a place of compromise, a crossroad of cultures, and thus a good place for a diplomatic session," Shogun finally said in a calm tone with a half smile. "French architecture, but Japan's sensibilities . . . both Japanese and Chinese tea and serenity in a city known for its lattes and excitement. A wall around the establishment to protect the gardens, but not enough of a barrier to keep out the beauty of New Orleans's diversity. I thought this would be a good place to have this very difficult conversation between Shadow Wolf and Werewolf leadership."

Sasha stopped walking. "What makes you say *difficult conversation*?"

"Because you honor-battled Dana to have it, and you haven't said two words to me on the way over since. If it was a casual request of me that you had, then we would have been engaged in walking discourse. Instead we've arrived here in companionable silence. I'm intrigued . . . but then you've always known that I was."

She dragged her gaze away from his and stared at the entrance. "You said they had a gift shop."

Although it had taken no more than ten minutes to enter the tea salon, hit the gift shop, and score a T-shirt, pair of sweats, and some rubber sandals, then hustle to the ladies' room to change, she also knew that the longer it took her to get to the bottom line, the harder it would be to just spit out what she needed from Shogun.

Blatant sexual tension always thickened the air between them whenever he was near; it was an invisible force that neither would confirm nor deny, but it was there regardless. That fact disturbed her to no end. And that it had risen within her like a beast when Hunter was at his worst, when he needed her most, ate away at her very soul. It shouldn't have been there at all, she silently admonished herself while changing into gift-shop apparel. Yet she knew it might be a bargaining chip Shogun would use . . . and if so, then what?

Sasha quickly shoved her glass-shined shoes into the shopping bag they'd given her in the gift shop, soles down, and then neatly folded her uniform to fit into the bag without squishing it. Her hat went on top of the pile. She had to stop stalling; this was ludicrous.

She looked in the mirror at the pale green T-shirt, which bore a white oval logo of the salon on its right shoulder and the name of the establishment spelled out in fine Japanese calligraphy below. "Not another humiliating public display," she said quietly into the mirror to her inner wolf, and then picked up the shopping bag and headed out of the fragrant, eucalyptus-bathed enclosure.

Even the bathrooms were pretty. If she knew anything about the male species at all, she knew she'd been lured to this place of calm majesty where he could get her to relax. Mental foreplay . . . good God she was in trouble.

Sasha stopped for a moment and looked around, fighting the roiling anxiety that trapped her. Dark mahogany-toned woods had been painstakingly carved with intricate patterns of dragons, birds, and trees. Open-air architecture surrounded her with exposed beams and carved pillars. Delicate rice paper screens separated rooms. Sasha looked through the center of the establishment to where patrons sipped tea and consumed Japanese sweets on bonsai-laden decks, or leaned on the rails enjoying the man-made waterfall below. Gently arching stone bridges created footpaths over small, gurgling streams in the back garden while sleeper steps allowed patrons to continue their meditative walks up to tiny, private mezzanines and ponds designed for tranquility.

Oh, yes . . . he'd truly brought her to an exquisite oasis, one that did anything but relax her. Sasha sighed; this was gonna be a tough meeting, indeed.

"Ma'am, your party is this way," a demure hostess in a kimono said, leading her to the booth that Shogun had selected. The woman's thick southern drawl was slightly jarring juxtaposed with the Asian motif, but her warm smile gently fused the cultures.

Sasha returned a tense smile and followed her, walking behind the young woman as if she were heading to the gallows. Dread settled at the pit of Sasha's stomach as she silently acknowledged all the issues that roiled within her. What if Shogun flat-out refused—or worse, wanted something from her that she wasn't prepared to give . . . how far was she willing to go to get a blood sample? Then there was the other issue—time was not on her side. What if she got the sample and Clarissa couldn't find out any more from it than Doc had from the infected version of Werewolf blood all these years? Truly, it was a long shot, so what was the point?

For the first time since the travesty had begun, she had to acknowledge that in two nights, Hunter might really have to die—and it might be for the best. She'd said it to herself enough times since his condition became evident, had thought it enough times, had even mentally admitted she'd probably have to be the one to put a silver slug in his head . . . but for some reason the reality was just now sinking in as she walked down the long, beautiful wood corridor.

Sasha slipped around the partially recessed rice paper privacy screen and joined Shogun at the low teakwood table, then accepted a hand-painted menu from the hostess. He glanced up from the menu he'd been studying and smiled, but the look in his eyes was too intense.

She set down her bag and took a seat opposite him. Sitting cross-legged on a large moss-green-embroidered pillow positioned on a hand-woven bamboo mat, she returned his smile and tried to appear much improved. But she wasn't.

"Now I feel better," she announced, opening the delicate, oblong menu.

"You look more comfortable . . . but your inner tension has increased," he said with a sly half smile. "But then, this is a place of compromise and dichotomies."

"Your server will be with you shortly," the hostess said, and bowed out of the room.

Sasha just looked at him.

"White tea perhaps?" he asked in a quiet tone. Merriment filled his eyes and spread across the flat plane of his handsome face when she didn't address his previous comment.

"Sure, that's cool."

"No, no, no. One must always be aware of one's choices." Shogun shook his head, but his tone remained pleasant and easy. "In my culture, we do everything with exquisite patience . . . tea is no different than good conversation. Although we are in a Japanese teahouse, they have chosen to present a variety of offerings, and you should understand the subtle differences among them. White tea comes mainly from China and is gleaned from handpicked new buds . . . it is rare, delicate, fragrant. A sensual experience, to be sure. It is not as bold in outright flavor as black teas, but its healing properties are second to none." He stared at her, amber beginning to rim his intense brown eyes. "It takes time to acquire white tea, which is only harvested in early spring, and cannot be rushed or it will be ruined . . . and is *never* rolled. It is still early spring and I am extremely patient, Sasha. Good tea, like good conversation or good company, cannot be rushed; I understand and respect this."

She stared at his intense gaze, watching his smile fade. She'd heard him loud and clear, understood the eloquent double entendre, and liked that he'd made his proposal in a way that would allow them both to save face if she declined. The man had class—truly unexpected from a Werewolf. Her own prejudices gave her pause.

"Then let's do white tea," she said in a quiet, thought-filled tone. One glance at the dizzying selection on the menu and her gaze met his again.

"Which one do you want, Sasha?" he replied in a near murmur, allowing the true question to hang in the air for a moment before glancing down at the menu. "Drum Mountain variety is harvested by the monks of a historic Buddhist monastery . . . that one is nutty, mild . . . whereas Darjeeling Silver Tips from the Makaibari Estate reminds me of vanilla and honey. Bai Mu Dan, or White Peony, is sweet, whereas Snow Buds reminds me of green tea—more robust. They also have a bouquet of red rosebuds, lavender, and fresh peppermint mixed with white tea that you can choose. Or we could share a pot of Silver Needles—highly prized for its origins. It is made only from tender new buds that are covered in white hairs . . . delicate, subtle, for quiet moments."

She stared at him dead-on until he slowly lowered his menu and set it aside. "I honestly don't know what I want. That's been the problem all along, I suspect."

For a moment they said nothing. Finally he nodded.

"I know. Sometimes too many choices can be stressful." Shogun laced his long, graceful fingers together and made a fist to rest his chin on. He leaned forward that way with his elbows on the table for a moment, studying her, and then sat back. "Let's go with Silver Needles, then? Something new, rare, budding in the early spring . . . for quiet moments."

She nodded but didn't speak as a server came in to take their order. She also didn't protest his selection of the Japanese sweets that were called *wagashi* on the menu, despite that fact that right now she couldn't stomach a thing. He could have at the steamed *manju* cakes filled with sweet red beans. Time had defeated her; two days wasn't long enough to crack a genetic code that had stumped scientists for three decades. She was grasping at straws.

A warm hand covered hers and made her look up.

"Your wolf is ravaging the edge of your menu and about to begin clawing at the finish on the table." Shogun took up her menu and passed it off to the retreating server before covering her hand again.

"I've got a lot on my mind," Sasha said without apology, her tone weary as she extracted her hand from beneath Shogun's warm touch.

"I know this situation is painful, Sasha . . . I didn't want this, no matter what you probably think. Not like this, anyway."

She stared at him hard, sensing for fraud, and found none. That only made her fight tears. "I know," she replied in a quiet rasp, forcing the moisture in her eyes to burn away. "I just don't know what to do—don't know where to begin. Part of me wants to turn over every gravestone in New Orleans to hunt down every Vampire to blame it on, or track every lead to possible demon-infected wolves that might be at large . . . but the evidence is so damning." Sasha rubbed her palms down her face. "In the human world, you can't just condemn a man to death on circumstantial evidence—but in the supernatural world, it's enough." She looked up at Shogun, searching his face for answers. "I was raised human, so my gut and my spirit . . . even my wolf can't make peace out of what could happen in two moons."

"They won't put Hunter to instant death unless he demon-wolf transitions, Sasha. If he doesn't, there has to be a fair trial, just like in the human world." Shogun's eyes never left hers as he spoke, and in the depths of his intense brown irises there seemed to be infinite compassion. "But I don't know how to tell you to manage your fear beyond a slow cup of tea with someone who cares," he added softly. "Waiting for the outbreak to happen or not is the worst."

"You sound like you've been here before," she said in a quiet tone, her gaze intense as she waited for corroboration of her hunch.

"I have . . . it's a genetic scourge in my kind. There's not one of us who hasn't had to worry over a beloved family member or friend. At one time or another we've all sat vigil for someone we loved, hoping for the best. Sometimes it was just a bad night and the individual was wrongly diagnosed or accused . . . then, again, sometimes, Sasha, it's simply a blood-red moon."

"I feel so helpless," she whispered, then sent her gaze out the unscreened window that overlooked the peaceful garden. Sunlight poured into their sitting space, bathing them both as she carefully chose her words. If only she could lift the burdens that were weighing down her soul. Yet it was a dream to think that she'd ever float free of it all. Soldiers didn't get to do Zen or bliss; wasn't in the contract. She'd never be worry-free like the sunbeams that were dancing along the carved shutters to cast prisms of shadows on the privacy screen guarding their booth.

"I don't have answers, and I need them fast," she finally admitted. "While I wait I have to gather evidence, but the other part of me wants to go to the holding area to just be there when it happens, if it happens, to do what has to be done—but *I've gotta* see it with *my* own eyes or I'll never rest, I'll always have the question . . ."

Sasha allowed her words to trail off. She hated feeling vulnerable, and she instantly pulled back everything she was about to say. Half of her wanted to go right to Hunter and simply hold him and weep. Another part of her wanted to go to Silver Shadow and beg the elderly shaman to conjure whatever medicine-man magic he could. The more rational human side of her, which she'd come to learn was ignorance masking itself behind arrogance, wanted a quick scientific fix—a magic pill—which was as absurd as hoping for someone to wave a magic wand.

Then there was the soldier in her that was pissed off, ready for war, and wanted to simply kill something and kill it good for the offense of giving Hunter the contagion. From the empathy in Shogun's eyes, she knew she didn't even have to say it; staring at him was like seeing into the soul of a fellow veteran. He'd obviously lived this pain before, as he'd told her, and knew the deal.

But she held all of that emotion in check, biting

her bottom lip when their server arrived. The young woman carried a bamboo tray laden with delicate ceramic Gaiwan painted with Dragon and Phoenix motifs set beside thin porcelain plates and a steaming, covered bamboo basket filled with fluffy white sweet cakes.

She had no appetite; reality and her partial confession had stolen it all. Sasha watched dispassionately as their quiet, efficient server set down carved chopsticks beside each plate and arranged the covered teacups before them. Next she set down a kiri wood trivet and hustled out of the room to return with a pretty Dragon-and-Phoenix glazed teapot to set upon it. As a finishing touch, their server removed a small jade bell from her kimono pouch and subtly left it by Shogun's hand. Somehow Sasha could tell from the demure smile the young woman offered that unless someone rang the bell, she wouldn't be back. New awareness thrummed through her, adding to her silent panic.

The young woman bowed slightly, accepting Shogun's nod and bow as her cue that all was well and she could be excused. Sasha watched the server retreat and discreetly secure the recessed privacy screen fully closed. Then she watched Shogun go through the painstakingly slow ritual of lifting the lid from his ceramic Gaiwan, breathing in the aromatic fragrance of the tea, and serving them each a steamed cake using his chopsticks.

"When you came to me at The Fair Lady, you had a request pressing against your spirit," Shogun said carefully as he went about the task of securing the woven bamboo top back onto the steamer basket.

"Yes, I did," she said, finally taking the lid off her Gaiwan to allow the heat to rise from her tea.

"I know you love him; that's been established and is respected. So tell me, what is my role?"

She stared at Shogun without blinking, watching him lift the delicately painted cup to his mouth with two fingers from each hand.

"I need a blood sample."

She watched him pause, but then fluidly continue bringing the edge of the china to his lips, evenly sipping from it before setting it down again.

"Am I a suspect now?"

"No," she said, shaking her head. "I'm a fool. I'm grasping at straws."

He motioned toward her tea, his eyes haunted. "Have a sip and let us speak as friends, if nothing else, then. Explain."

She nodded, bringing the tea to her lips to taste the subtly elegant flavor. Yeah—she owed him an explanation, even though she hated to have to go into it. "The tea is very good," she said with a weary sigh.

"It is, but now we're past word dances . . . now that you've asked me for blood."

He sat back. She set down her cup.

"You're right. It's not for what you think. We need to find a cure."

Seeming intrigued, he leaned forward. "We've already been hunted, studied as monsters, and this cure seems futile, even if you find it. If he's done what it appears . . . then?"

She raked her fingers through her hair. "I know. If he murdered that boy, then who cares?" She suddenly sat forward, hating the sound of the words that echoed in her mind and constricted her heart. "But what if, just like last time, it wasn't him—what if it was a Vampire setup or the handiwork of a demon-door escapee? If so, then . . . I don't know." She sat back and picked up her teacup and took a deep swig from it, briefly closing her eyes. "Like I said, I'm grasping at straws. Human scientists have only gotten their hands on, and studied, demon-infected Werewolf blood. They've never seen the healthy version. I want our lab to do comparison tests with that and Shadow blood . . . I'm looking for something, *anything*."

"If Hunter was set up, and he wasn't the one who gutted the human, then you hope to develop a vaccine for him and maybe others, to ensure that there's never a question in the future," Shogun said calmly, picking up a small, fluffy steamed cake and biting into it. "There's clearly a lot on the line here, which makes the dilemma interesting. High stakes."

Sasha briefly stared at the gooey sweet center in the dessert and then let her gaze sweep Shogun's glistening mouth as he chewed. "Yes," she murmured, closing her eyes. He was going to play hardball.

"There is nothing wrong with hope, Sasha. All men have hope in the face of seemingly impossible odds . . . that's what keeps us going. I suspect this is also true of the females of our species."

Shogun's voice had bottomed out on a gravelly murmur, and one look into his eyes told her they were back to word dancing. She took up a sweet cake and bit into it, allowing the chewy confection to cover her tongue while thinking, deciding. Was the long shot even worth it? The fallout from this could be disastrous.

"I need you," she said quietly, admitting defeat in their stalemate.

He gave her a sad smile and took up his tea. "How should I respond to that, Sasha? There's no politically correct way to dance around that remark." He took a deep swig from his Gaiwan and set it down, wincing as though he'd set down a shot of whiskey. "I need you, too."

Another stalemate. She nodded, sipping her tea as her shoulders slumped. "Okay. Name your terms," she said flatly, just wanting to get the whole thing over with.

He leaned forward and frowned. "Never like that," he said between slowly extending upper and lower canines, and then sat back.

"I'm sorry," she said quietly, truly sad that she'd offended him.

"You can have a vial of blood, Sasha," he said, clearly annoyed, "but leave me my dignity, at the very least."

"I am really sorry, Shogun," she said, dropping her head into her hands. "That was screwed up . . . said in all the wrong way . . . and you definitely didn't deserve that. I'm just stressed to the limit." She looked up to see him staring out the window, a muscle in his jaw pulsing.

"Is my kind so revolting to you that—"

"No," she said quickly, cutting him off and leaning forward. She waited until Shogun's gaze met hers before pressing her point. "It has nothing to do with anything like that. It's a matter of honor. Hunter is in prison, awaiting possible execution. I'm the only one, other than his grandfather, who's truly in his corner on this side of the silver-coated bars."

"He's a lucky man," Shogun said, his tone slightly bitter as he took another angry sip of tea.

"My head is so messed up right now, I can't even go there . . . and there's a part of me that's already grieving, trying to prepare myself for the worst. Then there's another part of me that's scared to death."

"You're afraid of me?" Hurt and shock muted Shogun's voice and haunted his eyes.

"Hell yes," she said quickly in a hissing whisper, sitting forward even farther and now talking with her hands. "I'm afraid that if I ever crossed that invisible line between us to do a casual exchange, I might not be able to find the boundary again. And if it turns out that Hunter didn't commit the crime and is released, then what? World War Three in the streets between Shadow Wolf and Werewolf Clans with lots of human collateral damage and Vampires having an I-told-you-so field day—all started over bullshit behind the pursuit of a woman who is conflicted? Yeah, that's enough to be afraid of—because wolves deal in absolutes. There is nothing *casual* about that."

Sasha sat back and sent her gaze out the window in search of any serenity she could find. "Never happen. Not a war on my watch caused by a stupid political mistake on my part. I can't even consider the ramifications of having a new lover until I bring closure one way or another to this case . . . until I know what's

happening with Hunter. So for the record, my trepida-
tion and lackluster attitude aren't about prejudice—
they're about reality. Everything I've just mentioned
is a real enthusiasm damper, all right."

"But unless I'm confused, you were still willing
to give your body to me in fair trade for a vial of my
blood," Shogun said slowly, his tone mellow and
thought-filled.

Oh, my, God . . . men. Sasha closed her eyes. She
didn't want to deal with the fine points of this issue,
didn't want to really delve into the complex layers of
emotions that striated this entire scenario, wasn't trying to deal with the thing that had always been there
but never fully explored between them. And the way
Shogun's calm, professorial response caused her
face to burn as she listened to him take a sip of his
tea made her crazy. Hearing him restate the barter so
bluntly really made it sound as bad as it was. Then
again, maybe the burn was coming from his intense
gaze . . . which she was sure she'd meet if she took
her eyes off the Roji garden.

"Yes," she finally whispered. "If it came to that."

"It won't," he said quietly. "Because you'd hate me
forever and that's not what I want . . . even though, at
this moment, I'm not sure that I care."

She looked at him hard now, wanting him to understand the tightrope she was balancing on. "More
than even your blood, I need your friendship for the
long haul. Our alliance has to stay intact while we
sort this all out . . . especially if it goes to trial at
the UCE. We have to keep a united front, but any
impropriety on my part sensed by the Shadow

Clans—or for that matter yours—will cause dissension in the ranks."

"Then how would sleeping with me to get my blood have kept that from happening in the first instance? This is so contrived, Sasha." Shogun took another sip of tea, but this time she could see the slight tremble in his hands as he did so.

"I don't know," she muttered and sent her gaze back out the window, feeling foolish when he swallowed a badly concealed smile. She'd never been a femme fatale, had never learned any tricks from the school of Mata Hari, and they sure didn't teach that at NORAD.

"I've never bargained like this before," she added with a disgusted grumble. "So I guess I botched the effort—my bad. I just didn't know that you'd go along with this for . . . oh, forget it."

"No," Shogun said, leveling his gaze at her. "I don't want to forget it—I want to clearly understand. You were hoping we'd have a conversation that would possibly lead to a discreet exchange that would never be mentioned again."

"Yeah, I guess, something like that." She focused on a bright pink clump of azaleas outside.

"Therefore, you should have been afraid, very afraid—because I would have done everything in my power to blur the lines, to ensure you'd remain conflicted and that you could never find that boundary between us and the so-called right thing again. Your wolf instincts were correct, Sasha. I would have been discreet and never told a soul. You know me that well, and I am honored that you do. However, I don't

think a onetime event would ever sate the hunger between us. That, *I know,* is a real beast . . . since it
frightens us both. And once escaped, then you'd be
correct. At some point, there'd be war between men.
But I would never place an ally under such duress for
a simple vial of blood. I have nothing to hide."

She slowly dragged her gaze from the window.
For a moment the smoldering, unspoken question in
Shogun's eyes stopped her breath.

"Then, for such a huge favor, what do you want?
I'm not trying to offend you. I just want to know."
She waited, watching him slowly inhale and exhale
as though finding it hard to pull in air.

"I want a permanent alliance, friendship . . . respect," he murmured, his gaze becoming heavy-
lidded as he sat forward and took up one of her hands.
"For you to come to me without an agenda and of
your own volition one day or night for more than
something casual, once you have closure with this
other tragic situation. For you to allow what has been
budding for a long time to be handpicked and satisfy-
ing, and rare, and gently steeped, never rushed."

The heat from his hand and the gentle brush from
the pad of his thumb grazing her knuckles radiated
warmth up her arm and throughout her belly. But it
was the look in Shogun's eyes that both frightened
and drew her.

"I don't know how this is all going to play out.
There are things I can't promise, because the future is
dicey. But you have my respect, an alliance that is un-
shakable, friendship, and a promise that if I ever

come to you like this again, it will be without an agenda."

His unblinking gaze captured hers. He swallowed hard, and she couldn't help stare at his Adam's apple and allow her gaze to trail down his throat. Sudden heat had spread from her belly to create moist longing between her legs. Horrified, she tried to pull her hand away from his, only to meet vise-like resistance.

"Don't stop the dance now," he murmured, his voice raw with passion. "I've never experienced this."

Almost afraid of what she might see, Sasha glimpsed the rice paper screen as Shogun closed his eyes, tightened his grip on her hand, and then clutched the edge of the table. Her shadow had betrayed her. Repressed emotions, tension, fatigue, grief, the need for comfort had all blurred the lines and started something she was unprepared to finish.

"The inner wolf never lies. You had to want this as much as I did," he gasped, dropping his head back, beginning to pant as bristles of blue-black hair began to sprout from his clean-shaven scalp.

"Our wolves can't do this," she said in a tense whisper, watching an onyx wash of silky black hair flow down over his shoulders to hang down his back. "We have to stop."

"I cannot completely shift until the full moon allows, but I can't stop my wolf from feeling yours, just like you cannot lie to yours about not wanting to feel mine," he said in a pained murmur between extended canines. "Oh . . . Sasha, what *is* this? You want my blood then open an artery. You asked me what I wanted—it was this—you wanting me like this, too."

Frozen, she watched her human female shadow on the thin privacy screen entwined with his across the room, though she'd never moved. His shadow held hers as her legs encircled his waist and she straddled his lap, his hands sliding up her back to find her hair while her face nuzzled his neck. Her shadow double on the screen grasped his shoulders, beginning to move to a slow rhythm that left no doubt in her mind that a line had been crossed, blurred, and several bridges burned.

"We can't do this!" she practically shrieked, and then dropped her voice. "I can't shadow-dance with you, it's not—"

"Oh, God, I'm not doing it," he said in a deep, agonized rumble, lifting his body now to each of her phantom shadow thrusts. "You are. Weres don't own this capacity, only Shadows do."

Panic made her clothes stick to her body. Unwanted desire created a confusing tangle of guilt, excitement, and horror that was impossible to sort out as Shogun's male wolf scent consumed her reason. As she glanced like a madwoman from him to the screen, the erotic display of both wrecked her.

"You have to let go of my hand," she said after the few seconds she needed to gather her wits, now realizing that his touch had triggered the outrageous chain of events. Everything else she'd been coping with had probably set off the madness, too, bringing her deepest subconscious desires to the surface while pulling his human-image shadow into an unwitting dance with hers.

He shook his head, his eyes pleading for her to understand, begging her to let him finish. As she glimpsed the screen, she did understand—the problem was, it was indecent. Yet he'd also asked for his dignity to be preserved early on in the conversation.

If he'd just let go of her hand long enough to break the shadow-to-shadow connection of his desire fueling hers and back again, her inner wolf could calm down enough to stop the shadow dance . . . her shadow would have the wherewithal to stop the inevitable embarrassment he'd endure with a wet spot in his khakis. However, he would be a tortured man. There'd be no getting around that, but at least he'd leave the tea salon and save face.

Leaning forward, halfway across the table, and now balancing on her pillow on her knees, she tried to corner whatever rational part of Shogun's mind was left. But as soon as he felt her lever in his direction, his grip tightened on the hand he'd been fiercely holding, his free hand was in her hair, his mouth on hers, creating a hot seal of dueling tongues before he broke their kiss, threw his head back, and moaned.

A hard shudder immediately claimed her. Shogun's stifled howl masked by a low moan sent a pulse of need through her that she didn't want to own. She couldn't look at the screen, no longer had to; she could feel her shadow's renegade spirit running roughshod over her will, her conscience, everything she knew was right or wrong. Shogun's touch melted her with searing caresses through their shadows, his skin burning against hers despite the actual distance separating their bodies.

Please don't make me do this, she begged her inner wolf—but there was no negotiating with the primal force once it had been unleashed. The stone-cut contours of his chest grazed her nipples with every undulating tide of her shadow against his. Gasping as the awareness strengthened until she could almost feel him inside her, she moved in torrid shadow waves while his hands palmed her ass, opening her wider on every upthrust until tears stung her eyes. Their bodies never touched, didn't have to—their shadows crossed boundaries for them.

She knew he could feel the realness of it all, even in shadow context; the agony in his startled expression told her he did as he struggled with sensations slamming him on two planes of existence at once.

Mouth open, tears streaming down his handsome, bronze face as he tried to remain as quiet as possible in a public tea salon—she knew. Her wolf was wild, feral, merciless, savaging his with passion in a shadow dance that he didn't have to tell her he'd never experienced before. His virginity to the shadows was evident in his sweat, in the way he gasped air like a man drowning, in his pulse. The dance had gone well past the point of no return, as had he, and she wouldn't have been cruel enough to let go of his hand to break the connection now. But it had to end.

"Give me your other hand," she murmured, trying to steady her breaths and regain some semblance of self-control.

He lunged for her, clasping her outstretched hand as though she were his lifeline at the edge of a cliff.

"Look at the shadows on the screen, not at me," she said quietly. "They tell the story."

"I don't know if I can," he said in a low, rumbling burst between pants. "This is driving me crazy—I need to hold you, even though . . ."

In a slow, sliding fall forward, she pushed him backward, each knee deftly navigating between lukewarm tea and expensive china, careful not to ring the jade bell. On his back, having tumbled over his pillow, he allowed her body to fuse against his with a groan.

"Look at the shadows," she begged him, kissing his face. "It can't go beyond this and can't happen again."

He nodded swiftly, finally understanding that she was trying to release his pain, was trying to be his friend, his ally without an agenda. The moment he looked, she felt his entire body seize, and her only recourse was to cover his mouth with a crushing kiss and swallow his howl. As soon as he stopped convulsing, she tore her mouth from his, shuddering hard, so they both could breathe.

After a while he stared up at her with sad eyes. "We'd heard about this . . . stories and lies that young males tell each other, always about what they cannot have . . . The forbidden mystique of Shadow females." He tried to force a smile to make it seem like what they'd just experienced was casual and no big deal, but his smile died quietly in the depths of his forlorn expression. "I never knew, never understood the divinity of it."

She moved a long, damp strand of blue-black hair from his face and tenderly cradled his cheek. He nodded and cradled hers.

"I know. Not now . . . not yet," he said sadly.

"Not now, not yet—with the possibility that, if there's been a mistake . . ."

"Then this never happened," he murmured, resigned, and then kissed her.

CHAPTER 8

Clarissa stared at the lab results, disbelieving. As resident psychic it had been easy to commit the treasonable offense of getting password codes to Doc's research. NORAD had thirty years' worth of pure gold, and time wasn't on her side. This was an emergency, she'd reasoned. Getting into Doc's local laptop system in Tulane was a breeze. There was no need to get Winters involved in breaching databases and going past security codes into files where he wasn't authorized. If anyone was going to do time, then it might as well be her.

Doc's time away from the lab with Sasha had provided the window of opportunity . . . it was just that now that she had the data, she didn't know what to do with it. God help her when Sasha brought in a sample of uninfected Werewolf blood. What was she gonna tell the captain—her best friend?

In New Orleans, if a breeze blew, it was thick, humid air that didn't cool. Sasha sat as still as a garden stone waiting for Shogun to come back from the men's room. Sure, it had been easy enough to slip from their screened booth to go to the gift shop to score him a pair of sweats . . . easy enough to hand him the blood-drawing kit that had been stashed in her military jacket pocket as he went to freshen up and change out of the khakis with the very revealing wet spot in them. Yeah. That was the easy part. But when he came back, she hadn't a clue where to begin.

This was *never* supposed to happen.

Something insane had unleashed itself from her subconscious. Maybe she could claim a psychological breakdown. A slow blink was all she allowed in the form of outward distress while pure hysteria was clawing at her guts.

She heard Shogun open the screen but didn't immediately turn to look at him. He came to her side of the table, slid into a squatting spoon fit behind her, and nuzzled her hair, then slipped a vial of blood into her palm. The transaction made her feel like a working geisha—albeit that had everything to do with her state of mind and not his treatment of her.

"I hope you find what you're looking for," he said quietly.

She nodded, her voice muted by despair. "Thank you, Shogun. So do I."

A sense of betrayal put tears in his eyes as he walked with purpose. Hard-soled loafers hit the polished floors of Tulane Hospital, his own footsteps almost foreign to his ears. He was there, but not—as though trapped in an out-of-body experience. A surge of hurt masked as rage made him hasten his steps. That someone he trusted so dearly could have done something like this was beyond his ability to fathom.

Doc leaned on the elevator button. The chopper could take him to the outskirts of where he had to go. From there he could go by jeep and would have to only hope that he wasn't being tailed. The late General Donald Wilkerson trusted no one, had everyone on the PCU team and Project Dog Star under surveillance. Maybe this new general was a little different; their styles were. Part of him still hated his dead boss. Then again, another part of him truly understood the man's philosophy of utter paranoia better now.

Bradley sat in the parlor on a burgundy velvet settee, his gaze sweeping the door, the drapery at the windows, the shelves and mantels loaded with exotic bric-a-brac. Unidentified herbs hung in dried bundles by the windows while crystal wind chimes reflected light through partially opened beveled, leaded glass. The heavy, pungent scents of incense and sage smudge clung to the ancient fabrics in the small, dusty room. Brick dust lined the doorsills. Tiny piles of salt waited silently in the four corners of the room. Pennies littered the floor, a hazard to any vacuuming— which, for reasons of the esoteric, had obviously never occurred.

"Sir, the Madame can see you now."

Bradley stared at the gaunt man with a sallow complexion, wondering if he'd once been a Zombie.

The only thing that banished the image was his perfect, genteel diction.

With a simple gracious nod, Bradley followed the man past a set of floor-to-ceiling burgundy-hued velvet drapes that led into a narrow dining room. An elderly woman sat in quiet repose at a small oval table before a crystal ball.

He studied the lines in her burnt-cinnamon face, and the bluish gray tint in hazel eyes that matched her bluish gray hair, searching for honesty. She offered a yellow-toothed smile and bade him to sit. Despite his dark arts expertise, being in Madame LaMonde's séance room was still a surreal experience. If she'd had on a church hat, she would've looked like a thousand other senior citizens he'd seen taking a stroll home on a Sunday morn.

But Madame LaMonde was renowned as a seer and conjure woman. Word on the streets in the Big Easy held that her place was a way station, of sorts, where spirits came and vented their concerns. Yet her frail composure, they said, was not to be taken lightly. Madame LaMonde had hoodoo not even the Vampires messed with.

Still, he couldn't make his mind sync up with the petite visage before him. There was no Gypsy scarf or door-knocker-size hoop earrings to give her stereotypical character, only an elegant pair of small pearl studs placed just so in her sagging earlobe skin. She wore a plain pink cashmere sweater with pearl buttons over her shoulders that was slightly too large for her frame. Her blouse was a neat white shell that housed her small, sagging breasts; beyond her earrings, she wore no other jewelry. That was all he could notice without seeming rude, and her genuine smile made him not want to appear that way. Were it not for the crystal ball on the table and a deck of Tarot cards, the meeting might have been with an elderly aunt for a cup of late-afternoon tea.

"Many, many questions . . . so many that the cards are restless," she said, motioning for him to sit down.

"Thank you for seeing me on such short notice, Madame LaMonde," Bradley said in his most polite voice.

She gave him a casual shrug. "If the spirits would have denied you, then we wouldn't be meeting. They decide, not me."

He had no answer for her.

She shoved the deck of well-worn cards across the table toward him with arthritic hands. "Shuffle them and cut them," she commanded. "Let your energy seep in, then we'll see what we have here."

He gave the cards his best casino shuffle and returned them to her.

She chuckled and clucked her tongue. "You work with the arts, have seen that which you cannot explain, but still have doubts. Too much education."

Again, he didn't respond to her accurate charge, though he felt badly that anything in his expression might have conveyed disbelief. But as if she'd read his mind, she gave him a kindly wave of her hand to let him know there'd been no offense.

"You know they ate that boy. He wasn't mauled,"

she said casually, laying the cards out on a Celtic cross spread. "There's a difference between being eaten and being attacked."

"Yes, there is," Bradley said in a noncommittal tone.

She glanced up and gave him a sharp look. "You know what kind of creature eats flesh. It weren't no dog. So why are you here?"

Bradley held her unfaltering gaze and leaned forward. "We need to know which one did it," he said quietly. "So there's no tragic mistaken identity."

"Ah!" Seeming satisfied, Madame LaMonde sat back for a moment and rubbed her bony chin, then studied the cards. "That's fair and honorable—just like it says here you are." Without warning she turned her head and frowned, her gaze studying something to her left as she squinted. "Really?" she said toward the empty space and then nodded.

"What, ma'am?" Bradley asked, his gaze following Madame LaMonde's for a moment and then settling on the elderly woman again.

She pointed down at the worn cards on the table, making Bradley lean in to follow her gnarled finger as he stared at the color-faded images. "See here," she said in a whispering hiss. "It's a queen. A female did it. A strong one with deep roots here. There's gonna be a war behind this, has to be. This just didn't set right with folks on the other side." She scattered the cards, flipping over image after image to prove her point.

Bradley sat back slowly, shock almost making it hard for him to breathe. He knew the Tarot well. Saw it, but Madame LaMonde confirmed it. Sasha was a strong female . . . she'd been with a male of the species who was demon-infected.

"She's close, nearby," Madame LaMonde warned. "Will do anything for her lover. There has been a sleight of hand, something was stolen from you—or from around you. Medicine, something important. Be careful these next two nights as the moon goes full."

Bradley closed his eyes. Sasha was close. Loved Hunter, that was obvious. Medicine had been stolen from the lab, and only a few people knew how and where the drugs were stashed. Sasha's mother was from New Orleans. A soft, pain-filled murmur left Bradley's lips. "Thank you for your trouble today, Madame. I've heard enough."

Sasha slid between the trees, shadow-hopping, catching passing shadows at a breakneck speed, her goal singular—she had to get the blood sample to Clarissa. After what had just transpired, she had to know for sure . . . had to get the only link to a possible cure into her best friend's hands and then had to go north to wait with the pack.

Winters stared at his computer screen. Warning code scrolled a silent alarm. After he'd almost faced court-martial for high treason when Vampires mind-stunned him and used him for a retina scan to break into NORAD's labs, he'd layered on so many additional fail-safes that no one could possibly enter the project's sensitive data banks without leaving a back-door trail. And the back door had just sounded.

His fingers flew across the keys, following, saving chunks of evidence as he burned it to a flash drive. How could Doc be accessing data from a system here when he was at NORAD? Winters watched the streaming files flying by on the screen—all genetic information going back to the beginning. Then it stopped.

Fear made him stand up slowly and glance around. He shoved the flash drive into his pocket. Although it was still daylight and couldn't be Vampires, an infected Shadow Wolf could come out of nowhere and rip him apart . . . or if he ran down the hall to the possible source of the breach, Doc's office, what if a Werewolf who had yet to transform was there waiting for him? Even in human form the demon-infected SOBs were strong as hell and meat-eaters.

He looked around again and mopped his brow. Clarissa was nowhere to be found, Bradley was out in the streets gaining intel; Woods and Fisher were on ammo-collection detail and due back shortly. Winters opened his desk drawer and pulled the cool metal of a Glock into his grip. "C'mon, guys, get back here quick . . . where are you?"

Sasha almost fell into Clarissa's arms from a shadow jump, but covered her mouth quickly with a hard press of her palm across her mouth before she could scream. She dropped the shopping bag that had her dress blues in it the moment Clarissa relaxed, and then opened her hand to fold the test tube of blood into it.

"Pure Werewolf blood from an uninfected host."

"Jesus H. Christ, Trudeau," Clarissa said in a low hiss, pulling Sasha deeper into the hallway alcove. "How'd you—"

"If I tell you, I've gotta kill you," Sasha said with a sad smile. "But it's the real thing."

Clarissa just stared at her for a moment.

"What?" Sasha whispered, becoming more alarmed as she stared at Clarissa's pained expression.

"I went back into the NORAD databases . . ."

"You did what?" Sasha said, now raking her hair with alarm. "If you tip off the brass—"

"I had to," Clarissa whispered in a harsh tone without apology. "You're expecting me to do in two days what Doc couldn't even do in three decades?"

"Okay, you're right, you're right,' Sasha said, beginning to pace. "What did you find out?"

"I first looked at mitochondrial DNA, the stuff that's passed from the maternal side, looking for similarities in genetic markers among you, Hunter, Crow Shadow, and even Doc. That would give me a stable human sample—Doc; a full-blooded Shadow Wolf—Crow Shadow; a half human, half Shadow Wolf—you; and a Shadow who has contagion in his system—Hunter. I was trying to see what genetic code switches were turned on and what were turned off. I knew Doc had to analyze this info, benchmarking it all against the infected Werewolf samples he'd had from Rod on back."

"Yeah, yeah, and?" Sasha said, growing impatient.

"And nothing," Clarissa said, dragging her fingers through her short bob. When Sasha's shoulders slumped, she held on to Sasha's arm. "Then I went the other route, through the markers on the Y chromosome, the male side of the equation . . . that's where I found a coalescence point that I keep going over and over, but it's blowing my mind."

Sasha grabbed Clarissa by both arms and pushed her against the wall, nerves at the breaking point. "Tell me. How bad is it?"

"I don't know if this is good news or bad." Clarissa met Sasha's eyes with her own, and the confusion in them made Sasha slowly back off. "I don't know how this affects Hunter at all . . . it may not even be relevant, and I'm not even sure that I have the right to tell you."

Almost ready to shake Clarissa, Sasha hugged herself. "Tell me."

"Crow Shadow is your brother . . . different mothers, same father."

Sasha blinked. She'd heard Clarissa, but the information took a moment to sink in. Now it made sense, the eerie connection she'd had to him . . . the way she could sense where he'd been abducted, where the Vampires had held him draining his blood in a French Quarter town house. Then pure horror filled her and she grabbed Clarissa's arms again. "Tell me, oh, my God . . . tell me I'm not Hunter's—"

"No, no," Clarissa said quickly. "You're not his sister or even a cousin."

Sasha let go of Clarissa and then rubbed her palms down her face, breathing into them slowly to keep from hyperventilating. "Okay, okay, I can deal with being Crow's sister. He's good people, we know Doc made me in a lab from donor sperm from the Shadow Clan." She searched Clarissa's face, seeing there was more.

Both women stared at each other for what seemed like endless minutes.

"Sasha," Clarissa said quietly, "Doc Holland didn't get donor cells from the Shadow Clan. He's part Shadow Wolf himself, and is both you and Crow's father."

"How long have we known each other?" Xavier Holland demanded. His voice carried on the cool April breeze and echoed through the mountain clearing. "Silver Shadow or Silver Hawk, whichever form you chose. Wolf or man, you owe me an audience. That at the very least!"

"You are right, old friend," a tired voice said behind Doc.

Holland spun and confronted his friend of many years. He was wrapped in a ceremonial blanket with traditional headdress.

"Before I die, I do owe you an explanation."

"I don't want you to die," Doc said, pointing at him and shouting. "I want you to tell me why you pilfered meds from my lab and didn't tell me! Why you wouldn't let me help if your grandson was rejecting the cure!" His voice broke and he dropped his arm in defeat. "Why? After all these years."

"Even in your righteous indignation you use the

words softly . . . *pilfer*, not *steal*. You and I are like brothers. That I betrayed your trust is something that weighs heavily on my heart."

"Then why would you not tell me . . . I could have tried something else, could have—"

"You are half human. You were raised by them, and incline more to their ways. This blood moon is the business of Shadow Wolf Clans, and I could not bear to see my longtime friend consumed by the tragedy of it. The pain in my spirit is enough to bear alone, but to give that to you would not have been the way of the wolf."

"Silver Hawk," Doc said, opening his arms, "something has gone wrong. I would have helped. Give me a chance! You know my history, you know my honor!"

"I do," Silver Hawk said quietly, tears shimmering in his eyes.

"Then remember the shunning that had a pain you can never imagine. I was denied a wife in this pack because of my heritage—half human, half Shadow Wolf . . . the kind that could not turn—likened to a damned familiar! Impotent to the change."

Silver Hawk closed his eyes as Doc's voice fractured in the forest.

"My own Shadow father abandoned my human mother, ashamed, and slipped into the shadows and was gone . . . *years* it took me to find my way home. Years! And based on my mother's so-called delusional outbursts that landed her in an institution, I followed the legend—I had to understand DNA. I needed to break the code in it for the sake of my own sanity. There's always a good outcome from the pain levied by the Great Spirit, you once said . . . and my knowledge helped this pack at an auspicious time, when your newborn grandson was convulsing. Tell me that wasn't Divine Providence of the Great Spirit! Tell me that was not my role as a familiar!"

Silver Hawk turned his face to the sky but did not open his eyes, allowing a rivulet of tears to leak from the corners of them. "So much pain, so many mistakes."

"My loving Shadow Dove was not a mistake while I was here working on your grandson. That is my job, yes, as a human doctor, but also as a member of this pack—to save a clan heir to the North American alpha was my responsibility. Is still my responsibility! But I was betrayed then, as now . . . My son was passed off as a beta, my mate was so ashamed she'd been with me. She would have rather seen Crow raised as a beta male, *lied* and said he was created by a full-blooded beta Shadow Wolf rather than a half-breed like me . . . a Shadow who couldn't shape-shift—and therefore shunned. All that intrigue so she could keep Crow with her. In the long run, I didn't blame her; in fact, I eventually applauded her guile once my ego got out of the way, because it saved my son from my fate. So I listened, I understood, and I bled from that truth told too many years too late to correct. We've known each other a long time, Silver Hawk. But you swore to me after I learned that truth that never again would you keep me in the dark about clan politics. You promised!"

"This isn't clan politics," Silver Hawk said quietly.

"It is not an attempt to keep you an outsider this time. It was a foolish attempt to spare you the grief of the ugliest part of our job as demon hunters. To put one of your own to death . . . with Sasha as your daughter, her my daughter-in-law, will break your heart three ways."

Silver Hawk leveled an empathetic gaze toward Doc. "You lost them both—Shadow Dove and Sasha's mother . . . one to a pack, one to an infected Were. Now you should break your daughter's heart and have to accept what her mate has become? Now you would have to know and live with the knowledge that another infected wolf could slaughter your daughter—who would not leave him until the last . . . until maybe it was too late. This would not be a lab accident at NORAD, the way Sasha's beloved mother died, Xavier. You and I both know this would probably happen when Sasha was alone with Hunter, trying in vain to help him to the bitter end. I had to give my grandson the medicine to stave off the inevitable long enough to keep her safe and to have him contained, while saving your sanity. This very thing drove your mother out of her mind—the human psyche is a fragile thing. And you wanted me to tell you all of this to break your heart again? No. After all you have endured, I would spare you that as your friend."

Doc looked away as the tree line around Silver Hawk became blurry. He was no longer angry, just suddenly very, very tired and his voice a mere rasp. "It was my decision to endure it, just as it is my sanity to lose. If Hunter was asking you to steal meds for him, then Sasha was already at risk. Don't you see that now?"

"Hunter never asked me to steal the medicine; I knew he needed it and did so on my own. He is no thief. I lied and told him that I had your permission when I saw that it was not working. Therefore, know that it is because I love you as my dear friend, who fought valiantly with human medicine and saved that boy's life, that I tried . . . but things have gone too far. I will deliver the death sentence, not his enforcer, not his mate, not his doctor, not the human military or a tribunal of Vampires. Me. I will take his life in the honorable way, and then I will leave my heartbreak in the mountain snow."

Tears stood in Doc's eyes and then fell. He shook his head. "Until the final silver bullet goes into his skull, let me try."

CHAPTER 9

Numb, Sasha watched Clarissa slowly walk down the hall in the opposite direction from the locker rooms. It took all of her strength to finally push her body off the wall where she'd slumped. She had to get to the hospital employee showers, put on her own clothes, ditch the telltale outfit from Chaya, and then put on the amber-and-silver amulet that would protect and guide her over the great distances she needed to travel through the shadow lands to reach the vast Uncompahgre forests.

Later, she and Doc could square up history. Before she said a word to Crow Shadow to acknowledge him as her biological half brother, she needed to understand just how much of this whole travesty Doc had revealed to anyone else, much less her. Things were spinning out of control; her entire life was yet again a series of half-truths. But she couldn't dwell on any of that now.

Sasha forced herself to hurry into the locker room, where she flung open her private locker to shove in her uniform and extract jeans, a T-shirt, Timberlands, and a gun. The outfit from Chaya went in the trash as she balled up her clothes on a bench, hiding the weapon. She jumped into a hard, hot spray of water and lathered quickly with shower gel.

Right now, she had to get to Hunter. Clarissa could reach her with a mental shout-out if anything critical had been discovered in Shogun's blood sample. Sasha walked forward on unsteady legs, grabbing a fresh towel from the wire hospital rack. Life as she'd known it had changed again.

She slipped into the teahouse men's room, a quiet blur of stealth. The scent of Shogun's sex wafted from the bamboo trash hamper where, upon inspection, she found his discarded khakis. A low growl of fury coated her throat and narrowed her gaze. She carefully rolled the pants in the plastic hamper liner to take with her and then left as quickly as she'd come in, but this time through the window.

"Dear brother, I trust from your change of attire that your diplomatic talks with the she-Shadow went well?" Lei said with a droll smile, watching her brother enter their suite and head straight for the bar. "Or not."

"Sometimes I despise you, Lei," Shogun said with a low, warning growl.

"I'm hurt," she said in a falsely contrite tone. "Although you despise me at times, I have always had your best interests at heart as your sister, and for you as our respected alpha leader. It is I who ensures your best interests and the best interests of the clan at all costs . . . I was even the one who suggested a meeting between you and Sasha Trudeau . . . now I am the culprit for any unfortunate circumstances that occurred during your meeting? How so? What went wrong?"

She looked him up and down and knit her brows until he looked away. "Did the she-Shadow attack you? Did you two fight? Is this the meaning of the change in clothing?" Lei bowed and lowered her gaze, hiding a sly smile. "Dear brother, no wonder you are annoyed at me. I apologize for the misunderstanding. And here I had so hoped she'd allow you to love her to strengthen the alliance."

Shogun turned away from his sister, abandoning the drink he'd been preparing, and stalked into his bedroom, slamming the door behind him.

"Holy shit," Winters said wild-eyed as Bradley came through the door of the lab. "Where've you been, dude? It's getting dark outside."

"Gathering intel, like I was ordered," Bradley said in a flat tone. "What the hell's the matter with you?"

"Somebody downloaded a shitload of classified project files while Doc was gone, and I can prove it wasn't Doc," Winters said nervously glancing around.

Bradley approached his workstation setup with caution. "You tell Clarissa, Woods, or Fisher yet?"

"No," Winters said, blotting his brow with a swipe of his arm. "But I'd feel a whole lot better if Sasha or our guys with the big guns were here right now."

"Sit down," Bradley said with a pained expression. He landed a heavy palm on Winters's shoulder. "Raise

Woods and Fisher on comm. Rissa, too—but not the captain. At least not yet. I heard some things in the street from a fairly reliable source. That, and what you've just told me, gives me the shivers."

Sasha looped the thick silver chain over her neck. As an afterthought, she briefly ran the pad of her thumb across the ancient etchings that were cut deeply into the huge hunk of sacred amber dangling from it. Just staring at it made her sad; Hunter hadn't been able to come near the amulet in the last week as he fought off the contagion—a piece of history from his clan handed down to champion alpha leaders throughout the generations. If he could no longer wear it, she had to return both amulets to Silver Hawk. Maybe she was no longer worthy to wear hers, either. In fact, after what had transpired at the teahouse she knew she wasn't.

"Great Spirit guide me," Sasha whispered, folding her free palm over the amulet she wore. "Take me to someone who has Hunter's best interest at heart, someone in the shadow lands who can show me the way, make me know the truth, and help save his life."

Clutching Hunter's matching talisman in her fist, Sasha wrapped the chain around her wrist and waited for her amber to begin its mysterious inner glow. She looked around the eerily quiet locker room and leapt into the first shadow she saw.

Sasha tumbled headlong and then flipped in a disorienting spiral to land crouched on her hands and feet, her senses primed the moment she came to a thudding stop on a weird carpet of meadow grass. The darkness was invaded by a strange wash of blue moonlight. Sasha stood slowly, readied for an attack that never came. Instead a beautiful silver-white wolf peered out between a stand of weeping willows. Spanish moss swayed from their thick boughs. The location was familiar but not. She sniffed the air as the she-Shadow lifted her nose and focused her attention just beyond Sasha's shoulder.

Sasha turned slowly. The potential threat made the hairs stand up on her neck. He was huge, majestic, coal black . . . his coat so shiny and dark that it almost appeared navy blue. The big male stalked forward, but his head was lowered in a submissive greeting. The shy female backed away a little, seeming unsure. Sasha remained as still as the stand of trees around her, a silent observer in shadow lands that echoed with ancient spirits. The scent and surrounding foliage slowly became familiar—New Orleans.

The moment the shy female transformed into her human self, Sasha covered her mouth to hold back the gasp. It was Hunter's mother. Her fragile beauty was breathtaking, and all Sasha could do was stare. The large male wolf who circled the woman's legs and then became man was not the beta male she'd previously seen cowering in the shadows. He was not the male Silver Hawk had blown away for allowing his daughter to be ravaged by a beast. This male looked like Shogun's body double, but a head taller and three shades darker.

Sasha backed away as the pair embraced; then she turned fully away, not sure she wanted to see what intimacies the spirit realm revealed. But as she stood mute, deciding, the temperature around her suddenly dropped. The instant climate change spun her back around, as did a feral argument between the huge black wolf and a new, vicious, golden-amber female wolf. A new scent stung her nostrils. Infected Were-wolf.

She backed up quickly and took cover, surprised to see that the foliage was gone. Her spine hit a carved pillar that was no longer a tree, causing her weapon to dig into her skin. She was trapped in a deep cavern, some underground lair. Gorgeous silk fabrics in reds and shimmering gold tones ensconced teakwood Asian furnishings. The gossamer drapes swayed in the places that the Spanish moss had just occupied only moments prior. From what she could tell, it looked as though she'd entered a sultan's tent beneath the earth while two wolves at extreme odds circled and snarled. One was infected; one was not. The tension between them was so thick she could taste it. One would soon lunge, instinct told her that, and she prepared to get out of the way, moving with them. Then something changed in the spirit journey.

The man stood before an exotic Asian beauty with tears shimmering in his eyes. He backed away from her as though she had the plague. She laughed, but the sound was harsh and hollow. Sasha moved in closer to follow them through a teahouse garden. Moonlight swept over them as he yelled *no* and drew a long samurai blade on her. A repugnant scent of demon death filled Sasha's nose, making her gag—just as the woman shape-shifted and leapt at the man, tearing at his flesh before jumping to a safe vantage point.

A demon-infected Werewolf threw her head back and howled. The golden-amber wolf then looked at the man and his ripped arm, oblivious to the long gash in her fur, and transformed. She held her shoulder wound laughing, insane, and naked. Her gaze held satisfaction as it assessed his bleeding arm. He dropped to his knees; she flashed an evil smile and faded into the garden. Sasha held her breath as the garden grass beneath her feet gave way to a thick carpet of snow.

Immediately she remembered this spirit journey—she'd taken it with Hunter before. She now knew his mother's wolf form. Saw it all happening again in slow motion.

Two demon-infected werewolves thundered into the pack lands. One was golden-amber, one black as midnight. The Shadow pack in wolf form was no match for a pair of demon-infected Werewolves . . . but the vision had been misinterpreted. The two weren't fighting as a pair. Warning barks rang out from the huge black wolf toward Hunter's mother, even as he struggled with what he'd become. Her husband, the beta male Silver Hawk despised, cowered at the sight of the huge male running headlong toward her. Then the golden-amber wolf broke free of her attackers and the huge male doubled back as though going after her to head her off. But in the chaos, confused Shadow Wolves separated the two. The female was gaining on Hunter's mother, who was now separated from the safety of the pack.

Sasha watched in horror as the big male was cornered and pinned down while mortally savaging many of the Shadow pack in an attempt to save Hunter's mother. History of the battle had been revised in error!

"No! He's trying to help her!" Sasha's voice rang out but the battle raged on all around her, every spirit locked in struggle the way it had occurred and oblivious to her. She knew it was futile; she couldn't get their attention, but the helplessness of watching it all unfold brought tears of frustration to her eyes.

Instinct, fight adrenaline, everything wolf inside her panted hard as her emotions rose and fell with the battle raging in the spirit vapors before her. Everything human in her grabbed her weapon as the deranged she-wolf headed for Hunter's delicate mother. It happened so quickly . . . Silver Shadow was over the ridge with a shotgun in human form. The Werewolf reared up on her hind legs as Hunter's mother stood on hers to meet the threat, her pregnant belly vulnerable. Silver Hawk screamed in horror as he released the silver shell, the shotgun report ripping through the icy glen. Silver Hawk's daughter dropped wide-eyed and stunned. The werewolf yelped, her coat grazed, and she fled. The bloody womb trapping an infant rolled into the snow with his mother's entrails. A huge black wolf cleared the ridge, saw the carnage on the ground, charged Silver Hawk—and this time the old man aimed dead-on, right between the eyes. The massive Werewolf lay dead, slowly transforming back to his human form. Seconds clicked by as Silver Hawk swung around to see his son-in-law cowering. He pulled the trigger and then dropped his weapon, racing toward the convulsing, womb-trapped child in the snow—Hunter.

Then the shadow lands went dark. Once again they became the mist-filled moonlit caverns of spirit and passage. Sasha wiped the sweat from her brow with the back of a forearm, shaken.

She glanced around, allowing the images to settle into her psyche. The exotic beauty looked so much like Lei, it was frightening—but at the same time she knew it wasn't her . . . just as the huge male resembled Shogun, but wasn't. Why was she being shown images of events prior to Hunter's mother's death and his infancy contagion?

The only thing she was sure of now was that it came from a female Werewolf linked to the Asian Werewolf Clan. The bad blood between that clan and North America's Federation had been legendary. Now, perhaps, she better understood why. But the only one she'd be able to trust with this information, the only one who was adept in interpreting the mosaic of spiritual images, was Silver Hawk. Sasha pressed forward, searching for a way out to the other side.

A translucent female image in a ceremonial white doeskin Native American dress stopped Sasha by stepping into her path. Sasha froze. Hundreds of shells and hand-tooled semiprecious stones gently chimed as the spirit moved, her jet-black hair a lustrous wash over her shoulders. A pair of haunted dark brown eyes met Sasha's gaze. She started at the regal features and the shimmering tears. She would know Hunter's mother anywhere now.

"This vision will kill my father. I have dishonored him," the ghost said.

"But your son . . . I don't know what this means or how to help him," Sasha said in an urgent, reverent murmur. "They'll kill him."

His mother closed her eyes. "This is my punishment—the choice of my father's death or my son's."

"What did you do that was so wrong?" Sasha cried out. "Talk to me!"

"I've pitted brother against brother, clan against clan, pack against pack . . . For my heart found its beat after I had taken a sacred vow. So did his. And now we watch the future unravel. One mistake, echoing through the glen. To save my son you must kill my father . . . perhaps even start a war."

Before Sasha could draw a breath the vision was gone. This time she ran, feeling the amulet heat her chest, guiding her to fresh air and moonlight.

Baron Geoff Montague smiled as he looked down at pants rolled in plastic, which were laid on a white linen tablecloth before him. He picked up his goblet of blood and offered the beauty beside him a gentlemanly nod.

"That, my dear, is nitroglycerine. Are you fully aware of the volatile nature of the game you are playing?"

Dana Broussard sat back and took a sip of Dewar's from her short rocks glass, peering at the Vampire over the rim of it. "Darlin', this is New Orleans.

Something like this in the Big Easy is more of an insurance policy than an explosive."

"But what brings you into a private Vampire blood club, unescorted in tense diplomatic times, to give us . . . a DNA sample, for lack of a better term, in khaki?" Geoff smiled and took a leisurely sip from his goblet, flashing her a subtle hint of fangs.

"To the shrewd observer, it could be tribunal evidence to show that there was cause for a dispute between sovereign wolf Federations. Our sources say that a female fed on that human boy . . . we know which male is currently carrying some form of contagion, as do you. Add two and two and do reasonable math, sugah, and we're now looking at his mate as an accessory to his contagion."

Geoff chuckled. "Are the Fae telling fairy tales again?"

"Nooo," Dana said with a soft laugh, licking away the amber fluid of her drink from her lips. "But the Succubae and Incubi are such gossips. Off the record, they say that Vampires might have a hand in tainting medicines that a heartsick old Shadow Wolf might have removed ill advisedly from the lab at Tulane."

"All is fair in love and war," Geoff replied with a nonchalant shrug.

"Especially when the Shadow went into places closed off to Vampires."

"Is it our fault that in his haste the old Shadow Wolf stockpiled the meds he stole in a nonsecured location?" Geoff chuckled and took a deep swig from his goblet. "A little tainted blood never hurt anybody."

"You didn't." Dana laughed hard and covered her mouth. "You had old infected blood from the Dexter incident, yes?"

Geoff gave her a gallant wave of his hand. "Waste not, want not. We cleaned up the streets of New Orleans. There was so much bloodshed and carnage, it would have left the human world simply aghast. I'd like to think of it as recycling, as well as our way to bring closure to an outstanding debt."

"You poisoned the big alpha Shadow?" Her eyes widened and she shook her head, laughing harder. "That is positively *evil.*"

Geoff bowed, "Thank you, milady. But if I hear it again, I will categorically deny the charge."

"What happens in New Orleans stays in New Orleans."

The twosome shared a smile.

"Well," Geoff finally said with an aristocratic, bored sigh, "now that we understand our mutual contempt for the same adversary—and since the enemy of my enemy is my friend—how do we make this mutually profitable as a co-endeavor?"

Dana swirled her drink around in her glass. "The Shadow Wolves are more dangerous to you than we Werewolves are," she said flatly. "They hunt any entity that preys on humans, which includes Vampires who take a human life. But they've been weakened from the last war with Dexter's demon-infected pack and by the fact that they have the North American leader already behind bars. It's just a matter of time before they can pin the murder of that human on his mate. That would leave a clear path for a single ruler of both regions, since there's already an alliance. The Werewolf Federation would be ever so grateful." She gave him a meaningful look.

"Ah . . ." Geoff said, wagging a finger at her and clucking his tongue. "But at the United Council of Entities Conference just last month, the Fae stood with the wolf Federations, as did our feudal members from The Order of the Dragon, the Mythics, Phantoms . . . this is a delicate dance, milady."

"The Fae have never helped us, except that one time at the recent UCE Conference—and they wield no consistent power. Once they see Max Hunter go down, they'll panic and lose cohesion, trying to hedge their bets. The others will fall in line with us after the Fae waffle, like they always do."

"You make an interesting proposal," Geoff said, twirling the stem of his goblet between his fingers. "I'll take it up with my management . . . however, I'm quite surprised to see you at the helm of these negotiations. I would have rather suspected Lei to come to me like this. Help me understand what's created such a sudden change."

Dana's easy, sensual smile faded to a harsh line the same way the coquettish teasing left her eyes. "That," she said, motioning to the pants, "is an insurance policy, like I said. Lei is playing all ends against the middle after having promised me a mate-seat as premier alpha female at Shogun's side. But she's clearly hedging her bets. I saw that this afternoon. However, this new turn of events"—Dana motioned toward the plastic-sealed khakis again—"ensures that my competition goes down with her mate, and my position is left unchallenged. *That's* what's in it for me."

The Vampire set down his goblet and tossed his thicket of brunette tresses over his shoulder, his blue eyes burning with passion for the game. "Tell me, darling," he said with a smooth lilt, leaning forward and lacing his graceful fingers together beneath his chin. "What's in it for *us,* then, pray tell?"

"Let's begin with what's in it for *you,*" Dana said evenly with a wicked smile.

"I like the way you think," Geoff crooned. "Here's to southern belles and steel magnolias." He lifted his goblet.

"You would bring your cartel a foolproof way to divide and conquer the wolf ranks, culling out the most dangerous element within it—the Shadow Clans, in particular, the North American leadership that was responsible for the deaths of François and Etienne, to name a few."

When Geoff sat back, Dana chuckled. "You thought I forgot? Werewolves have long memories, too, and can hold a grudge. Don't you all say fair exchange is no robbery?"

"Indeed."

"Well, Baron . . . This blood feud over a woman, if not addressed, could cause a civil war between the immediately involved packs, one that could last generations. But the larger clan structure wouldn't allow that. They'd see the danger and call for an alliance to restore the peace. Therefore, regardless of the lovers' triangle, the nonguilty party—the wolf who had no hand in the murder of the human, and the wolf who was not contagious—would be the final ruler. This is the way of the wolf in a co-leadership scenario. One wolf goes down, but in order to keep the power base intact at the UCE and the new, fragile alliance in effect . . . regardless of improprieties, the Federations would call for unity under the already selected co-ruling alpha—Shogun. See how simple that is?"

"Brilliantly devious," Geoff said with a sly half smile.

Dana preened at the compliment and leaned in closer, causing the Vampire to follow suit. "Shogun is already positioned to take me as his mate, once the she-Shadow is discredited. The last thing he'd want to do is create a feud with the North American Werewolf Clan—my daddy's people. Once he and I are in power, we'd be very, very grateful if the Vampires would help rebuild after any collateral damage and restrain themselves during the wolf hunt. There'd then be a formal inquiry into the infected, discredited Shadow Wolves' true motives when the Vampire lairs were attacked, which would shift UCE members' opinions, perhaps enough to restore the cartel to equal bench seating again. Backroom deals could be struck—but accord would be facilitated. All this you'd bring to your management—something I'd suggest you'd do *after* your position as the bearer of good news was locked in."

"I am one of the members of the UCE tribunal that will ultimately investigate this human mauling incident," Geoff announced proudly. "They have a wolf rep and a Fae rep. The three largest voting bloc members will make the determination about the contagion and the murder."

"I know," Dana said coolly, staring at Geoff without blinking. "Representative Dugan is the Fae ambassador, since he owns the B and B where they stayed and was thus elected to the investigative tribunal. Anyone from the packs of Shogun's or Hunter's immediate family is exempt from participation for obvious conflict-of-interest reasons. However, since this is New Orleans, sugah, and it is indeed where the atrocity occurred . . ."

"Nooo," Geoff said, beginning to laugh. "This is beyond rich."

"Oh, yes, honey, my daddy is the next in line. And nobody messes with Buchanan Broussard."

CHAPTER 10

"She didn't do it," Clarissa said through her teeth, rounding the desk to get in Bradley's face.

"How do you know?" he asked quietly, his voice sad and no longer accusatory. He glanced at Winters, Fisher, and then finally over to Woods, who was next in command if Sasha went down in battle, before returning his gaze to Clarissa.

"I just know," Clarissa said, daring the others with her eyes to dispute her. "I'm the resident psychic, and I don't care what that old bat you visited in the streets of New Orleans said. Sasha is innocent!"

Spirit time and earth time were so different that she'd become disoriented. Never before had she gone into the shadow land pathways and gotten so turned around that she couldn't find her way out. The amulet in her hand was now so warm that it was almost too painful to hold it. But she'd never leave it here where it could be lost forever.

Quickly unwinding the looping silver chain from

her wrist, she shoved the large piece of amber-and-silver jewelry into her front jean pocket with effort. The moment she looked up again, the huge black wolf from the previous vision quest slowly stepped out of the mist and began to circle her.

Their eyes met; Sasha didn't move. But she was completely prepared to fight, if it came to that.

She turned with the large predator. "Who are you?" she shouted across the divide.

"He's been poisoned," the wolf said, standing on his hind legs.

Sasha shivered at the sight of the Werewolf transformation. The demon-infected ones could talk in wolf form, their hind legs bent back unnaturally for them to stand like men . . . it was sickening to see. The moment the realization hit her that a demon-infected Werewolf was in the shadow lands, Sasha drew her weapon.

"I am no trespasser. The one you seek lurks in the demon realms," the wolf said, eyes glowing gold as he backed into the mist and vanished. "I was slaughtered with right in my soul. Help my second son."

Sasha almost dropped her gun as her arm slowly lowered at the same time her jaw went slack.

Lei glanced up at the moon as she strolled quietly through the teahouse gardens. The sound of flesh ripping and the scent of new blood perfumed the air, luring her. A pair of glowing eyes met hers as the huge she-wolf looked up. Blood splattered her golden-amber coat, and she growled a warning for

Lei to back off until she'd finished with the body. Lei leaned against a granite lantern and waited, staring at the long blond hair on the ground that was now matted with blood and garden soil. A discarded, ripped kimono lay nearby, as though a paper wrapping for the naked body that was being gorged upon. Such a shame . . . so young, but Mother needed to eat.

The female wolf looked up and snuffled the air, her massive fangs glistening with blood. "Where is my son?"

"We both know that it would not be good for Shogun to see you like this."

A low growl threatened the peace.

"He thinks you're dead, dear Mother," Lei said calmly without a hint of fear. "The clan believes the Shadows killed you, too. You know this. So why have you been asking for him of late?"

"Because *that bitch* that has smitten Shogun just went into the shadow lands, and his father's spirit dragged mine there to show her the truth. I took the demon oath and made the ultimate sacrifice to strengthen our rule, not to diminish it—but your father was shortsighted and could never understand this, not even after he transitioned to demon greatness from my bite. Fool!"

Lei ducked as the partially eaten human body whirred past her and landed with a slick thud against the small stone path. "What is your bidding tonight, Mother? How do I keep our clan strong and honor your vision?"

"Right now, I need you to find Shogun . . . to dispatch

my warrior—my son—to protect his own reign! That whore whom he lusts for cannot be allowed to get to her home pack with my ex-husband's truth."

Lei pushed off the stone lantern and leveled her gaze at her mother. "Shogun will never attack her, even though he is the firstborn heir . . . even if he knew that Hunter is the bastard son, the second son, a half-Shadow, half-Werewolf abomination to his pure-blood Shadow pack." She spat, slowly transforming. "Shogun is like Father, believing in diplomacy and alliances, rather than brute force. Mother, it will be me who ensures that the son who disgraced your marriage will never rule or co-rule with my brother, no matter the mistakes of our father."

"Good," the demon wolf snarled as Lei dropped down onto all fours. "I tried to claw Hunter from his mother's womb, and yet he lived. That fornicating bitch took my husband, your father . . . and now another one like her has two half brothers in her clutches, forming an alliance between my bloodline and my archenemies—when they should be on the precipice of war. Sacrilege! I want her stopped before she delivers the message of mistaken identity and misunderstood intent."

Lei threw her head back and howled a rallying call, and then looked at her mother. "Sasha Trudeau is as good as dead."

Shogun's attention jerked his sightline over his shoulder. He'd know his sister's rallying call anywhere, and it bristled the fine hairs on his neck. A

meditative walk through the semi-abandoned Ninth
Ward had come to an abrupt halt. The moon was
full, he was alone—in seconds he was pure wolf.

He threw his head back and called his six best
lieutenants. Lei was still his sister, still a member of
the pack. If something had sent her on a hunt, then it
was something that was a threat to their family.

Houses became a blur; streetlamps, intermittent
flashes of yellow light. Lei's signature drew him to
the teahouse. But a dead girl's body stopped him in his
tracks. He recognized the hostess from her hair and
scent, which was all he could judge by; gone was her
once pretty face. Six strong enforcers skidded to a halt
beside him, assessing the damage and scenting the air.

The residue of sulfur told them all Lei had chased
whatever it was through the demon doors. If she
had, she was lost. Were-demons would shred a solo
wolf who didn't own the contagion. Lei was many
things, but demon-infected she was not.

Shogun briefly closed his eyes.

His lieutenants stood in wait, ready for war. This
had to be redressed. Another human had been eaten.
His courageous sister was now lost to the forbidden
zone. There was only one wolf he knew of who had
been infected. She must have come to feed here after
she'd gone back to her den in the basement of Tulane
Hospital. That's where she'd emerge from the demon doors with his sister's blood on her hands. She
and Lei had always been at odds. It was no secret.
She'd go back to her pack, her familiars, to the labs
that were working on her cure. That was the way of

the wolf, demon-infected or not. That's where he'd corner her and put her out of her misery. Then he'd take great pleasure in exterminating the bastard that gave her the dread disease.

Even though it broke him in two, Sasha Trudeau was not above pack law.

"Did you hear that?" Fisher said, going to the window toting an M16 loaded with twenty-millimeter silver shells.

"Yeah," said Woods, silently signaling for Bradley, Winters, and Clarissa to move away from the windows and doors.

Both soldiers sniffed the air. Another distant howl made Woods's ears lay back against his skull. Clarissa shivered and glanced around the lab with the others. Winters eased back toward his workstations. Bradley crawled to his desk and yanked open a drawer, coming away with wolfsbane to begin making a circle in the center of the floor with the dried leaves.

"Oh, shit, oh, shit, oh, shit," Winters whispered with a squeak. "We've got incoming." He pointed to the crouching images on his flat-screen monitors, which were picked up on the hallway sensors.

Clarissa nodded and motioned toward the windows. "Get away from there and into the circle," she hissed through her teeth five seconds before Woods and Fisher dove toward safety, sending her sprawling as the doors burst open and glass came crashing in.

Huge, snarling Werewolves thundered into the lab, their massive heads swinging as though on pivots, searching. Monitors, tables, chair, stools, anything in their wake became instant rubble as Woods and Fisher squeezed off rounds trying to protect Clarissa. But they just moved too fast.

Rage-filled beasts were up on a lab bench one second, down the next. Lights were shot out of the ceiling as airborne wolves dodged machine-gun fire, raking the walls with massive claws. Clarissa found a desk to hide beneath and curled herself into a fetal ball. Woods was up on his feet, the muzzle of his weapon now breaking the plane of Bradley's circle. It happened too fast to stop.

Bradley yelled *no*. A Werewolf claw reached out and grabbed Woods's gun, pulling him in a flip out of the circle along with his gun. A beast was on his chest. Fisher couldn't get off a shot without shooting his own man. Winters took dead aim with a Glock nine-millimeter. The beast that was about to rip off Woods's face dodged the shot and crashed into the desk where Clarissa had been.

With Woods out cold and Fisher's machine-gun ricochet sure to kill Clarissa, Winters tossed the marine his weapon. But a heavy desk hurtled forward to knock the soldier out cold, barely missing Winters and Bradley.

Seven angry wolves surrounded Clarissa. Glowing eyes and pitch-black coats glistened in the darkness. A gaping maw with razor-sharp teeth snarled a low, steady warning to her. Saliva and hot breath leaked into her hair as she cowered on the floor. Fear had slicked her body with adrenaline sweat. Her panicked heartbeat drowned out the sounds of sirens in the distance and pandemonium filling the hall. She slowly opened her hand and held out the vial of blood Sasha had given her. A series of close, fierce barks made her yank back her offering and squeeze her eyes shut.

"Where is she?" a booming voice demanded just behind her skull.

"I don't know," Clarissa whispered to the floor, tears running down the bridge of her nose, blinding her. "She left hours ago."

"Blood is in the air, sir," a sly Phantom said, whispering in the baron's ear and then glancing around the blood club.

"Do tell," Geoff murmured, smiling at the company of several Vampire females who graced his table.

"Yes, and you heard the hunting-party howls . . . now human sirens."

Three alabaster beauties with crimson smiles leaned in toward the vaporous form.

"Secrets?" the brunette crooned. "Oh . . . Geoff, I love secrets involving bloodlust."

"What do you think it could be?" a willowy blonde asked, her pupils dilating to eclipse her pale blue irises, leaving only the depths of pure darkness.

Geoff waved the server over to bring another round of private-label new blood for his guests, and then studied the insistent Succubus. "If you find out what's happened through the network and bring it to me first, I promise a handsome reward."

The Phantom nodded and slid against him in lazy repose. "May I join your bed tonight, as well, sir?"

Geoff chuckled. "That was part of the handsome reward. I don't think any of these ladies would be offended if you shared their bodies while I shared them."

A breathy kiss sealed the deal, leaving a vaporous trail behind.

"Human death in the district is so titillating . . . ," an auburn-haired beauty seated to his left crooned. "Do you think the wolves have eaten another one, Geoff?"

"I do hope so, my love. That would be perfect."

"You saw what happened!" Bradley yelled. "We have to call this in!"

"We call nothing in till we talk to Doc!" Woods shouted back, his finger in Bradley's face. "Me and Fish almost got smoked by our own in Afghanistan because the brass thought we were contagious. Never again. The only man that saved our asses was Doc, then after that was Trudeau—her contact's people made it all good . . . fed us, protected us, laid down their lives to make sure it was all good. So we wait for the word!"

"We need a damage-control strategy fast, bro," Fisher said, looking out the window. "Got tell the civvies something reasonable."

"Attempted robbery," Winters said quickly. "Druggies heard we had heavy meds in the labs, we came in here, there was gunfire, a fight, they ran down the fire exits—we covered the contraband."

Woods pointed at Winters. "Good looking out."

Clarissa remained numb, staring at the unaccepted

vial of blood in her palm. "They weren't coming for this," she said quietly. "Didn't want the pure Werewolf blood back. I don't understand."

"What?" Bradley whispered, the low resonance of shock in his voice stilling the group dissent. "You've got pure fucking Werewolf blood in here?" His chest rose and fell in hard breaths as his voice escalated. "Are you insane? No wonder we got rushed by beasts—get that bullshit out of here before another search party comes for it. Next time we might not be so lucky!"

"Everything here is destroyed. I have to get this sample back to NORAD to run some tests stat. They didn't want the blood," Clarissa said calmly, going over to the destroyed tables in search of anything she could use, without success.

"If they didn't want the blood, then what the fuck did they want?" Woods shouted, his nerves filleted.

She looked at the group. "They wanted Sasha."

The moment she hit the soft padding of moss-covered earth, she knew she was home. Sasha breathed in the fresh spring air and allowed it to thread through her body to chase away the eeriness of the shadow lands. Moonlight bathed her in luminous peace. With freedom surrounding her, she longed to move, to run, her inner wolf begging for a chance to dash through the underbrush and hunt wild game, but she needed her human form.

There was a mission greater than releasing her wolf—she had to get word to Silver Hawk, then had to get the pack to grant her an audience alone with

Hunter. She only had this night to hear his side of the story . . . or to witness his change on the first true night of the full moon. Tomorrow night, if he was still alive, a tribunal would hear the evidence and decide his fate. Then it would all be over.

Extracting Hunter's amulet from her jeans pocket, she looped it over her neck, allowing the moon to recharge it as she ran. To sweat and move and leap and stretch her muscles felt divine. Something was calling her wolf harder than she'd remembered in a long time, harder than she'd wanted to admit. But now warning chills were coursing through her, panic easing into what had been an exhilarating run. She saw it in her peripheral vision, a blur in the dark depths of the woods. Her Glock was in her palm as she spun and fired, clipping tree bark. A familiar scent filled her nose. It was demon.

Sasha turned 360 degrees in a quick blur of motion. Glowing eyes lit up the tree lines around her. She was surrounded. A huge golden-amber wolf lunged, its demon-infected, gnarled jaws snapping as she ducked and came up firing. A yelp told her she'd gotten it, but she knew it wasn't dead. Instantly she was rushed. She knew two of the wolves—the huge amber creature was Lei; the smaller auburn-hued one was Dana. Sasha drop-rolled out of the way, blew away two females with timber markings, and was up in a flash, hauling ass.

Deft footfalls broke fallen branches behind her. The angry pants of the hunt drove her forward, sweat slicking her palm, human fatigue making her gun heavy. A flash of glowing eyes and a blur cut her off with a lateral move. Two seconds too late, and she went down in a skid right toward the jaws of the beast—but she went down squeezing off rounds that flung it out of her way with an agonized howl.

A dead click from an empty magazine put her up on her feet just in time to see two blurs barreling toward her. The amulets came off, one in each fist; swinging them like nunchucks, she was able to silver-stun both female attackers, adding a flying kick to their heads to back them off.

A pump-shotgun report made all combatants go still. A rallying howl from the Shadow pack narrowed Lei's gaze and sent the injured demon-wolf into the shadows with Dana.

Silver Hawk burst through the clearing, leveling his gun and turning in a full circle before acknowledging Sasha.

"The amulets never lie," he said out of breath.

Sasha nodded and rested both hands on her knees.

"Bring me a human body," Lei's mother demanded, clutching her side as they limped through the demon doors. "Here, to be injured means to be cannibalized." She looked at the intense moonlight in the passageway. "I cannot hide in here until I am healed, but must eat before the disk of transformation goes down. Then I can return. Avenge me once and for all, daughter. Once and for all!"

"How many were there?' Silver Hawk asked, helping Sasha collect her weapon.

"Four females. I got two," Sasha muttered, still gulping air while stashing her spent weapon in the back of her waistband.

"Four infected she-demons?" Silver Hawk said, retracing their steps through the brush as though he was still tracking them. "No wonder they were bold enough to cross into Shadow territory."

"No," Sasha said, holding Silver Hawk with her gaze. "There was only one infected female . . . the others were clean Werewolves."

"Those are very serious charges, Sasha," Silver Hawk said. "You must be sure."

"I am," she said lifting her chin as several pack enforcers came through the stand of trees toting heavy artillery. She gave them a look that told them they were very late to the party. They lowered their weapons and their eyes, ashamed, but said nothing. "We need to talk, privately. A lot has gone down."

Silver Hawk nodded. "I know, Shadow-daughter. Yes. I know."

CHAPTER 11

He'd heard the call to arms. Knew he wasn't hallucinating. Sasha's voice was unmistakable, her howl was a chill that ran through his skeleton and shook him to his core. His mate was in battle, outnumbered. Werewolves were in the glen. The pack was on the hunt; his grandfather had transformed from his human form as Silver Hawk into his wolf-self, Silver Shadow. There was another howl that he'd never forget, one etched into his cellular memory. The bitch that slaughtered his mother. Gunfire. A full moon. Hunter's wolf would not be denied.

Silver-coated bars be damned. He was Wolf Shadow, stronger than he'd ever been. His guards didn't understand. Doc's voice was becoming distant, their conversation murky. Bear Shadow's eyes told of his confusion. It wasn't Sasha! That wasn't the female he smelled. Sasha wasn't a demon-infected Werewolf breaching the shadow lands or the pack's borders with other female Weres!

Chaos. They had to lower their weapons. He was

suddenly wolf and hadn't remembered even shifting. No, he wouldn't allow Doc to inject him—the meds made him fuzzy, lethargic, sick! A warning snarl ripped up Hunter's throat. The scent of gunpowder wafting off silver shells stung his nose. Doc was so close to the bars. The others were yelling as he moved in toward the opportunity. Yes, old man . . . Just a little closer . . . Hunter's ears lay back against his skull. That's right, Doc, reach out . . .

In the blink of an eye it was all over. Deafening gunfire echoed all around him. A tranquilizer dart filled with meds whizzed through his coat but didn't nick his skin. Doc had blocked the light and cast a shadow.

That was all he'd needed to break free and be gone.

She sat across from Silver Hawk at the ancient, knotty-pine table in his cabin. Pack enforcers surrounded the house, guarding their remaining leadership. A dangerous threat of war was in the air. Werewolves from the Southeast Asian Clan had breeched territorial lines to set up an unauthorized hunt against the alpha's she-Shadow mate—long before the UCE tribunal or trial, long before Hunter's possible contagion turn—and they'd aligned somehow with demon forces. A demon-infected she-wolf was leading the hunt.

Old wounds revealed themselves as memories of past slights returned with a vengeance. Dissension rippled through the pack. Were it not for their respect of Silver Hawk, chaos would have hit the streets of New Orleans in the form of a swift retaliatory strike.

Sasha rubbed her palms down her face as she studied the lines in Silver Hawk's weathered brow. Bits of the vision began to finally fit into place, like the tumblers of a lock coming together to open a secret vault.

Slowly, with a heavy heart, she slid his old amulet toward him across the wooden surface. It was the one Hunter normally wore. As she stared at it for a moment and then looked up at the elderly Shadow Wolf, his brown face seemed so much like the amber piece with hard-etched lines that told a mysterious story of life, death, time . . . Her soul ached that she had to hurt him and cut him deeply with the truth.

"I took a spirit walk earlier today," she said quietly as Silver Hawk took up the amulet but didn't immediately put it on. "I know Doc was here . . . I can still pick up his scent. Where is he?"

"With Hunter as part of the moon watch," Silver Hawk said in a sad tone, glancing out the window as he finally looped the amulet over his head.

"Good," Sasha said, just above a murmur. She paused and waited until Silver Hawk's eyes met hers again. "I'm going to share some very hard truth with you, and then I will ask you to do the same."

He nodded, but didn't commit. "Some of that truth does not belong to me."

She nodded. "Same here, but we'll make do . . . as pack leadership, as friends, and two who understand a heavy heart."

He closed his eyes and nodded. "All right. Tell me, and I will tell you."

Sasha leaned across the table and gathered his hands within hers, reveling in the leathery, kind warmth that emanated from his ancient, healing hands. "Your daughter loved another man . . ."

Silver Hawk nodded, but kept his gaze lowered to stare at their joined hands. "This I can believe. The beta was cruel, not just physically but also emotionally, once he'd won her." The old man looked up, his eyes burning, the edges of his irises beginning to change into wolf's. "I had never known hate until then. But she wouldn't leave him."

"She couldn't," Sasha said softly. "By then, she was pregnant."

Silver Hawk drew a deep breath and released it slowly. "I know. I told her it didn't matter. She and I would raise her child, but—"

"It wasn't her husband's," Sasha said as calmly as possible, squeezing Silver Hawk's hands to steady him when he stopped breathing. "She was afraid, and ashamed, and didn't know what to do."

When Silver Hawk tried to draw away, Sasha tightened her grip. "She loved you so much, she couldn't let scandal rip you to shreds."

"I wouldn't have cared," he murmured thickly. "She was all I had left in the world . . . my heart."

Sasha nodded. "But she respected you as not just her father, but also who you were to the entire North American Clan . . . this would have caused an international incident."

"Who," Silver Hawk said, drawing away from

Sasha's hold with a hard break and then standing. "Tell me not those who took her life!" He went to the window and then turned slowly, his eyes flickering dangerously near a wolf transformation. "Tell me who fathered my grandson, who is linked to my pack by blood and deceit."

Sasha was on her feet and had rounded the table to stand before the pain-racked old man. "Use your shaman sight. Go with me now in spirit to the edges of the shadow lands. Let her tell you. It is not what you think."

She held out her hands to him, waiting for the rage to subside, waiting for him to be escorted to the truth. After what felt like a long time, a pair of callused hands slid into hers. A pair of haunted eyes stared at her, issuing silent thanks for being there and not making him have to face this alone.

Wolf eyes set in human faces and backlit by inner moonlight met. Amulets warmed and glowed. The shadow paths opened around them where they stood. Secrets whispered until the spirits parted the mist. A shy young woman came near, her beautiful face streaked with tears. Her voice was as soft as her doeskin dress. Her eyes were pained, but she never looked away as her father swallowed away his tears.

"My husband beat me, and I knew you would eventually kill him. I didn't want that; it would fracture the pack, but I had to get away that night. He was insane, furious that his marriage to me didn't elevate his rank and had still left him locked out of the UCE Conference. All betas had been left at home in the pack lands. Only enforcers could go. I was not that. Although I was your daughter, I had married beneath my station—so I was left home to be beaten while you weren't around. As it got worse, I finally ran that night. I had my mother's amulet . . . I was a child of alpha Shadows. I could cross realms he dared not. And I exited in a tea garden, shaken, beaten, afraid . . . and that's when I was found and helped by the most unexpected source of tenderness."

The spirit looked away as though seeing it all in her head as she spoke. Sasha could feel Silver Hawk's hands tremble within her own, and understood the emotion only too well.

"He was oddly tall for his region," the apparition said in a faint murmur. "And he proudly explained that as a blend of peoples—from the Hindu Kush to Mongolia, Korea, and the highlands of China—he fit no stereotype. I saw only that he was regal, majestic, and kind. We talked into the night about his fascination with our mixture of French, Haitian, African, a world of people and cultures under one human skin. How the hatred was so insane, how there needed to be accord among nations. We sipped tea and shared stories—he fed me, gave my weary spirit sanctuary, and then touched the bruises on my face as though he'd just seen them until I cried."

She looked at her father, her eyes pleading for understanding. "And he vowed to protect me till death and beyond, to never make my father have to give his life in my stead—he would do that for me. That's when he traveled with me through the dangerous shadow paths to confront the man who'd beaten me.

My husband, the man you warned me not to marry, was threatened by one who didn't come under the laws of our pack or our lands. He was told that if he touched me again, he would die. He never laid a hand on me again. I never let him have me again, as only one warrior was worthy of that, but by the time I was ready to seek divorce I was already with child. He never hit me again."

"But he also never lifted a hand again to help save your life," Silver Hawk whispered thickly.

"No, Father, he didn't."

"The huge black male was trying to stop the murder," Sasha added quietly.

Silver Hawk stared at her as images careered through his mind. "I now see. I shot the wrong wolf . . . perhaps also shot a man who'd already seen vengeance. Then again, I have no regrets about that latter issue, regardless."

"The golden-amber one, the wife . . . That's who killed your daughter, and that's the one who got away again," Sasha said, squeezing Silver Hawk's hands. "Your son is a blend of two clans. The Werewolf Southeast Asian Clan and North American Shadow Clan."

"He is the one they will one day call Shogun's half brother," the spirit murmured. "That is why my son is so susceptible to the contagion. Forgive me, Father, for the dishonor. The weakness to the dread disease comes from the Werewolf line . . . as you know, our Shadow Wolf blood has long been immune to it. Hence I now personally understand why marriages across the lines were forbidden."

"Oh, daughter . . ." Silver Hawk's voice trailed off in a pain-filled whisper.

"Father, I know that among our people, to be with a Werewolf is worse than ever being with a beta of our own kind. But my heart crossed the bridge into his world, just as his left his people to meet mine. I could not tell you this while I lived. My child, my son, I wanted to hide from this disgrace behind a loveless marriage. I had not the courage for truth about this. My shame has followed me beyond the grave. Forgive me for the heartbreak I've caused you."

"You are wolf and human. You are my heart and my soul, just as Hunter is. There is nothing you could do that would dishonor me. Let your spirit rest free," Silver Hawk said quietly. "We will make peace, if peace can be made."

"I don't know how possible that is," Sasha said quickly, hating to disturb the deeply private communion, but needing Silver Hawk to understand the risks. "Lei is in cahoots with her mother. The wife didn't die when you shot her years ago, just as I only wounded her now. She's still feeding after all these years behind demon doors. Our only chance at dealing with a rational party from their ranks is Shogun." Sasha's eyes widened as the implications slammed into her brain. That option might have been left as a burned bridge at a teahouse!

"Then we must set up a meeting," Silver Hawk said calmly, his tone resigned. "If we can send healing to Hunter, he must sit down with Shogun, brother-to-brother, just as the prophecy foretold: *When the wolf would be one, brought together by one born of them, yet made . . . strengths of both warring wolves sealed in one skin, with one heart, therein lies peace.* That bridge between clans is Hunter. The one born of them, yet made, is you, Sasha. You have brought the two brothers together. They must meet in peace. I am an old man now—I have made many mistakes born of anger and war. Now is the season to be still."

The spirit nodded, beginning to fade, but her eyes met Sasha's with an unspoken understanding. She clearly knew the warring wolves sealed in one skin also meant the conflict going one within a woman trapped between two brothers. Panic made Sasha's hands moist within Silver Hawk's hold.

"We have to alert Doc," Sasha said after a moment. "If one of Hunter's gene sets is imprinted, if it can't kick in when there's been trauma to the primary one . . ." Her words trailed off as the image of the huge Werewolf male that was Hunter's real father jumped into her head. "Oh, my God . . . his father said he'd been poisoned. It makes sense that his Shadow blood couldn't beat this thing. He wasn't pure Shadow, and whatever they tainted the vials with—most likely contagion—was weakening that one barrier till it collapsed. He's been shooting up with a dose of diseased Werewolf blood without even knowing it!"

"Father . . . you left the vials just inside the door of their room while they were sleeping," Hunter's mother said, disappearing as she looked at Silver Hawk with sad eyes. "His mind saw you when you called him awake . . . but never once saw the sleight of hand. Beware those who call themselves friends."

Silver Hawk again closed his eyes and shook his head. "We will need proof of this deed, just as we will need proof of Hunter and Shogun's combined heritage. None of it will be accepted at the tribunal without hard evidence. A shadow land spirit walk is not something any of the judges can do to verify authenticity, thus it is inadmissible."

Sasha nodded. "I have a blood sample from Shogun that can give proof of parentage. Now all we have to do is prove a poisoning."

The elderly shaman opened his eyes and gazed at Sasha. "I kept one vial of medicine that I gave back to Doc, just in case it got bad and Hunter came here. He's with Hunter now at the containment cells. If the medicine is tainted, we can show that . . . but they may think that I did it to save my own grandson."

"Maybe," Sasha said. "But we might be able to build a case on enough circumstantial evidence to discredit anyone who might have poisoned Hunter's meds. If we can initially buy some more time with that, I've got a lab team that can give hard, indisputable data. There are eyewitnesses to Lei's treason with a demon-wolf—her own mother."

"You don't understand. None of those who actually saw the infected she-wolf will be allowed to testify. Lei's treason is unsubstantiated unless there's an eyewitness not from this pack."

"Damn . . ." Sasha blew a stray wisp of hair up off her forehead with a puff of breath. "All right. Then I'm going to have to draw that bitch out of hiding in New Orleans before it's all over, or go in behind a demon door and drag her mangy carcass out into the streets. Either way is fine by me."

Silver Hawk stared at Sasha, his eyes asking what he never verbalized: How had she gotten the blood sample from Shogun? Just that quickly they were no longer in the shadow lands but back in the cabin where the vision quest had begun. The unspoken question hung in the air like a silent partner. Sasha stared out at the moon.

"I should take you to Doc now . . . and to Hunter," Silver Hawk said, his weary gaze sliding away from Sasha. "And I will make my best healing medicine with the Great Spirit. That is all I can do at this point."

Hunter lowered his nose to the ground. Fresh tracks, some human, some wolf. He separated out the scents. His grandfather. Sasha. Two dead Werewolf females. Two heavier ones, thicker in body and build. Sulfur trail meant they'd come by way of demon doors. He studied the strange two-paw tracks left by the demon-infected wolf that walked on hind legs.

A new snarl filled his throat as the scent flashed back memories in cascading horror within his mind. Spent shells littered the forest floor. Blood painted new grass and leaves crimson. Sasha's blood wasn't amid the carnage, nor was his grandfather's. They'd been victorious. They'd walked away on two human feet. That's all he needed to know.

He stared at the demon door within the shadows. His own pack would come for him through the shadow lands, not understanding. There wasn't time to explain while the trail was hot. Someone had to stop the infected she-alpha hunting the she-Shadows of his pack. This was old history that had to end this generation.

Hunter threw his head back and howled.

"Look," Bradley said in a tight British brogue, dropping all formality as he walked around the wrecked room. "We've got maybe ten minutes, max, before local police get here—and that's only because NOPD lost eighty percent of its staff after Katrina and still hasn't rebuilt. Any so-called security guards from the hospital aren't equipped to deal with M16 gunfire report, and aren't coming up here. So I suggest that we figure out where we're gonna set up shop next, people. I think we can safely assume that we'll be booted out of this facility, *at night,* under a full moon, with very pissy Werewolves afoot in search of our missing Captain!"

Fisher rubbed his palms down his sweaty face and looked at Woods.

"Okay, we head for the truck after we explain whatever we have to tell the locals, and we give Cap the bill when she gets back here," Woods said. He glanced around. "Me and Fish picked up a UAV, micro version, from the base. We can send up that unmanned aerial vehicle, which is mounted with seven cameras." He looked at Winters. "It's got synthetic aperture radar with resolution down to four inches. Should be able to spot a field mouse as incoming with that."

Winters nodded and stared at Bradley. "Yeah. It uses microwave versus photos. If they've got a laptop with software in the truck, I can watch our backs with it while we head to NORAD."

"We picked up all the new shit that Doc authorized to be shipped in for our use only," Fisher said, glancing around the small, shaken team. "Sonic guns that give those bastards with extra-sensitive hearing instant migraines. This thing called the Dazzler—which has lights that cause temporary blindness. And a SWORDS—a strategic weapons operation deployment system."

"In English, Fish," Clarissa said, losing patience. She dragged her fingers through her hair and stared at him hard.

"Small robot on tractor wheels . . . three feet tall, machine-gun turret on top—runs by laptop and two joysticks. Better than sending a man in the dark to get his face ripped off. Even got a few uniforms with GPS embedded that monitors a soldier's bio, so if we've gotta do caves, tunnels, swamps on this frickin' detail to go in and lay down some IEDs, hey."

"I don't know about improvised explosive devices or all that other technological crap," Bradley said, walking to the center of the room and standing in the circle he'd made. "Call me old-fashioned, but when all else failed, the wolfsbane worked. You gentlemen can have at the conventional weapons. Give me a moment to gather up more forest-friendly deterrents and a little brick dust."

"Stop being such a smacked ass, Bradley," Clarissa said, clearly annoyed. "We're all freaked out. I am. At least you didn't have them circle you, single you out, and open their jaws over your fucking head! So cut the misery. We work as a team. Before we leave, I'm taking saliva samples out of my hair, off the floor, looking for wolf hairs, anything I can put under a microscope for the future so we can build biometric dossiers on all these creatures. The National Civilian Labs might also be able to play a role—because who knows what they've inadvertently cataloged?"

"What the f . . ." Woods's voice trailed off as he stared up at the ceiling, drawing the attention of the others.

Small colored lights like multihued fireflies gathered and dispersed like dancing dust motes in the moonlight.

"That's so—"

"Shush!" Woods said quickly, cutting off Fisher's comment. "Listen!"

Silence settled on the group. All eyes followed the lights, which seemed to be gathering closer into one small miasma of glowing particles.

"They want the Druid?" Woods said after a moment, tilting his head. He looked at Bradley with total confusion.

"Who's *they* and why *me*?" Bradley said, hedging.

"You're not gonna believe this, bro," Woods said, his eyes following the lights. "Fairies—"

"What?" the group said in unison.

"Honest to God," Woods said, his eyes wide with wonder, seeming mesmerized by the lights. "They're pissed off because somebody ate a girl in their gardens. They claim it wasn't Sasha." He placed a hand on top of his head. "They refuse to testify for fear of reprisal, but say they were double-crossed and want a dark arts specialist they can trust, someone who can reverse an enchantment spell at the teahouse."

"You seem . . . distant," Lei said, giving Dana a sidelong glance as the male body vanished into the bayou thicket with her mother.

Dana stared at Lei for a moment. "Not distant, just tired. I lost two very close friends tonight."

"Their sacrifice was worth it," Lei said coolly, beginning to walk back in the direction of the road.

"I hope so," Dana said, standing in place and not following Lei.

The stillness and the comment behind her made Lei turn around. "I sense hesitation on your part to complete our very worthy cause."

"You sense confusion," Dana said carefully. "I don't understand why you would bribe the Fae into creating an enchantment spell to draw Shogun to me, and then offer those same services to Sasha Trudeau?"

"Ah, you have been walking in my garden and listening to the complaints of meddlesome Fairies, I see."

"They are disgruntled about your mother feeding in their gardens—that was sacrilege to them. Their complaints were loud enough to overhear." Dana folded her arms.

"That was a grave mistake, but you have met my mother. She is not to be denied. The gardens were her favorite refuge while here at conferences. My father had the spot made for her, years ago, while they were still . . ." Lei's voice trailed off, the wistful tone left it, and the familiar hardness returned. "Why both you and Sasha, you ask?" Lei placed a graceful finger to her lips, appearing to contemplate Dana's question for a moment while staring up at the moon.

"My brother is shrewd," she finally continued. "If I were to appear openly against Sasha, he would immediately sense duplicity. But if I encouraged his fleeting fantasy, even said his bond with her might strengthen the alliance . . . if something unfortunate happened to her, there would be no obvious blood on my hands."

"I understand why you asked for aid from the Fae to get him to come to me," Dana said, lifting her chin. "But I don't understand why it was necessary for you to make her willing to accept his advances."

"Jealousy clouds judgment, Dana," Lei said with a smile, clucking her tongue. She wagged a finger as she spoke, beginning to make a wide circle around the weaker female.

"Take a page from *The Art of War.* Think. Suppose my brother believes that Sasha truly cares for him and wants him intimately, and the only thing standing in his way is her North American mate. Way down deep in his subconscious, beneath all the honorable rhetoric, is still a man . . . is still a wolf who wants what he wants but cannot readily have—her. That is enough to incline him to war if the slightest opportunity presents itself. The opportunity has presented itself. The Fairies will get over it. Their garden refuge will eventually get cleaned up by the Gnomes." Lei's eyes narrowed to a threatening glare. "And *you* will get over it, Dana. All of this was a necessary step to place you where you've always wanted to be—at the top beside Shogun. And then you will owe me. Power often requires sacrifice."

Geoff stood in the garden staring down at the naked, mauled female at his feet. His Vampire henchmen hissed as he slowly rolled her body over with a dark-charge from the tip of his forefinger.

"Look at this mess," he said shaking his head. "A beautiful face gone, body torn to shreds, viscera everywhere, organ meat eaten. Completely savage. A positive natural disaster and waste of a gorgeous woman's body. She could have been elegantly drained of blood and life and then reawakened later as one of us, but I couldn't even tell you what this woman-child looked like."

One of Geoff's henchmen stooped down and closed his eyes, then sent the images he perceived into the minds of the other vampires around him. He looked up at Geoff, complete black overtaking his green irises in the moonlight.

"Dana Broussard was here," the lead security lieutenant said. "She helped with the feeding of the demon one . . . so did Shogun's sister. Max Hunter and Sasha Trudeau had no hand in this murder. But it may be a sign that all wolf packs in the region are out of control, boss." He smiled a gleaming porcelain-white smile that made the others around him join him with toothy grins.

"The Fairies won't tell, even if it's happened in

their own backyard," another handsome security lieutenant said. He flipped his blond mane over his shoulder with an aristocratic toss of his head. "It's like
they've adopted the foolish human thug don't-snitch
policy. All the better. You're on the tribunal, so it is
whatever you say it is—as a lead investigator."

"I don't think we'll have any issues with Dugan,"
a tall, athletic brunette said, slapping five with the
first henchmen as he stood. "Not after he relaxed his
B and B security to let us in . . . ah, a man's soul for
the price of silver. A piece of the casino action will
do it every time."

The Vampires standing around Geoff laughed in
low, wicked unison, slowly becoming vapor.

"It's been a long time since we've had an open wolf
hunt. Should we alert the Cartel? Your call, boss," the
group leader murmured on the night air.

"Not yet," Geoff said, choosing his words with
care as he straightened his French cuffs beneath his
suit before dematerializing. "One must be strategic
to avoid outright war. I need more information and
we need plausible deniability, as always."

Footfalls pounded the front steps and porch. Wolf
calls ripped through the night sky. Sasha and Silver
Hawk crossed the room just as the front door burst
open. Bear Shadow and Crow Shadow panted hard,
sending puffs of breath in white clouds into the frigid
mountain air. She could see Doc running down the
path leading to the house. Sentries littered the porch
and parted for the doctor.

"He's escaped," Bear Shadow said, seeming confused that Sasha and Silver Hawk were meeting calmly. "Went right into a shadow like one of us."

Crow Shadow looked at Sasha and then at Silver Hawk, lowering his pump shotgun. "How can this be when they said he had the dread disease? His containment cell was covered in pure silver. But we scented female demon-wolf . . . we thought . . ."

Silver Hawk raised a hand. "She did no harm and was with me. Ten pack brothers who guarded my cabin know this—Sasha is not the she-demon scent on the wind."

CHAPTER 12

"If he got past the bars and went into a shadow," Sasha said, clasping Silver Hawk's arm with repressed hope, "that could mean his Shadow blood is rejecting the contagion." She gazed around the table of the closed session with the pack's senior leadership to lock eyes with Bear Shadow and Crow Shadow before looking to Doc to corroborate her theory.

"If what you're saying is so," Doc said, glancing around the pine table, his eyes holding Silver Hawk's then Sasha's, "Hunter came from two genetically strong parents. That's why I need to get to the lab. If his father's gene set isn't imprinted, even though he was a strong alpha Werewolf clansman, and if his father was more impervious to the contagion that the average Werewolf, Hunter might stand a chance. His mother's Shadow heritage definitely gives him the advantage—which is why it's so odd that he didn't shake the virus. Before, when he was infected in battle, it was harder for him to recover—due to his father's genetics, as we now know. But he did recover.

His body has to be strengthening its autoimmune system against the contagion."

"I want you to take a look at Shogun's blood," Sasha said, her gaze boring into Doc's. "On the vision quest it was clear. Shogun's mother got infected—which means that on his matrilineal side, there's the imprinting weakness. His father Turned much more slowly after a deliberate attack by her to infect him; he even retained some of his original inner wolf long enough to try to help Hunter's mother. To me that means Hunter's mother was pure Shadow—and had the immunity. A strong gene set. Hunter's father, although Werewolf, also had a very strong immunity. Over the past week, Hunter was inadvertently dosing himself with contagion, but he's still got Shadow Wolf capabilities."

"It could be working like snakebite anti-venom— a little toxin helping the body to build up its own natural defenses against it." Doc peered around the table. "Or it could be a time bomb inside him, waiting to explode."

"He's fighting it," Sasha said quickly. "He has to be."

"He's bigger, Sasha. His wolf is insane," Bear Shadow said quietly. "Stronger than I've ever seen him."

"And he's on the run," Crow Shadow said, rubbing his hands down his face in frustration. "We tracked him to a demon door, too, then nothing. He's gone behind the dark doors without his amulet, where none of us can follow him."

The room fell quiet for endless seconds.

"He thinks it's all over . . . he went after Shogun's mother on a suicide mission to protect our pack and to avenge his mother," Sasha whispered, horrified.

Silver Hawk shook his head. "He went on a mission to protect you."

"Muttering Fairies, disgruntled Gnomes, and double-dealing Elves," Woods said quietly in the truck's cabin, glancing at Fisher as he drove. "What's next?"

"I don't know, dude, but from the one camera that wasn't destroyed, I got it all downloaded on digital and erased before the local boys saw this sick shit and had flippin' heart attacks," Winters said, his hands rapidly moving across the laptop balanced on his thighs. "Talk about breaking the supernatural news to the general public . . . sheesh! Werewolves busting into the lab, Fairy lights. I don't know if I'll ever be able to enhance the audio enough to actually hear what they said, but your relay to us is good enough of a translator, Woodsey. For now, I'm shipping these files to a secure hub up at base. Got the rest on flash drive," he added with a wink. "Never can have enough backup."

At every turn, his search for Sasha had ended in frustration. Shogun scented the bayou air. Female Werewolf was clear and present, familiar in an eerie way, but not Sasha. Probably a security lieutenant. A growl filled his throat as pain entered his heart and shattered it. He had to stop her, but didn't want to see her like this. His lieutenants' snarls pushed him forward. He was a clan leader. He had to do what he had to do, much as he hated it.

Following the infected female trail mixed with the distinct odor of dead human blood and remains, he tried to jettison the horrifying image of Sasha's infected wolf feeding off that kill. Until he saw the carnage, he wanted to remember what Sasha's human form looked like. Forcing himself, he thought of her soft, milk-in-tea complexion . . . her dark swath of thick, shoulder-length hair . . . her piercing gray eyes and full, lush mouth. Her graceful hands and sensuous curves. An athletic body that was lean but also soft . . . female . . . woman. She owned a touch that could make a man betray his honor; her kiss stole reason and supplanted it with dangerous dreams. Her wolf was equally as majestic. Vital, with a silvery, glistening coat washed blue-white under the moon when she changed.

The mental vision carved at Shogun's soul as his wolf bounded over logs and through the overgrown marsh on the hunt. That someone, something, gave her the contagion . . . a careless male . . . ate at his insides until he had to stop and howl.

Her son was hunting her? Noooo . . . Paranoia lifted the she-demon's head from her human feast in the bayou. She moved deeper into the swamp. Shogun could never see her like this.

Hunter barreled through the demon-door opening, barely escaping the dangerous caverns with his life. The scent of a Werewolf militia fused with infected she-wolf immediately stung his senses, and was obviously enough to keep what was chasing him in the darkness at bay.

Death. Human death floated on the thick bayou air. The she-demon had added a male militia to her previously all-female hunting party. He suddenly lifted his head and snarled. Lei's scent was there, as was Dana's . . . but that Shogun was there and had obviously double-crossed him, too, meant war.

"Would you like to see me add gasoline to a bayou flame, darlings?" Geoff crooned from the vapors, slowly materializing out of the mist with the three beauties whom he'd been dining with earlier.

They gathered in close, whispering with excitement and watching a plastic bag containing rumpled pants in his hands. He then snapped and showed them a red plastic biohazard hospital bag. Confusion marred their serene gazes. Geoff threw his head back and laughed at their lack of understanding, snatching the sound from the air and transforming it into the hoot of an owl. It was his private and very fulfilling joke. Dana was a fool. The Cartel dealt in absolutes. Sharing rule with werewolves? Never. There was no such thing as compromise.

"We'll have our open wolf hunt yet, darlings," he said in a confident murmur. "Watch as both leaders become infected from their own lusts."

He moved through the bayou, a blur of black shadow painted on moonlight-swept foliage, and then was gone. But a scent that nearly stopped his heart brought

him to a skidding halt. Hunter went back to the pile
of leaves and pawed at it, his body trembling from
rage and fear of what he might uncover. When it
wasn't the body he feared most, he slumped a bit and
sniffed harder.

Sasha's female essence was trapped in green
sweatpants that had been shoved into a red hospital
hazmat bag. Shogun's male sex scent was trapped in
clear plastic-wrapped khakis. Hunter backed away
from the pile of clothing, not breathing for a moment.
He circled the discovery and then loped away at a
much slower pace for a moment. When . . . how . . .
why? That she'd done something like this was beyond comprehension.

Then dark thoughts besieged his mind. What if
they'd moved on her, the Werewolves as a clan . . .
forcing her to accept the loss of her mate, coercing
her into making a snap decision so that the power
bases remained intact with the wolf Federations.
What if all this had been part of a huge setup? He refused to believe Sasha had just left his bed without
cause. No. They'd been working on her for the week
he'd been sick. Memories of the night they last
fought chiseled at his reason. The scent of his rival
imploded it.

In a flat-out run, trees were blurred lines, moonlight a streak. Five huge male sentries turned in unison bearing saliva-dripping fangs as he broke through
the bramble. Their lead alpha was airborne before
they could even crouch. He met Shogun in the air in a
feral lock of claws and teeth.

The fight was so vicious and moved so quickly

that the others could only circle, barking and snapping. There was no way to enter the fray without possibly injuring their own pack leader as thick, muscle-laden wolf bodies slammed against ancient trees, felling them with the sheer force of momentum. Underbrush was uprooted, mud and bayou bottom slung against onlookers along with spent saliva and blood.

Werewolf howls went out for more reinforcements. Local Shadow Wolf packs sent rally calls for war. New Orleans at night awakened. Fae archers tossed back drinks hard and pulled away from the bars. Clarissa, Bradley, and Winters leaned forward confused as Woods slowed the truck, tilted his head with Fisher, and made a U-turn. Those supernaturals with more delicate sensibilities, like the Fairies, Pixies, and Elves, shut themselves away. Gnomes closed their doors; Mythics hid. Vampires smiled and began taking odds using Phantoms as go-betweens as they festively moved out into the night. The Order of the Dragon bouncers mounted Harleys and peeled away from curbs. Sasha stood stock-still hundreds of miles away from ground zero.

"We have to go through the shadow lands," she announced in disbelief. "Our clans just went to war."

She leapt into the first shadow that would have her, Bear Shadow and Crow Shadow on her flank with four agile lieutenants. The others were quickly following with Silver Shadow—who also wore an amulet—and Doc, who had to make the perilous journey wolf-escorted and protected in his human form.

Were it not for his hidden Shadow heritage, the density change would have been too abrupt and could have sent him into shock, killing him. Even Fisher and Woods could never travel that way, given their natural timber wolf mix . . . the shadow lands demanded that only their kind could enter. Sasha prayed as she ran through the mist-filled pathways that Doc would be all right.

Her internal homing was to her familiars' panicked vibrations. It dropped her out in the bayou, so close to the battle she could smell it before she heard it.

The crash that missed her and her men was surreal. Hurtling wolf bodies locked in mortal combat twisted and leapt as a single thousand-pound animal, then fell, splintering fallen logs and anything beneath them. Gators quickly fled banks to get out of the battle's way, but positioned themselves to be rewarded by its spoils. Before she and her pack could gain their bearings, what seemed like an endless stream of huge Werewolves sailed over rocks and ground cover coming straight at them.

Lei was on Sasha so quickly she'd knocked the wind out of her, but Sasha pivoted just in time to keep her throat from being ripped out. All around her Werewolves and Shadow Wolves were paired in mortal combat. But a hail of silver-tipped arrows sent the combatants seeking cover in growls and yelps.

In the distance the thunder of motorcycle engines rumbled—then just as quickly as that stopped, the bayou lit with what seemed like flame-throwing blasts. The Order of the Dragon had arrived. Wolf eyes glowing with hatred filled the shadows between trees. Two badly wounded alpha leaders still circled each other snarling as they shape-shifted into their human forms. Arrows pierced their shoulders, calves, and thighs, slowing them, making them drag in huge inhalations and release them with trembling growls.

"You made her sick!" Shogun shouted, pointing at Hunter with a hard snap of his arm. Blood coursed down his stone-cut chest in rivulets from multiple open wounds.

"She is not a carrier!" Hunter shouted back, his thickly muscled arm pointing in a hard snap to match Shogun's. "Your mother is a carrier, and a murderess—not my mate!"

"My mother died more than two decades ago. The past is dead. Our argument is here and now!"

"No," Hunter said with a growl. "Your mother lives, even though she murdered mine. Same scent, same bloodline—now that I've spilled yours, I'd know it anywhere."

Archers raised their weapons, but Sasha leapt before the retinue that fell out of the shadow lands. Doc stood with a pump shotgun, looking bewildered. Sasha quickly reached over and lowered his weapon before the aggressive stance caused an attack.

"This is bullshit!" Shogun shouted, watching the other Shadow Wolves come out of the shadow lands and shape-shift into their human forms.

"It is truth," Silver Shadow said once he'd again become Silver Hawk.

"They lie!" Lei shrieked, pacing. "They would say anything to deflect the truth from Hunter."

Dana rushed to Shogun's side as he stared at Sasha

for a moment, but he pushed her away. She snarled and spun on the Shadow pack. "You bit him," she said, openly accusing Hunter as she studied Shogun's wounds, aghast.

The entire Werewolf clan that was assembled slowly backed away from Shogun and Hunter.

"No!" Lei screamed, rushing at Hunter, but several lieutenants held her back. "You're a carrier. My brother is the future!"

"Hunter is immune," Doc said flatly. "He's throwing off the virus. His Shadow mother probably gave him the gift of life . . . the immunity to the contagion." He looked at Lei and then Shogun with sad eyes. "Your mother and father did not pass that to you. I'm sorry."

Shogun looked down at his wounds and then at Hunter and snarled. The entire Werewolf pack snarled. Archers raised their bows as new tension swept the clearing.

"The blood sample you gave Sasha might hold a miracle," Silver Hawk said, his gaze nonjudgmental.

Hunter quickly looked to his grandfather, then to Sasha, at the same time Lei and Dana jerked their attention toward Shogun.

"You did what?" Lei said with a dangerous snarl.

"It was for him," Shogun said, ignoring his sister and staring at Hunter. He laughed a cold, bitter laugh and shook his head. "Ironic." He then turned his attention to Sasha and released an echoing yell of pain as he began ripping arrows from his body, each silver-tipped projectile sizzling as it came out dripping gore. Breathing hard, he flung the offending instruments on the ground. "I hope it was worth it."

Hunter followed suit, staring at Sasha. The glen was silent save the yells of agony of each man. When it was all over, the elder shaman stepped forward.

"I was on the spirit vision quest and saw what happened, Shogun," Silver Hawk said. "The history you have been given is not accurate, and we must end the lies here tonight."

"You are the liar!" Lei said, gaining barks and jeers from the Werewolf contingent.

"Let him speak!" Shogun shouted, resting by placing his hands on his knees. "If I am to die by the silver bullet, then at least let me hear the truth first!"

"Your mother didn't die at the hands of the North American Shadow Clan," Sasha said, choosing each word with extreme care. "Your father did inadvertently—trying to save Hunter's mother from her attack. It was a battlefield accident in the heat of battle. He was Turning from his contagion, yet trying to save Hunter's mother when he was shot—but they weren't both shot. Your mother was maimed and fled. She was the one who made the demon pact, but your father wouldn't go along with her methods. They argued, and she intentionally attacked him so that he'd Turn. She was the one who attacked Hunter's mother, and your mother still lives and is feeding. Lei came after me in the Uncompahgre with Dana, two female lieutenants, and your mother. I don't care if the evidence is inadmissible at the tribunal—out here under the moon, the truth is what it is."

"You'll stand here and allow her to disparage our parents, our history, our *everything* after she's made a fool of you?" Lei yelled, her voice now shrill on the dense night air.

"That's not my intent, and you know it," Sasha said quietly, looking at Shogun. "I saw your father in the shadow lands. The things that happened in history were tragic. But both you and Hunter might have a common element in your blood that could save you . . . we don't want you to become infected, Shogun. I'll bring everything I have to bear to stop that, if I can."

Sasha spun on the crowd and glared at the Vampires milling in the background of it. "Hunter's meds were tampered with. I'll prove it, one way or another. But I know he didn't kill any human. I don't think Shogun did, either—and *I* damned sure didn't. Somebody, however, didn't bank on there being a silver lining to our détente—Shogun selflessly giving me a blood sample." She gave a dangerous smile. "I have a clean version of his blood that Doc can look at and study, since we obviously don't need it for Hunter now. What we found out in the shadow lands was that Hunter had been injecting himself, unknowingly, with infected Werewolf toxin—but he'd clearly built up an immunity to it. He must have, if he got out of the silver bars and shadow-traveled all the way from the Uncompahgre to here!"

There bayou was so quiet that even the crickets and bullfrogs had stopped their night serenade. Sasha looked from Hunter to Shogun. "If Hunter and

Shogun share lineage, then maybe Doc can come up
with something that can stop the virus from taking
you over, Shogun. Maybe Hunter's blood can wind
up saving you—just as you gave yours to try to save
him." She looked at the Vampires hard and finally
spotted Geoff in the crowd. "One thing is for sure,
though—somebody had an agenda. When we find out
who switched the meds and started this whole thing,
oh . . . trust me, there will be hell to pay."

Hunter rubbed his palms down his face as Fae
archers lowered their bows and Dragon bouncers
withdrew. Vampires fell back deeper into the mist,
watching and very unhappy about the turn of events.

"She speaks the truth," Silver Hawk said, first
looking at Shogun and then Hunter. "We must come
together as one, break bread, and discuss the facts.
Shogun, you are blood of our blood. There cannot
be war between brothers." He looked at Hunter with
moist eyes. "I spoke to your mother. The history we
have all known until now has been revised."

A tall redheaded male with a massive barrel chest
wearing hunting fatigues parted the Werewolf pack.
"Buchanan Broussard—member of the tribunal and
North American local clan alpha, presiding." He
looked around the glen and then called, "Is the baron
present? Dugan!"

All eyes turned to the UCE tribunal members, who
made themselves known by stepping forward. Baron
Geoff Montague cleared his throat and nodded from
a spectator's position in the back, but pushed his
way forward with a look of disdain, brushing off his

designer suit's lapels. Dugan elbowed his way forward, his roly-poly frame and scowl further dwarfed in the moonlight by the looming shadows of taller entities beside him.

The large redhead who had called the impromptu meeting to order walked in a circle like a strutting rooster and then stopped short to gaze around the assembled supernatural crowd. "In addition to the personal affront to my daughter's honor, which I don't even want to discuss in mixed company, there are still multiple offenses that must be addressed. And our local family has to be made whole."

Buchanan cocked back his pump shotgun and spoke in a loud, clear bellow like an evangelist. "First off, we got a contagion spreader. That's a felony if ever I saw one, regardless of who specifically ate the humans. See, we have to take that as a serious offense, because we can't have the other UCE members thinking wolves of any variety can't handle themselves in a civilized manner. Ain't fittin', and just ain't done. We don't need to give *anybody* any reason to start a full-out wolf hunt." Buchanan shook his head. "You know you got the dread disease as a carrier of it in your bloodstream and you go after an innocent man who's protecting his pack? Ain't right."

"Finally, some semblance of justice," Lei growled, pointing in the Shadow packs' direction.

"Well now, hold on, little lady—I ain't quite finished. We've got an unauthorized attack at Tulane Hospital by your brother and his men, which was a little over the top. We don't operate gangland-style in this neck of the woods—or at least we're trying hard not to. Happens from time to time, but we try to keep the humans out of it. That's a misdemeanor. But then, there's the other not-so-small problem." Buchanan sighed.

"What crime have we committed beyond some stupid misdemeanor?" Lei yelled, setting off the Southeast Asian Werewolf Clan in a series of discordant growls. "We will pay for any damages!"

"It's more than that, Lei," Shogun said quietly.

Buchanan nodded. "Yep. Sad but true. As much as it breaks my baby girl's heart, until that man there does twenty-four hours and a full moon, we've gotta make sure there's no cause for alarm. Right now, we've got two half-eaten dead bodies down at the morgue. That's gonna create a human witch hunt—and we know they'll be sure to turn us in so it's a wolf hunt." He sighed hard again and shook his head. "Then we've got all kinds of allegations of collusion from mates, and family members, and what have you. Seems to me, the big Shadow and his mate need to be incarcerated under house arrest—since they're no immediate danger, as long as he don't go biting folks. The alpha brother from our Southeast Asian contingent and his sister mayhaps need a watchful eye—but that boy who got bit gotta go in chains after the Doc looks at him. Then we best be scouring this bayou to find us that alleged she-devil, if in fact she exists. And for the record, I really hope she do—because it would break my heart to have to put a slug in anybody who came out to this here yard party tonight."

"I'm not going anywhere!" Lei shrieked, snapping and snarling as local Werewolves came through the trees.

Sasha and Hunter were immediately surrounded, but there was no resistance to their capture. Silver Hawk simply nodded and remained composed while the Shadow pack parted and fell back, allowing them to be taken into custody.

Buchanan Broussard raised his shotgun and pointed it at Shogun's head. "Son, while you're still in your clear and right mind, please tell your sister to go with us nice and easy, and I suggest you do the same."

CHAPTER 13

She had to get to her squad. Being incarcerated now was not just inconvenient—it was potentially life threatening. Sasha kept her eyes straight ahead as she and Hunter were separated from Lei and Shogun. Sasha and Shogun briefly shared a look. Hunter unfortunately caught it. Shogun saw that he did. This was so not good. She said a silent prayer for a temporary truce. Silver Hawk, Doc, and the others trailed behind them. This was crazy!

But another dark reality slithered into her consciousness—her human squad was at extreme risk. If anybody had an agenda . . . Sasha stopped walking at the same time Silver Hawk came to an abrupt halt.

Several Werewolf guards and Fae archers whirled on her and Hunter, also edging around the older shaman with care. Huge Werewolf sentries immediately stepped back and took aim. The crowd of witnesses backed up. Nerves were a hair away from tragedy.

"My human military squad," Sasha said. "I want them protected. If my evidence gatherers—"

"You mean tamperers!" Lei screeched.

"My guys might have the key to saving your brother's life, so shut up!" Sasha yelled back. "Don't you see we could all be getting played? The Federations could have been set up for internal warfare."

Hunter and Shogun shared a silent glance. This time the look in their eyes didn't contain hatred but something unfathomable to anyone other than them.

"More importantly," Silver Hawk challenged, "the incarceration should be handled by both Federations, not one."

"We'll sort it *all* out at the tribunal," Buchanan said with a good-ole-boy drawl that gave away his Texas roots.

"No," Silver Hawk said, his voice even and lethal. "I have experienced broken treaties before, as well as kangaroo courts, when young Lion Shadow was injured in the battle with Dexter, along with many of our most able Shadow Wolves. It would leave a serious void in our forces if our current alpha—Hunter— were to mysteriously meet a catastrophic end." The old man raked his wise gaze through the crowd, his seer senses keened enough to make everyone around him nervous. "That would be no different from us demanding that you remand Shogun to our custody without oversight . . . although I think he'd fare better in our care than yours."

"Old man," Buchanan said with a snarl, "this ain't no time and place to be casting aspersions. Not with tensions running so high."

The veiled threat seemed to make Silver Hawk become more aggressive, and he landed a hand on Hunter's forearm to keep him out of it, since Hunter was such a ready-made target.

"My age makes me see things from the position of experience," Silver Hawk said coolly. "You too lost many of your warriors in the battle with Dexter that broke out in the residential vistas of New Orleans one full moon ago. As it was, North America had only an older Werewolf alpha male left . . . you. The Southeast Asian Werewolf Clan had bested all others to the death, and you were the only one with wisdom enough to defer. Thus you are still standing and next in line if Shogun falls—if ever there was a time for a coup."

"You have a lot of nerve spreading rumor and doubt, shaman," Buchanan growled. "You best water your own garden!"

"I want a neutral party to police us while we're under house arrest. Fae or Order of the Dragon, not Vampires." Silver Hawk crossed his arms over his chest.

Begrudgingly, Buchanan tossed his pump shotgun to the nearest Dragon as Fae archers repositioned themselves to surround the two senior potential combatants.

"Suit yourselves. Do as you like," Buchanan said angrily, drawing his local pack near him. "We've got nothing to hide. But if one of them infected sonsabitches escapes, the blood is on your hands. The spectacle that erupts into the streets and the human death toll will be yours to own, not ours! With all these here fine folks watching, I completely absolve myself, my pack, and my clan from anything to do with any of this—y'all hear?"

"We've got a camp over in the Ninth Ward," a burly blond Dragon in full biker gear shouted out. "Believe me, we do Dungeons and Dragons better than any of you can imagine. Escapes won't be a problem."

"No. Too visible now," said a tall, handsome Fae captain of the guards. "That Hollywood guy, Brad Pitt, is doing major charitable work there rebuilding homes . . . cameras are everywhere. You've seen the pink tented houses. It's a solid media goodwill effort and what we *do not* need is exposure on TMZ or *Entertainment Tonight.*"

"Can you picture it?" a pretty Phoenix said, her eyes blazing. "An all-out battle caught on *Access Hollywood*? Spare me."

"They might think Pitt was filming for a movie, though," a Dragon yelled from the rear of the crowd.

Voices of dissent rang out, but when the Vampires stepped forward, parting bodies from sheer vapor, the group fell silent again, waiting. Baron Geoff Montague raised an elegant hand and turned to address the crowd like a mesmerizing politician.

"If our characters hadn't been so assailed," Geoff sniffed, "we could offer our Vampire lairs—they're hidden within sprawling estates that are impenetrable to sunlight, and could thus be arranged to block moonlight as well. Veritable fortresses in affluent neighborhoods on high ground that didn't even flood during Katrina. Concrete vaults in the—"

"Thanks, but no thanks," Hunter snarled. He then

whirled his attention to Dugan. "And I'm also not big on going back to the B and B where my meds somehow got tampered with."

"What are you trying to say, laddie?" Dugan yelled. "I should be the one offended to have a . . . a . . . toxin junkie hiding out in my establishment!"

Hunter spun on the voice and snarled so deeply that several clicks from weapon hammers echoed through the clearing.

"Not a problem to respect the requests of the accused, who also have legitimate concerns. Our objective is to be neutral and to see that justice prevails," the Fae captain said, motioning for several crossbow-toting archers to move forward. "We have our own enchanted compounds in the forests and bayous."

"Where?" Shogun snarled, his gaze distrustful.

"If I tell you, I'd have to kill you," the Fae captain said without a smile. "But rest assured, laddie, stealth is what we do. Any more complaints before we move out?"

Loud silence was the crowd's unified answer. A pump shotgun barrel nudge from a nearby Fae guard prompted Sasha to begin walking again, but not before she sent Bear Shadow and Crow Shadow a meaningful glance. The two lead enforcers gave her and Hunter a look, then peeled away from the larger group as her mind began to shut out the surrounding chaos to focus on Woods and Fisher. Her familiars needed to know what was happening, needed to know to look alive to stay alive—and to be careful not to shoot the wrong wolves.

* * *

"I might be a team shaman-in-training," Winters said to Bradley in a loud voice to get his attention over the truck's diesel engine, "but I'm better on kinetics." He glanced at Clarissa, whose gaze was far off. "Like, I can't do what she does, but I've got the heebie-jeebies. Now, in my world, heebie-jeebies, after all the shit we've seen, should be a valid thing. Ya think?"

"Shut up, Winters," Fisher yelled through the partition. He nodded toward Woods, whose gaze was much like Clarissa's.

"Then, if the man is having a familiar vision, shouldn't you take over the wheel before we catch our deaths by vehicular homicide?" Bradley yelled at Fisher.

"Sasha wants us off the streets ASAP," Woods said in a faraway voice.

"I like how the captain thinks," Winters said, growing nervous with the others.

"Send in Bear Shadow and Crow Shadow as armed guards . . . get the blood sample to a base, any base we're close to, and use the protocol code to give Clarissa and Winters unrestricted access to systems . . . use that to deploy a don't-ask, don't-tell special-ops cover so MPs let us through with Bear and Crow, and will cover us in a firefight." Woods finally slumped forward, holding the wheel tightly, then wiped sweat off his brow with the back of his forearm.

He looked at Fisher the instant Clarissa braced herself. Both soldiers drew weapons at the same time, making the truck violently swerve. Something heavy hit the roof. Bradley picked up the M40 Remington rifle that had been at his feet, pointed up, and fired. Clarissa got to the center of the truck holding a nine-millimeter just as an arm came crashing through the side.

"Vampires!" she yelled, squeezing off rounds as Bradley and Winters scrambled away from the back flap.

Something landed on the hood, causing Woods and Fisher to open up their clips and send silver shells through the windshield. Glass spiderwebbed into a frosted pane as both soldiers made a direct hit that sent burning embers over the front of the vehicle, blinding them to the road. Within seconds, two predators had opened the back flap, scrambling like fast-moving crabs.

But before they could reach out their razor-sharp claws, the vehicle lurched hard, then pitched and came down hard, still hurtling forward from momentum as Woods fought against a hard rollover. The sound of metal scraping asphalt screamed from the bottom of the vehicle only seconds before the axle came through the floor, goring one Vampire. A huge dark wolf sailed through the flap before the second Vampire could disappear, tearing out his chest cavity with an angry growl. The truck came to a groaning stop. The smell of gasoline changed wolves into men. No words were necessary, no further shots fired as Bear Shadow grabbed Clarissa and Winters, practically tossing them by the scruffs of their necks to Crow Shadow on the ground, and then got Bradley out.

Woods and Fisher had already bailed and were on

their way around the side of the vehicle when the group started running a breakneck hundred-yard dash. A huge *kaboom* and a flash of heat sent the group onto their stomachs in the marshy grasses along the side of the road. Flying debris and shrapnel whirred over their heads, and the sound of rounds going off and metal hitting concrete added into the impact.

For several minutes, nobody moved. Finally Bear Shadow and Woods lifted their heads.

"Everybody okay?" Woods shouted, his worried gaze assessing the group.

One by one squad members gave verbal confirmation and began to move.

Fisher was on his feet with Crow and Bear, helping everybody up. His gaze went toward the destroyed truck. "All that fucking new equipment we just hauled—damn!"

"You're lucky no civilians were driving near that, or we'd be pulling dead bodies out and explaining to grieving relatives, man. You can get more weapons, but damn," Bear Shadow said in a low rumble.

Fisher raked dirt and leaves out of his hair, still shaken. "They blew the tank, man. They were gonna burn us alive in there. Fry us!"

"Only after they figured out you had the sample and any evidence for the trial still on you," Crow Shadow said, winded. "Vampires can smell blood even better than we can. They knew it was in the truck—so you and the truck were obviously a problem."

"Trial?" Bradley peered around, his gaze moving like a ferret's.

Bear Shadow nodded. "The United Council of Entities tribunal. Right now they've got Hunter, Sasha, the doctor, Silver Hawk, and—"

"Hold it," Woods said, checking his clip. "That's bullshit! They've got the captain and our man, Doc, plus two friendlies? Do they know they're fucking with the USMC? In two seconds I make one call to the Joint Readiness Center over at Fort Polk NAS about two miles up the road, plus Barksdale AFB, and I say a missile-ready F-18 plus a coupla Black Hawks—"

"It might come to that," Bear Shadow said, holding Woods's forearm as he whipped a cell phone out of his pocket. "But not yet. Right now they're being held by neutral and fair parties. Sasha was clear—she wanted us to get the sample to the lab, evidence secured, and eventually Doc back to help come up with an antidote for Shogun." He hung his head, his massive shoulders a network of sinew beneath a fall of onyx hair. "But we were too damned late."

"Saving our asses wasn't such a bad thing, dude," Winters said, still glancing around like a nervous rabbit. He whipped a flash drive out of his pocket. "If you need Fairy testimony, I've got the tape from the Tulane incident on digital."

"Let's say it sometimes pays to have second sight," Clarissa said, extracting a vial of blood from between her ample breasts. "Sorry, guys, it was the only place I could think to stash it where I couldn't get pickpocketed by a Phantom, or have it break."

"I could kiss you," Crow Shadow said with a weary sigh.

Clarissa smiled and gave Crow Shadow an appreciative once-over. "And I might let you."

"This blast probably already has MPs en route— I'm calling in," Woods said. "We need to get a lift to NAS and get these guys to a computer fast." He looked at Bear Shadow and Crow Shadow. "Thanks for the assist. Seriously. That's the third time you've pulled me and Fisher's asses out of the fire."

"You're family," Bear said, grabbing Woods's forearm in a warrior's embrace. "You're pack. That's what we do."

Winters shook his head. "All this is real cool, most appreciated," he said, nodding toward the quickly approaching headlights on the road. "But I suggest they do their Shadow thing and meet up with us later dressed in stolen uniforms or something. It's gonna be harder to explain what happened to the authorities if these guys are buck naked."

As quickly as the crowd had gathered, it dispersed. The Fae retinue of guards and soldiers marched the group forward, seeming alert but also at ease. Their confidence in being able to handle the situation had a strangely calming effect. As bizarre as it was, Sasha felt a low, buzzing peace fall over her, as though she'd been lightly sedated. She glanced around; even Hunter and Silver Hawk's lids appeared heavy. When she glanced at Lei, the woman was practically stumbling through the underbrush, as docile as could be.

Enchantment . . . whoa. She'd never underestimate the Fae's military prowess again in her life.

Sasha tried to rub the haze from her eyes as the

group proceeded forward in a steady, quiet march
through the bayou. Then suddenly the captain of the
guards drew a small pouch out of his vest pocket and
began flinging a golden dust out before them. Tiny
sparkles shimmered in the moonlight and gently
floated down to coat the ground in a multihued glitter.
Sasha again rubbed her eyes as the path they'd been
on split, trees and underbrush landmarks appeared to
move, and the scent all around them became a gentle,
floral, and thoroughly untraceable foreign odor.

"That is awesome," she said, suddenly giggling.
Oh, yeah, whatever they flung around definitely had
an effect. Shogun had slapped Hunter five?

"Glad you like it, lassie. A little Fairy dust and
enchantment is good for the soul," the Fae captain
said. "If I told you Welcome to Oz, that would be
too corny, so how about Welcome to Forte Shannon
of Inverness?"

His piercing blue eyes seeming to twinkle with
delight at her compliment as he walked forward
straight, tall, and proud. He then flung his long spill
of brunette ponytail woven with silver bands over his
shoulder and began running in a dizzying zigzag pattern while the other Fae archers held up their hands
for the group to wait.

To the amazement of the uninitiated, a cobbled
path opened in the moonlight shrouded by mist. The
Fae captain stood in the middle of it and called out in
a loud, strong voice, "Lower the drawbridge!"

"Oh, shit . . . ," Sasha murmured in complete rap-
ture as a huge, stone thirteenth-century-like castle
slowly became visible.

Turrets and catwalks were populated with milling soldiers. A massive moat filled with muddy water and clearly ravenous gators yawned before them. Slowly, a wide iron plank groaned open to bang against the stones close to the Fae captain's feet. Then seemingly out of nowhere, three unicorn-riding guardsmen galloped forward.

Sasha stared at the black, chestnut, and snow-white horses, each bearing a silver-lance-carrying rider whose long tresses matched the slightly glowing coats of his mount. It was almost worth getting locked up to witness this, she thought with another quiet giggle. The buzz that came along with it wasn't half bad, either.

"Sir Rodney," the rider on the black unicorn said, trotting forward. He bowed and his unicorn bowed, then the Fae captain returned the graceful gesture. "Your orders?"

"No harm is to come to any of these guests. They may be under our house arrest, but my instincts say there's been foul play. Too many were eager to see their demise. I have been in contact with good Ethan, who owns The Fair Lady in town . . . be sure that he, his lovely wife, Margaret, as well as his children are also brought in under protective custody. The Fairies will not testify, as you know, but they've been thoroughly mortified by events that have taken place in their gardens. That is a matter for later." Rodney turned and looked at Shogun with sad eyes. "But this guest may have the moon sickness. We hope not, but we must be prepared for that eventuality, as much as I hate to remand him to the lower chambers."

"We'll prepare the dungeons—"

"Dungeons? Dungeons!" Lei shrieked. "Do you know who this is? He is a VIP, the . . ." Her voice trailed off as Sir Rodney extracted a fistful of shimmering powder and blew it through the small hole he'd made between his curled fingers and his palm.

"Please keep that man as comfortable as possible during his unfortunate stay . . . as well as his sister," Sir Rodney said with a weary sigh. "She, however, may need restraints when she wakes up."

He looked at Sasha, Hunter, and then Silver Hawk, pointing toward Xavier Holland. "That man is a doctor. One of the best. The contagion that the Southeast Asian Clan leader received was through an accidental infection during battle between two males—this was a domestic, personal issue that no one should be put to death for, especially since frightened Fairies had a hand in it. We, the Fae, have an obligation to assist in righting this wrong. The doctor has been separated from his lab and his human medical colleagues . . . maybe if we afford him what he needs, a catastrophe can be averted. Ethan's wife, Margaret, can help— bring her here. She's an adept healer."

Just that quickly, the rider of the black unicorn turned with the others, gave Sir Rodney a swift nod, and galloped off. Sasha watched the ground, perplexed. She heard hooves clatter across the cobbled path, but their hooves never touched it as they rose steadily and disappeared into the moonlight.

"That is just soooo cool," she murmured, gaping behind their misty trail.

The moment they stepped onto the heavy iron drawbridge, Sasha felt she'd gone back in time. A small, bustling medieval village lay behind the high, protective fort walls under a winking blanket of stars. Soldiers peered at them with curiosity, as did gawking Elves, sparkling plumes of Fairies, grimy little Gnomes, and a few irate miniature Trolls. Tiny bodies were everywhere, all holding handmade brooms and pointing small sticks at them, only lowering the wands once they'd safely passed their vendor stalls or storefronts.

Tall, proud Elves frowned their disdain as the group went by, and a few Hags gathered their damp toads and bundles of struggling, tied bats in close as though the passing prisoners might swipe one to eat off their stands without paying. That's when Sasha realized that the two battling male wolves had transitioned back into their human forms naked. It was a natural occurrence in the wolf packs—but in the Fae community, seeing two buff prisoners of war promenading under archer guard in the raw had to be scandalous. A smile tugged at her cheek. Oh, yeah, she *had* to be high on fairy dust. Everything around her was so absurdly surreal, she wanted to laugh.

"Once inside the castle, you'll be able to rest," Sir Rodney said in a cheerful tone. "It's been a long while since we've had prisoners. We generally remain neutral in all disputes, and most are solved with mortal combat anyhow, so there's normally no one to bring in for a stay."

As they walked, he motioned with his chin up to a tower that seemed miles away. Two huge, shadowy things with long necks and tails and bat wings were circling the endlessly tall structure in the mist, but were so distant that Sasha squinted trying to make out what they were.

"Griffin Dragons," Sir Rodney said with obvious pride in his voice. "Pets on loan to us from The Order of the Dragon—they don't transform into human form, you know. Though they do enjoy . . . uhmmm . . . remains. Make for great guard dogs. But they'll be so disappointed that there won't be anyone staying in the tower to play with. We always ask for the scraps after battles for them, of course. Our way of recycling and being environmentally responsible to the forest, our mother."

Glances of instant understanding passed among the members of the leisurely imprisoned group. Even Lei seemed to gather that Sir Rodney was offering them a quiet threat. It was no doubt his way of diplomatically explaining that any breach of conduct and the offender could be eaten alive or hunted down like a mad dog by a hulking Griffin Dragon. Given the size of what was flying around the tower in the mist, even a deranged, demon-infected Werewolf would be kibble for one of those monsters. Same deal with the moat— the thick bodies moving through the mud were bigger than anything she'd ever seen in Louisiana.

He didn't need to tell them twice. Sasha nodded

and her gaze met Sir Rodney's with open respect. She'd definitely never underestimate the Fae again. In truth, this little walk through their world was growing on her. She liked their style as much as she liked their easy, down-home manner. Their magic was outrageously effective. It was just the Trolls and Hags she wasn't sure about. She wondered what other ethnic groups resided here, but decided now wasn't the time to ask.

The retinue of guards brought them to a halt before massive, wooden castle doors that slowly opened. Several Gnomes rushed out with long silver spears, then bowed and stepped aside once they saw Sir Rodney.

Again, the group merely gaped as they entered a great hall with an apparently endless vaulted ceiling that almost kissed the sky. Huge lanterns flickered as though powered by the dust of Fairies. Wide, polished slate sections created a mosaic pattern of beauty on the stone floors. Stained-glass windows with knights in battles flanked the spiral staircase and gracefully moved through scenes as though reenacting an age-old epic. A warm fire roared from a huge walk-in fireplace tended by little people who seemed in a perpetual hurry. Empty silver suits of armor saluted as they passed the foyer into the great hall. Music from lyres and flutes sent a joyful noise through the castle from an unknown source. That alone almost made Sasha fall asleep where she was standing, were it not for the rumble in her stomach caused by the delicious scent of grilling meats.

"These men will show you all your accommodations," Sir Rodney said, splitting the group of guards into two sections with a wave of his hand. Half the retinue guided Sasha, Hunter, Doc, and Silver Hawk toward the stairs. The other half moved Lei and Shogun toward a heavy stone door covered in iron bars and huge locks.

"Baths will be drawn in your rooms, platters of food brought to you all. New clothing. Medical attention to tend your wounds . . . we have expert healers on staff. Rest, after what you've experienced, is important."

He looked at Shogun with compassion. "We will treat you equally as well, my friend. Don't worry. Food, baths, comfortable bedding—albeit behind bars and away from moonlight—will be afforded you and your sister. We will allow the doctor to visit, and the others . . . I take it you all have much to discuss. But we need to be sure certain precautions are observed. No offense ever intended."

"None taken," Shogun said, proudly lifting his head and staring at the dungeon door. "I actually prefer it that way."

Torn, Sasha gazed at Shogun's profile, then slowly dragged her eyes away. Conflict ate at her. A part of her stood with Hunter and her Shadow family, yet she couldn't help her feelings for Shogun, even though they defied definition . . . each one impossible to describe even to herself. All she was sure of at the moment was that she couldn't abandon the man to the fate of an infected Werewolf Turn.

No matter what, he was a friend, and deserved a much more dignified end than that.

CHAPTER 14

Sasha didn't argue when the guards insisted that they each go to their own rooms first, then call for an escort if they wanted to visit another prisoner. As house arrest went, this wasn't bad at all. Even Hunter seemed all right with it once they'd explained that he would indeed be able to confer with his family members. Cooperating was easier than resistance at this juncture.

Sasha made quick work of jumping into and getting out of a steaming tub of luxuriously soapy water that almost melted her bones. It left a smooth, creamy residue on her skin. The Fae knew how to do enchantments, all right, right down to hand-tooled leather pants and an ivory silk blouse with billowing sleeves. Wasn't her style, the blouse, but felt fantastic on the skin.

Hand-cobbled boots that the Elves left fit like a soft glove. Although they'd confiscated her firearm, they'd given her a small silver dagger engraved with mesmerizing Gaelic symbols—they obviously trusted her.

Or they knew whom she'd most likely want to see . . . it had to be Sir Rodney's way of ensuring that she didn't become collateral damage at the hands of a Werewolf contagion outbreak.

Sasha tried not to gulp as she stood by the table, shamelessly shoving forkfuls of grilled pheasant into her mouth, along with wild rice and the sweetest carrots and peas drenched in butter she'd ever had in her life. If anyone was watching her, it was a total lie that she was eating so fast to get quickly to a conversation with Hunter and Silver Hawk, or even Doc. Any of those talks were going to be hard and emotionally draining. The raw truth was she was famished.

Still . . . she had to talk to Hunter, had to find out what he had learned that could help his case. Had to address whatever had sparked the bitter fight in the bayou between him and Shogun—as though that were a secret now. Had to admit what had happened in the teahouse, and had to talk to Doc . . . her father. From there, she had to go to Shogun and help the man while he was still lucid. If she went to him first, no one had to tell her that it would get ugly in the family.

Sasha closed her eyes as she pushed the last forkful of her dinner into her mouth. She grabbed a handful of grapes as she crossed the room to pick up the wide belt that had a dagger scabbard built into it and threaded the buckle, pulling it tight over her hips with one hand. Thinking, dreading, she popped the grapes into her mouth and then stopped as sweet juice exploded on her tongue. It was so good it literally stunned her.

Tiny chiming voices pelted her ears and dancing

opalescent lights made her dizzy as she opened her eyes. For a second she stared down at the grapes. "What the . . ."

"Miss, miss!" a tiny voice cried out. "We are so sorry!"

Although she was looking at the grapes, the voices seemed to be coming from somewhere near her ear. Disoriented, Sasha's gaze tore around the room and stopped on a sparkling, moving miasma of tiny dust motes.

"Dugan tricked us."

On guard, Sasha tilted her head as she stared into the moving lights, slowly making out the gnat-size Fairies. Straining hard, she listened with wolf ears now.

"Dugan tricked you?" she said softly. "How?"

"Oh, our gardens," the miasma wailed. "Our beautiful, beautiful gardens are ruined forever by blood!"

"Okay, take me through it slowly. What happened?" Sasha popped another grape into her mouth and tried not to swoon from the flavor.

"Dugan told us if we enchanted you, he could keep our gardens safe from the beast. But that didn't work. She still came there after all those years . . . back to where she had been before," tiny voices cried out in unison.

"All right," Sasha said, growing peevish as she cast the grapes on the table. She pointed at the floating lights. "What did you guys do to me at the teahouse?"

"We enhanced what was there," the small voices wailed. "Nothing bad . . . just like the grapes' sweetness. We only made it better, we meant no harm. We just wanted to be safe. We don't like Lei. We don't like Dana. They called the beast there and fed her there, but Dugan said you'd keep her away . . . just like Shogun would. We wanted you both to like the garden and to stay near us to keep us safe. We don't want you to leave with the other big wolf, Sasha . . . Shogun likes the garden. It was his father's. Please stay in New Orleans with us, *please*. The Vampires here are so mean to us. They kill people sometimes, too!"

Sasha slapped her forehead and closed her eyes. There was no denying the chemistry between her and Shogun, but an enhancement spell was so not what she needed to be dealing with right now. Hunter was gonna have a cow. Frightened Fairies were not going to make a good alibi to a jealous male wolf who mated for life.

"You guys should have just asked me," Sasha said in a weary tone, opening her eyes and pointing at them as though they were naughty children. "Bad Fairies!"

A collective wail rose up from the shimmer, and she used their distress to press a point—after all, they'd given her some serious intel. Dugan was in on it, supposedly trying to keep Lei and Dana out of their gardens; plus, Lei and Dana had been caught luring an infected Werewolf there and feeding it. She'd already gotten word that Vampires had gotten Dugan to remove his defenses against them at the B&B so they could do a bait-and-switch with Hunter's meds . . . but she needed to know what their angle was. And why would Dugan want her and Shogun to hook up?

"You guys owe me, you know that," Sasha warned. "You've really pissed off the big wolf, and now an innocent man got infected in a fight that didn't have to happen." She raked her damp hair and folded her arms over her chest.

The colorful, shimmering cloud seemed to burst like Fourth of July fireworks, sending sparklers everywhere before coming back together.

"Oh, Sasha . . . we saw. The Forest Pixies told us. The baron got your clothes and Shogun's and left them for the huge Shadow. He was so upset . . . oooohhhh . . ."

"The baron, huh?" Sasha's hands were on her hips. She cocked her head to the side. That definitely linked Geoff Montague with Dugan. To her way of seeing it, the only thing that bringing her and Shogun together and then leaving cold-blooded evidence like that for an out-of-control, possibly demon-infected Shadow to find would accomplish would be to start a wolf war. "Hmmm . . ."

Sasha looked off toward the windows, studying the moonlight in the leaded, beveled glass. Have both leaders go into mortal combat, and that leaves the wolf Federations on both sides weak . . . allowing the Vampire Cartel to step back into power. Her mind was on fire as it tracked data points. Everything made so much sense. Once wolves were weak again, the Fae would fracture into special-interest groups, just as the Dragons and Mythics would.

Dugan was a businessman, one who'd suffered severe losses after the hurricane. She just wondered what the Vampires had promised him. Maybe it was just a smart move—somebody hedging his bets to help the old boys' network that never forgot a slight or a friend. Sorta like helping out the mob before they asked for assistance and being considered a good egg when they rolled on an area. She could figure out what his angle was later. At the moment she needed hard evidence to get both Dugan and Geoff off the tribunal and possibly convicted themselves.

Narrowing her gaze on the distraught Fairies, Sasha walked in a circle around their throbbing cloud of shimmering dust.

"First of all," she said, trying to push as many guilt buttons in them as she could, "you have a man's execution on your hands if we can't come up with a cure—so I want a full-scale, all-out effort to help Doc and Clarissa come up with a cure, even if it involves cheating with a little magic."

"We'll help, Miss Sasha, we'll help. Oooohhhh . . . We never kill people. It is against all that we believe in—we never meant for him to get hurt!"

The cloud burst into tendrils of sparkling rain all around the room. Maybe she'd gone too far. This could be a Fairy feint, she wasn't sure, but she kept up the bad-cop voice just to whip them in line.

"And now that you potentially have an innocent man's life in limbo . . . I want whatever you can find out on Dugan and his Vampire connection to Geoff. If you have a tainted needle, a vial, anything they used—heard a conversation—"

"Pixies can help us lift heavy things like vials and needles," the Fairies said in quick squeaks. "But we cannot testify . . . noooo . . . oh, noooo . . ."

"Why can't you testify?" Sasha said in a flat, monotone voice, totally annoyed.

"Because they'll all know we helped you, and we never get involved."

"But you *are* involved! You did a spell and that backfired. So cut the don't-snitch crap!" Sasha walked around the room as the cloud dispersed into fleeing dust motes. As she chased them, she could hear them squealing like they were having mini nervous breakdowns.

"All right, all right," Sasha finally said, standing still as the Fairies gathered their composure. Making them run screaming into the night wouldn't solve jack.

"I won't press testimony if you can bring me intel and evidence in the next twenty-four hours that can help. I've got several problems that you guys helped create and therefore need to help fix—let's start with a man in a dungeon who is very, very sick, plus one down the hall who is very, very hurt. I've got a she-demon wolf looking for me, and Lei and Dana are feeding her in your gardens . . . gotta find that bitch fast and make sure the other two do time for loosing that on the general public. Something like that can't happen again."

"Oh, oh, those poor young humans," the Fairies said, swooning. "Wood Sprites can help you find the demon. They will tell us where her lair is—they don't want her in their bayou any more than we want her in our garden!"

"What about Lei and Dana?"

"No, no, no, we saw but cannot testify . . . ohhh!"

"You could do a truth-enhancement spell—an enchantment to bring out what's already there," Sasha said, calmly, watching the miasma settle down. "Let them tell on themselves at the tribunal. That way, you stay out of it, and it's evidence against a coupla bad Werewolf chicks who you want out of your garden, anyway—not Vampires whom you're deathly afraid of."

She took the Fairies' lack of immediate response as a possible yes and pressed on, knowing they were considering the repercussions of going against Buchanan Broussard's family by setting Dana up. The teeny folks did have a point; he seemed like a real bastard.

"Listen," Sasha said in a weary tone that was no act. "I've got two huge wolf Federations about to go to war over the bull, and a local yokel angling to get him and his daughter installed as the next clan leaders. *That* would be lovely—picture that," she added with biting sarcasm. "Then, if that weren't bad enough, I've got a squad on the run that needs protection. And if all of this isn't enough to make your head hurt, think of it this way . . . if the wolf Federations go to war, and you'd better hope they don't, the Vampires will be in prime position to take over not just the UCE again, but also New Orleans. The math is real simple—either help me or you're screwed as not-so-innocent bystanders. I'm going back up to the North Country when this is all over; you guys have to live here. This is your neighborhood."

Sasha watched with great satisfaction as the shimmering lights stopped moving about for a moment, gathered together, and then took on a dark gray hue that she could only interpret as outrage. "Face it. You got played," she said with a dramatic sigh designed to add a little inspiration for them to

step up. "Hate to tell you, but, your man Dugan hung you out to dry."

Hunter stared at his grandfather across the table in his room. He ate; the old shaman ate. Words seemed to elude them.

"This is not like Sasha," Silver Hawk said. "There was something else involved, no matter what you found in the bayou."

Hunter looked up from his plate, his gaze level with his grandfather's. "From all that you've told me, even my own mother made choices like this," he said in a bitter tone. "That's how I got here. She chose someone over her life mate, who was a wrong fit. Couldn't blame her, just like I can't blame Sasha . . . Sasha thought I was dead to her, a junkie to the antitoxin, maybe even Turning . . . as good as dead. So she made a logical choice. I suppose my half brother was that." He shoved another forkful into his mouth as his grandfather's eyes slid away from his.

"Son," the old shaman said quietly. "There is more to it than you know, I'm sure. Let her tell you in her own time. Your words are raw now, just as your heart is raw. Let both heal before you speak pain that will leave her heart injured. That is all I ask. I am tired. I am going to see if I can help my friend Doc, and then together two old men will endeavor to save a young man's life. The rest of it—the healing, the bringing together of blood brothers and justice—is in the hands of the Great Spirit."

Silver Hawk stood. Hunter abandoned his plate and stood as well. The two looked at each other for a long while, and then the old man simply embraced him.

Doc looked up quickly from his meal as a knock sounded at his door. Silver Hawk had promised him he'd return soon after he talked to Hunter, but if he was back already that was not a good sign. Standing slowly, he called out for the person at the door to come in. But seeing Sasha enter his room as two guards left her and closed the door behind her thoroughly shook him. He hadn't planned on talking to her alone until the morning . . . until his beaten, fatigued brain could rest and come up with an explanation that her pain-filled eyes demanded.

"Hello, Dad," she said in a quiet monotone. "Mind if I sit down so we can finally get to the truth?"

Whatever had been in the bathwater stung every silver wound like hell. Cooked meat, the stench of roasted pheasant and—of all things—vegetables, was about to make him hurl.

Shogun lay across the bed panting and naked with sweat rolling off his overheated body. Goose down was too hot. The duvet, the linen, the silk pillows all made him want to howl. He needed to be outside. Needed to run, to hunt, to kill something . . . to taste blood! His claws dug into the comforter, shredding it as blind rage propelled him up off the sumptuous mattress to begin flipping furniture, hurling the privacy screen at the bars that had enclosed the tub, a toilet, and a small dressing area, and then crashing anything else in his huge cell that wasn't nailed down.

He could hear Lei screaming for the guards to come assist him, but her voice was shrill enough to make his head throb.

"Make that shrew shut up!" he bellowed. "Put her on another side of the castle! I don't want her near me—she betrayed me and the family!"

"I didn't, I didn't," Lei said sobbing as guards opened her cell to move her quarters. "Don't take me away from him—only I can help my brother now," she shrieked, fighting against air as the Fae guards stood back and sent enchanted vines to bundle her into acquiescence on the floor. "I did what I did for you!"

"My mother is alive—where?" he shouted, a sudden intense desire to pack-bond with the demon-infected overwhelming him. "All these years you knew, and kept that from me! I had a brother and you knew, bitch!" Shogun shouted through the bars, watching them carry his struggling sister somewhere he couldn't see her.

A lonely, agony-riddle howl crept up his throat as his hands sought his hair. Tears stung his eyes. He was Turning . . . God help him, he could feel it.

The sound of Shogun's howl made Sasha hug herself as she stared across the table at Doc. She knew she should have gone to Shogun first, but she'd told herself that she needed to speak to the medical professional on the team to better understand what she was dealing with so they could both go together. The moment she'd opened the door to face Doc she knew she'd again told herself lies. This was about unfinished business and needing to understand why any and all of it had gone down the way it had.

Doc had stopped speaking when he'd heard Shogun's howl. The pain in his eyes made her finally reach across the table and clasp his hand. That simple gesture made tears well in both their eyes as Doc squeezed her hand back.

"I'm immune, too, Sasha," Doc said in a quiet rasp. "Like my mentor, Lou Zang Chen. We'd both been scratched over the years by patients—soldiers we were harnessing down after they'd been brought in half eaten during the Colombian incident. That was before we realized how the contagion morphed, how a man transitioned. But that's also when we discovered that he and I shared a hidden secret. We both wanted a cure. We both had wolf DNA in our blood and both had pure human mothers."

Sasha dragged her fingers through her hair. Somehow, talking to Doc about DNA and cures was so much easier than discussing the subject they both were so obviously avoiding.

"But if I'm half human from my mother's side, plus one-quarter Shadow from you—because you're a fifty–fifty mix of human and Shadow," she said, studying the grain of the wood in the highly polished table between them, "then why is my wolf so strong?"

Xavier Holland let out a long, tired sigh as she looked up and met his weary gaze. "All I've ever been able to attribute that to is dominant and recessive genes being the roll of the dice, Sasha. It's just like in a family of brown-eyed individuals—a startling pair of green eyes or blue eyes can show up, or even a vastly different skin color." He opened his hands, as though imploring the heavens to give him an answer. "There's been no adultery in those cases, only what old folks used to call a throwback trait—something that probably got many an innocent woman stoned or beaten to death. Pure human ignorance of the vagaries of genetics . . . such a waste."

"Why didn't you, me, or Lou Zang Chen Turn, though? There's something among the three of us that we're not figuring out," she said, her gaze trailing away from her father toward the waning moonlight." She looked at Doc. "I got infected, you got infected, he did, too—and we all had varying degrees of Shadow Wolf and human in us."

"His wolf was very far removed," Doc said quietly. "Only an eighth or less . . . yet he didn't Turn. That genetic riddle has stumped me my entire career."

"I wish we had blood samples from your mentor," Sasha said, raking her hair.

The deafening silence made her quickly look at Xavier Holland.

"We do," he said in a thick, shame-filled murmur. "We kept all the bodies from that lab accident."

"Frozen?" Sasha's eyes were so wide now that it felt as though they might roll right out of her skull. "All of them?"

Doc nodded and looked away. "Yes. *All* of them."

"My mother . . ."

Doc closed his eyes. "I will never let you see . . . what was left. Don't ask me that, Sasha."

She stood and went to the window, drawing in

ragged breaths. Nausea made her stomach roil. Science and the military knew no bounds.

"I won't ask you to see her," Sasha finally said. "I don't ever want to see her like that—I've seen her in the shadow lands in spirit, whole and beautiful. That's enough for me. But I'd like to go back to NORAD with you and Clarissa to look at Dr. Chen's blood, comparing that with Shogun's and with ours . . . there's gotta be a marker, something."

"For three decades, Sasha, I've turned over every stone. What can we possibly find now at this late hour? As much as it breaks my heart to say this, Shogun probably won't make it tomorrow night. It's gone too far too fast in his system."

"Then we're gonna turn over those stones one more time." She spun and looked at Doc's dejected expression. "We've never had pure, uninfected Werewolf blood in the lab before, right? We didn't even know the species existed thirty years ago—not till earlier this year. I got infected and fought it off, just like Hunter eventually fought it off, just like you did, as well as your mentor had in the past. My instincts say we're on the verge of a cure . . . have to be. And during the last UCE Conference, what got the Vampires expelled was that they'd sent in an assassin to hit General Donald Wilkerson. We learned then that they didn't want a vaccine to be widely distributed that could make the taste of human blood so offensive; Vampires would begin to starve to death. Even money says this is part of the issue. Power. Resources. Territory. It all fits the profile of vampirism."

Doc nodded and then rubbed his palms down his

face. "It would be an effective strategy to get the wolf packs fighting with each other, huge Federations at war . . . makes it easy to call for an all-out wolf hunt to quell the violence. They get back in power, based on all you've told me about how this council works. Meanwhile, any chance of developing a cure is diverted. Humans are more focused on wiping out the scourge than developing vaccines or genetic medicine—forget harmonious living when there are monsters threatening mankind. Meanwhile, the Vampires continue to feast, unrestrained. It's a beautiful plot, strategically brilliant."

Sasha walked in a circle, nerves strung tight. "All I need is evidence to bring to the UCE to stop a wolf hunt, as well as to avert a war. The Federations still don't fully trust each other—you saw that very fragile peace out there in the bayou. Shogun and Hunter have to sit down at the table together to show a unified front . . . but that means Shogun has to heal."

"It also means Hunter has to heal, Sasha," Doc said quietly, his gaze containing empathy. "He's been shot in the heart with a silver bullet."

She looked away. Doc didn't have to tell her that she'd been the one to pull the trigger.

"I know . . . ," she finally said in a subdued tone. "I wanted to give Silver Hawk a chance to have the private talk with him about his mother and his heritage, first."

Both she and Doc knew it was an evasive tactic, but he was good enough not to call her on it.

"They've had that talk," Doc said gently after a moment. "Now it's time for you two to have one."

"It's time for you and me to have one," she said, staring at Doc as new tears brimmed. "Why didn't you tell me? Why foster care?"

"So they wouldn't know," he said just above a murmur, holding her gaze. "Sit with me, Sasha. Don't stand across the room like you're ready to bolt. If I'd let them know what I'd done, and what was in my DNA spiral, I would have been taken off critical research . . . they would have studied me like a lab rat. Human thinking is so ignorant. Then there would have been no way I could have worked on cures, could have continued what I had to do. I would never have been in a position to protect you from madmen like the late general. Fear creates this ignorance we struggle against in the human condition; power madness and glory seeking magnifies it."

"But I missed grandmothers, aunties, family, connection . . . all because . . ." She covered her mouth and choked back a sob. "Dad, I just wish I had known." Her statement was simple, nonjudgmental, and filled with old pain that had never really gone away. Hurt had dissolved anger, and she couldn't even pull back as Doc rushed to embrace her.

"Oh, Sasha, Sasha, my sweet pea . . ." Doc's warm hug finally made the tears fall, and she put her head on his shoulder. "Child, I was your shadow . . . I was coming for you, wherever they'd taken my baby girl. I was never going to let them take you from me."

"What were my people like? My grandmother, all those I missed?" she whispered thickly into the warmth of his shoulder.

"Your grandmother, my mother, was a tall, dark-skinned beauty. They say her grace captivated my father, your grandfather, from the very beginning. I inherited his Shadow resistance to the virus. I had enough proof of that, knew I could fight it off . . . so that's why I made you from me and no one else. I had truthfully hoped you'd be a flawed Shadow like me—unable to shift so you'd appear normal, be human enough to always blend in . . . just have the instincts. I didn't know what a majestic gift the inner wolf was until I saw it in you. I had been brainwashed, prejudiced, by my own human condition . . . forgive me, daughter. God forgive me."

"I just wanted to be like every other kid, every other person . . . For so long I knew something was wrong with me, but nobody would just tell me the truth."

"That, among many things, is one of my deepest regrets." Doc buried his face in her hair as he hugged her harder. "Don't you see, that's why I used my DNA . . . that and because I loved your mother so, but would never violate her marriage or her trust—or my best friend's trust. They were gonna make you, one way or another. I wanted you made with a fighting chance at being so-called normal . . . human. You were never just a lab experiment to me. *Ever*."

He let out a hard breath as he stroked her back. "They say my mother was a fighter, a loving, high-spirited gal who could see things." He paused as though the memory was more painful than he'd realized, and then he let out his breath in shuddering increments. "I never got to see that part of her. They'd caged her like an animal in a mental institution, because she wouldn't stop telling stories about the wolf

people. In her last days, when I went to see her, she
was broken . . . they'd institutionalized her long
enough and given her enough meds that it finally
stole her spirit. Imagine what they did to a poor,
supposedly mentally ill young black woman in Jim
Crow Louisiana. They weren't kind to the wealthy,
so can you imagine the conditions she'd endured?"

"Oh, Doc . . . ," Sasha murmured, now hugging
him to lend support rather than absorb it.

"Then one night," he said in a sad, far-off voice,
"she just slipped away peacefully. Silver Hawk came
to me, then . . . I was just a young man. He said that
Wolf Shadow had come to escort her to the shadow
lands. He was Silver Hawk's best friend, my father,
and it's how we gave Hunter his wolf name."

"You've been friends for that long," Sasha said
quietly.

It was more of a statement than a question as the
longevity of the relationships began to sink in. She
now better understood why Doc was probably there
when Hunter was born. It made sense that he'd want
to be close at hand when Silver Hawk's daughter
delivered—only no one had expected the camp to
fall under attack.

"If your father and Hunter's grandfather were
best friends, I understand the connection . . . the research, how you as the son of his friend would have
a bond." Sasha shook her head even as Doc hugged
her. The pack loyalty was staggering.

"It all goes so far back, baby girl," Doc said in a
slow rumble of emotion. "Wolf Shadow, my father,
aka Storm Walker when in his human form, had tried

to keep Shogun's demon-infected mother from eating Hunter's mother's remains. He died from the battle. Severe blood loss. Silver Hawk told me that my father's spirit had come to my mother at her deathbed in the hospital so she wouldn't die alone, and to carry her to the shadow lands . . . and to atone for leaving her—and me. He did love her, but he just couldn't reconcile her humanity with his wolf or the traditions and taboos of the pack. Hunter's grandfather and I have sat in many a sweat lodge together, discussing all this to bring us both peace through understanding. Silver Hawk and I have been fast friends ever since."

"I can see that," she whispered as Doc pulled back to meet her gaze.

"Silver Hawk gave me the yen for medicine . . . said I had a purpose to fulfill, a calling to answer. A destiny. Once I saw you, I knew that was true. He also showed me that my mother was anything but insane."

Sasha looked up into the exhausted face and eyes that had always been there for her. So much bloodshed and violence; so many lives shattered from hatred . . . Shogun's mother had also killed her grandfather, not just Hunter's mother. She now understood the explosive nature of it all—history was a time bomb. But anger had fled her, deep sorrow filling the void as she touched her father's cheek. She stared into the eyes of an imperfect man who'd tried to do his best in an imperfect, very human world.

"She's happy, Dad. I saw groups of people in the shadow lands . . . Mom, too. Hunter took me there. We went together before the conference. I saw people whom I didn't recognize on a porch in New Orleans . . . they were all smiling at me. They invited me in. My mother was sitting in a rocking chair. A tall, dark, beauty was in the screen door, and she waved at me. I think that was Grandmom."

"That was my mother's house in New Orleans," Doc said, allowing tears to fall without censure. "That was her, in the screen door. That was her rocker. Promise me, when I die, that you'll take me there to the shadow lands . . . I want to be with my people, and I'm so very, very tired, Sasha."

"I promise," she said quietly. "But that won't be for a very long time. We have lives to save and people to help. Don't quit on me now."

"All right, baby. For a little while longer."

He closed his eyes as though trying to see the images that had been in her mind, and they stood that way for a long time, just holding each other, not talking, but feeling. Now so much of it made sense. Missing pieces to her life's puzzle began to fit, just as smiling spirits fit with Doc's description and the images that flitted through her mind. His people, who were also her people, were in that rowdy, love-filled house. She'd been surrounded by spiritual protection from the moment she'd been conceived—and it didn't matter how she was conceived, now that she knew she wasn't a throwaway child. She'd meant something to many whom she'd never even met . . . meant so much to the man hugging her, who'd devoted his life to protecting her from those who would have done her harm.

CHAPTER 15

He'd been there and couldn't listen to the suffering any longer. It grated his soul, knifed his gut, was like a scraping down his skeleton—the howls of a Turning man.

Hunter called for an escort. Four archers immediately came. They said not a word but watched him warily. He understood why. Wasn't offended in the least. No one was above suspicion when so much clan leadership power hung in the delicate balance between injured parties.

The long, somber walk and endless corridors gave him time to think. He watched silently as stone doors were heaved open, silver-coated iron gates unlocked, and a labyrinth of passageways cut into granite beneath the castle revealed themselves. Every fifty yards, alert guards with silver weaponry hailed his escorts, keeping a hard line of vision on him. Another baleful howl made the hair stand up on his neck as they entered the formal dungeon chambers.

One massive cell carved into the granite cavern

and gated by silver-coated iron bars stood on either side of a twenty-five-foot expanse. In the center of that, guards amused themselves with cards at a small table laden with silver coins and ale. But the moment they spotted Hunter, they jumped to their feet and gathered up their weapons.

"It's all right," one of the escorts said. "This one is a head of state—just wants to visit with the howling one . . . to maybe help him. They're brothers."

Shoulders relaxed, heads nodded in agreement, and then guards sat back down—but remained watchful. Hunter looked at the empty cell.

"Where's Lei?"

One of the guards at the table shrugged. "She pissed off 'er brother and was making 'im crazy—so we moved her to a locked room on the other side of the castle. Made him calm down a bit, till he ate."

Even though he hated Lei's guts, relief wafted through him. If she hadn't Turned or been injured, that was one less thing for the Southeast Asian Clan to blame him for.

"You came to gloat?" Shogun said between his teeth, staying clear of the bars but rising slowly from a hidden position behind overturned furniture.

For a moment, Hunter just stared at him. That was all he could do. Shogun's hair was long and clotted together, as though trying to dreadlock. A thick beard covered his face and was beginning to spread over his chest and forearms. His eyes were a sick yellow-amber, and elongated upper and lower canines distorted his face. His hands were huge like his shoulders

and chest had become, his fingers gnarled as though
stricken with arthritis; yellow nails were razor-sharp.

Wild tufts of hair covered his knuckles, and the
sour stench that wafted from his sweaty body almost
turned his stomach. He watched as Shogun struggled to stand up tall and then stalked away. Hunter's
eyes remained on the knotted spine that curved his
back, hunching his shoulders. Deep remorse ate at
him and stole his voice. He wrested it back as
Shogun turn toward him and growled.

"I didn't come to gloat. I came to apologize to
you for this . . . I'm sorry."

Shogun's chuckle created a low, demonic sound in
the cavern. "Why be sorry, brother? You will right-
fully head both Federations after they put a silver
slug in my skull tomorrow night. You get the title and
the woman." He looked past Hunter's shoulder to the
gaping retinue of guards. "Give this man a drink so
he can celebrate an almost bloodless coup!"

Hunter turned to the guards. "Did you feed him?"

"Yeah," one of them said with a shrug. "All the
prisoners got pheas—"

"Raw meat!" Hunter thundered. "A goat from the
village outside, a damned deer from the bayou, a cow
from a local farm—warm, still twitching—did you
feed this man tonight?"

Two guards stood as the others looked around
confused.

"If you doom my brother to death I'll hold you all
responsible!" Hunter shouted, sending guards running.

"Why, brother," Shogun said in a dangerously low tone. "I didn't think you cared."

"I do," Hunter said, going close enough to the bars to speak to Shogun without being snatched.

"Why?" Shogun growled.

"Because you were never supposed to be infected."

"That's what they all say," Shogun snapped, and began pacing.

"I smelled demon-infected she-wolf in the bayou . . . Lei, Dana, had been there with your mother's scent. I am no liar." Hunter's unblinking gaze met Shogun's. "I thought they were after Sasha."

"I thought you'd infected her," Shogun said between his teeth. "I wanted to find her myself . . . wanted to be the one to end her misery if you had— and then I was coming for you."

"As well you should have—if I'd done that to her. But you saw for yourself tonight that I hadn't."

Shogun paced away from the front of the cell.

"Then, out of nowhere, in a pile of leaves and mud I found your clothes."

Shogun rushed the bars and then backed off. "Impossible! You lie!"

Hunter shook his head. "Khakis wrapped in plastic . . . hers was a T-shirt, green, and matching sweat pants that said CHAYA." He moved closer to the bars than advisable and kept his voice low. "How would I know what you were wearing when you were with her if I'm lying?" Hunter banged on the bars. "Think, man, even in your condition . . . I know in my soul you weren't out there in the bayou with her—so somebody is playing games!"

Shogun circled the cell's interior, growling. "We were at the teahouse . . . miles from where you found them." He looked up at Hunter. "I had thrown them in the trash. I would never disrespect her like that or break her heart by throwing what happened in your face . . . if it's any consolation, she did that for you—not for me. She wanted a vial of my blood to save you. I wanted her, and made her have tea with me." He shook his head and laughed bitterly. "She did. And I never laid a hand on her." He looked at Hunter. "On that, I am no liar, as you say. So rest easy, my brother. Werewolves don't so much care about the fine point . . . we don't split hairs on the subject like Shadow Wolves."

"None of that's important," Hunter said, staring at the rough-hewn wall. "The alliance is at the core of it all—that's the focus."

"Now you're not only lying to yourself, but lying to me," Shogun said with a hollow laugh. He threw a chair at the back wall, shattering it, and bent with a painful howl as a wave of agony overtook him. "You were about to kill me, alliance be damned, because you thought I'd been with her!" Shogun released a bone-chilling howl and then dropped down on all fours, panting. He gave Hunter a dangerous side-long glance. "If this hadn't happened, I would have competed with you until the end of time for her—*brother*. Know that."

Hunter watched Shogun stalk away, hearing him loud and clear. Yet as he watched the man before him, he shuddered to think that that was what Sasha had witnessed. If he'd been like what

Shogun was now—and he had at points—then he couldn't blame her if she'd sought a mate who was free and clear of the dread contagion . . . who could live with the disgusting transformation? But she'd stayed and loved him and fought for him and with him . . . and had even offered her body in exchange for a blood sample to give to Doc to possibly save his life. And now he'd killed a man due to misplaced jealousy and being a disease carrier, all over a shadow dance.

Guilt lacerated him as he listened to the footfalls of anxious guards returning. He could smell the fresh blood in the dank dungeon air. He watched Shogun spin and begin to pace, eyes wilder from the scent. Time was running out for an innocent man.

"You have to eat. You have to hold on to your human," Hunter said quickly. "We have to stand as one. We have to both lead the Federations and find out who did this."

"You lead," Shogun said, panting through elongating canines, his eyes beginning to glow. "I'm finished. You won."

"No! Together," Hunter said emphatically, pounding the bars with his fist. "I didn't want to win like this—and I never wanted Sasha by default, either."

"Nor I," Shogun said, his hands trembling.

Hunter quickly looked over his shoulder. "Where is that man's food?"

He stepped away from the cell bars as two Fae guards lugged in a freshly killed deer. Shogun charged the bars and then fell back with a yelp that became a roar as his skin popped and sizzled.

"How the hell are we gonna get it in there?" the lead guard asked as they all stood, weapons at the ready.

"Give it to me," Hunter said.

"Bull," one of them said, dropping the antler end of the carcass on the floor.

A crimson tide slowly spread at their feet, sending Shogun into a frenzy. Hunter stooped down, grabbed the animal by one hand, and yanked it into a shadow with him, then was gone. He appeared behind a blind of destroyed furniture inside the cell and was back on the other side before the dead deer hit the floor and Shogun rushed him. Blood covered his clothes; shotgun barrels and crossbows moved from him to Shogun and back as edgy guards scrambled away from him. Shogun covered the deer in a possessive, snarling crouch before tearing into its belly and coming away with entrails. Hunter turned to stare at the guards, who stood with mouths agape.

"For the love of God, man . . . you could've been slaughtered in there!" the lead guard shouted, slapping gun barrels away from Hunter's chest. "What did you do that for?"

"Because he's not heavy. He's my brother."

The howling had stopped. She didn't know if that was a good omen or bad one. But she'd left Doc to go have the conversation she needed to have. Problem was, the armed escorts told her Hunter wasn't in his room. That was all they'd say. Her assumption was that he was still in heavy conference with Silver Hawk. Were else could he have been? She knew all too well that hearing your lineage wasn't what you'd assumed all your life was not a quick and casual conversation. Especially if you were clan leadership and not just the son of a beta as previously assumed—but the progeny of the taboo combination of Werewolf and Shadow Wolf. Her mind could barely take it all in.

Sasha walked in a daze, headed for the dungeons. There were things she needed to say to Shogun, things she needed him to understand before the last vestiges of his human were gone. Questions she needed to ask. But the sight of Hunter surrounded by four armed escorts, shoulders bent from fatigue, clothes bloody, made her snarl.

Gun barrels pointed at her and she squared off on her escorts, prepared for battle.

"What have you done to him?" she demanded. "You tortured the man!" It was a statement, not a question.

Hunter began running toward her as bewildered guards backed up and began calling for reinforcements.

"No, Sasha! It's not what you think . . . don't call your wolf!"

Too late. Powerful jaws locked around the closest forearm, ready to rip the limb out of the socket if the man didn't lower the weapon. Hunter was in front of her in seconds, ripping off his silk shirt and shoving it close to her nose. He kept one hand up, his body blocking positioned archers who were readying on catwalks and staircase banisters to get a shot off.

"She saw the blood; back off and she'll come back

to herself," Hunter yelled. "She's my pack enforcer—thought I'd been attacked by your men in the dungeons."

No one moved. But the scent of deer blood slowly broke through the fury haze in Sasha's mind. Her jaws slowly relaxed until the stricken guard could yank back his arm and flee. She looked up at Hunter. He stooped down and encircled her neck. In the span of a slow blink she was on her knees hugging him.

"I thought—"

"I know," he said, helping her up.

Weapons lowered. Guards muttered curses. Hunter swept up her clothes.

"How is he?" she asked tentatively, placing a hand in the center of Hunter's chest, all modesty gone.

"Not good. I fed him, that's the best I could do until morning . . . he'll hopefully sleep off night one."

"But by tomorrow . . ."

Hunter shook his head and placed an arm around her shoulder to begin walking them back toward his room, ignoring their escort.

Sasha stopped abruptly. "I should go speak to him, let him know he's not alone . . . we're going to try all we can."

Hunter's palm cradled her cheek. "I'm saying this in all sincerity—he's not himself. If it were me, I wouldn't want you to ever see what I'd become." Hunter let out a long, weary breath. "That was part of the thing that killed me about what happened between you and me. If you go down there, Shogun will forever lose face in his mind. There are some things, Sasha, that a man never wants a woman to see. Right now, if you care about him at all, even as a friend, you'll allow the man his dignity."

What could she say to that? She accepted her clothes back from Hunter and slipped them on in the hall-way. She watched the guards dispatch a message to send him a clean shirt and pants, along with more bathwater, and was left awed at the efficiency of the castle's miniature staff. The tall Fae guards looked so weary that she actually felt sorry for them, and as she and Hunter entered his room, she wondered if they'd seen this much action in a hundred years.

She waited by the door for his clean replacement clothes as he stripped off his boots and bloodied pants—and didn't say a word as he sat down heavily on the side of the bed and hung his head. She knew where he was at.

Silence whispered through the room as small Elves took out spent bathwater and refilled the tub. Fresh clothes with a new leather scent, along with a thick, warm, white terry towel, were carefully loaded in her arms as nervous castle staff slipped past her and shut the door with a bang. Both she and Hunter waited until they heard the tumblers turn in the locks, courtesy of the armed guards just beyond the door.

"Did you talk to your grandfather?" she asked quietly, bringing his clothes to a wooden chair by the steaming tub.

Hunter nodded and stood, his majestic dark frame rising from the edge of the bed like a shadowy moun-tain in the mist. "Yeah . . . did you talk to . . . Doc?"

"Yes. And it's okay to say *my father.*"

"You're not angry with him?" Hunter hesitated, waiting for her reaction.

Sasha shook her head. "When you listen, put your own hurt aside, walk a mile in another person's shoes . . . and see their humanity, their fears and flaws, you come to understand that they did the best they could at the time they could."

Hunter stepped into the tub and she watched the thick network of sinew move in graceful ripples beneath his mahogany-hued skin.

"It is wise, because I suppose we all do that . . . the best we can at the time we can."

"Yeah," she murmured, taking up his clothes and towel again and holding them in her arms as she sat on the chair staring at him. "I'm sorry."

"Don't be," he said, not looking at her and lathering soap in his hands. "I'm sorry."

She hesitated. "Why?"

His gaze met hers and then slid away. "I finally saw, really understood, what you were dealing with when I went into that dungeon." He spread the soap over his neck, arms, and chest in a hard scrub as though washing away more than animal scent and blood, and then doused it off in large, angry splashes. "You lived through my contagion purging more than once, and are still here. That's enough for me, Sasha. Don't define it."

"I need to explain what happened," she whispered.

He stood up like a sudden dark geyser in the tub, glistening wet, sculpted and beautiful. "I already know and apologize for that as well," he said, lathering the bricks of his abdomen and then his thighs,

flinging water and soap everywhere in an agitated
flurry of jerky movements.

"Shogun told you?"

"Yes," Hunter muttered, turning away from her
and looking around for his towel.

She studied his back, the power of it, and the way
long, lean muscle flanked his spine to dip low in the
small of it to quickly rise into a stone-cut, gorgeous
ass. She stood slowly, almost mesmerized, carefully
placing his clothes onto the chair and walking forward with his towel. When he finally turned to face
her, she enfolded him in the thick terry cloth.

"It was a shadow dance . . . encouraged by the enchantment of very bad fairies. I know it sounds like a
line, but I didn't trade sex for blood."

"You would have," he murmured, staring into her
eyes. His voice held no judgment, just very deep pain.

"Yes," she nodded, "for you, I would have."

Two large, warm, slightly callused palms gingerly
held her face. A kiss so tender that it brought tears to
her eyes took her mouth, the consumption of it gentle and reverent.

"I love you, Sasha Trudeau," he murmured against
her lips and then pulled back to stare into her eyes.
"I'm doing the best I can at the time I can."

She nodded and sniffed, splaying her hands
against his damp body through the terry towel. "Me,
too."

"A shadow dance is almost more intimate
than . . ."

"Shush . . . ," she whispered, closing her eyes and
laying her head against his damp chest. "Until I . . .

Hunter, I didn't realize that until after. I thought in human terms it was better, less of a betrayal, I—"

A swift kiss stopped her words. He pulled back and stared at her. "I know. We do the best we can at the time we can, and look at what I'd left you to confront alone . . . contagion of the worst sort. You were not raised in the ways of the wolf. You didn't know."

"I swear—"

Another deep, punishing kiss stole her breath as hands that held her face slid up and into her hair.

"I know," he whispered harshly against her cheek as he broke their kiss. "And I thought I'd lost you forever when I came upon planted evidence in the bayou—I'm so sorry, Sasha."

Powerful arms enfolded her as he stepped out of the tub, his towel falling away, crushing her body against his.

"Do you realize what I've done? I've taken an innocent man's life on the ruse of Vampires. A man whom I respect . . . my brother will die tomorrow night because that demon contagion he fights was within me. Great Spirit, lift this damnation."

"It wasn't your fault," she said quickly, holding him close, her hands spreading healing touch against tense muscles in his shoulders and back. "You both rushed each other, one way or another, you both would have fought. The blame lies with the ones who orchestrated this entire horror."

His breaths were coming in short, agonized bursts of pain as he nodded and nuzzled her neck.

"First light, I'm going to ask for an escort out to rendezvous with my human squad. Me and Doc need to get to NORAD by chopper and bring every technology we have at our disposal to bear on this problem. Meanwhile, you and Silver Hawk can do what you can to keep trigger-happy UCE members in a fallback position . . . and maybe our combined clans can get some ground intel to provide evidence at the tribunal."

This time when he pulled back to look at her, there was something very different from hurt and remorse burning in his gaze. Amber rimmed his irises; his wolf was ready for war. And she knew from past experience, as well as natural instinct, that an adrenaline-boosted testosterone rush played itself out very strangely in the species called male.

Her mouth became an instant target, as smooth full lips consumed hers with an urgent brutality. Teeth and tongues went to war, dueling, struggling, tangling in a breathless twine. Rough hands battled blouse buttons and pant fastenings, each small victory won heralded with a deep moan. She was walking backward, giving ground, stepping out of her boots then pants in frantic tugs. To be conquered now would slay all the demons in her mind, erase time for a moment, and obliterate every problem they owned.

A blanket of muscular heat covered her as she fell back into goose down and surrendered. His shadow strangled hers with pleasure, a triumph that she knew he needed—a sign that he was back to himself and would never be lost again. Arching, reaching, she fisted his spill of midnight hair, allowing him to claim territory and plant himself within her hard. Out of respect for the fallen, the one in the dungeon, who was still a prisoner of war, they both swallowed a war cry and buried their faces in warm shoulders . . . mouths burning skin, teeth grazing it, both agreeing to that as a compromise, a treaty made on the fly as they moved to one accord, palms splayed over backsides and hip flesh till heads lolled back, eyes sealed shut, and bodies braced for the imminent blast.

He took her mouth before she could cry out. Her legs fought his waist, circling it, squeezing it, lifting her to slam her belly against his, breasts bouncing, nipples hard and throbbing . . . it was mortal combat that made him tear his mouth away from hers to gulp air, arms trembling not from his weight but his need to release—and she saw it a second before it happened, catching the cry, muffling it like a silenced gunshot, a stealth assassin, killing him softly, killing him swiftly, cruelly . . . brought down hard in the prime of his life, her life . . . his fists pounding the mattress for mercy and just one breath as her palms held his face. He dropped, hot stone against her sizzling, wet heat. She let him go, her arms rubbery masses at her sides. She stared up at the ceiling, dizzy and sated. His haggard breaths told her that he was all right, too.

The only thing that disturbed her, but she decided not to mention it, was the twinkling miasma of colored lights that scattered with a delicate, pleased giggle. *Damn those Fairies*!

CHAPTER 16

"I understand why it has to be this way," Hunter said, pacing to the dawn-filled windows, "I just don't like you being out there with me being in here. If anything happens to you, Sasha . . ."

"I know," she said, stepping out of the fresh tub and wrapping a new towel around herself. "But they'll never let you out of here to go with me, which I don't want anyway. Your hands have to remain clean. You have to have deniability, just like the Vampires have now. Hell, I barely got them to agree to let me out of here with Doc to collect our evidence, and only could under the proviso that Sir Rodney is our discreet bodyguard. How we're gonna get him into NORAD is anybody's guess. But traveling by day oughta cut down on some of the Vamp shenanigans."

Hunter kept his gaze out the window. She came up behind him and hugged him, wondering how the Fae managed to include pastel-hued, mist-covered mountains in their oasis.

"You know the Vampires have human helpers, and

the Cartel isn't our only threat, Sasha." Hunter issued her an annoyed, sideline glance. "There's at least one North American Werewolf alpha whom we know wants both Shogun and me executed at midnight, plus a strong member of the Fae Parliament who's hedging his bets on our deaths, which leaves me suspicious of any of the Fae, regardless of surface hospitality . . . and there's still a very dangerous demon with vengeance in her black heart." He turned to Sasha and placed a palm on each of her shoulders. "So you be careful out there, Trudeau. Come back to me in one piece, or I swear I'll personally hunt you down till I find you."

"You little bitch," Buchanan said between his teeth, kicking in the motel door. "Took me all night to find you, but sure as rain you knew I was gonna."

Dana was up and countercircling the angry beast before her. "Daddy, you listen here, I'm not gonna be treated this way when what I was doing was for the good of the entire family!"

"What you was gonna do was sell my ass all the way from where I'm standing to Georgia's Chattahoochee River, darlin'. At least that's what it looked like to me," he hollered, making a lunge for her and missing.

"You think I'd do that?" she said, placing a hand over her heart. "I'm appalled."

"Then why'd you run? Only the guilty run!"

"I ran and found me a place where I could eat and go to sleep in peace because I didn't wanna hear any of your drunken bullshit last night!"

"You're gonna be dog meat in a minute. I'll kill ya quick as look at ya, and make another one that look jus' like you, sweetie pie. You know that."

"See, that's exactly what I'm talking about and why I took to a motel," she shouted, not seeming the least bit afraid of him. "Violence only begets violence. Sometimes you gotta use your head! And what I know is, it's easier to install my father as alpha if I marry the man and then a tragedy befalls my husband . . . but, noooo. You just had to come all out in the bayou when I *told* you I had learned a thing or two from my mama."

"Your mama was a whore!"

"Absolutely true," Dana said without shame or apology, folding her arms over her ample chest. There was no fear in her eyes. "So I learned from the best."

Her father straightened and came out of his rush stance. After a moment he smoothed the bristled hair that had risen on the back of his neck and smiled a toothy grin. "You was gonna do that for your old pa?"

"Till you messed things up and got my future husband arrested!" She turned away from him with a pout.

"Aw, now sugah-lump, I'm sorry. Don't be like that."

"How'm I supposed to be, Daddy?" She whirled away from him with tears in her eyes. "This just ain't working out as planned and you don't trust me—I'm hurt," she wailed, shrugging away from him as he tried to approach her.

"You jus' as purty as your mama used to be, you know that," he said in a husky voice.

"Don't even start that," she said, gathering up her belongings. "You messed things up! Even if Shogun had the contagion, I woulda been his mate, then the clan coulda put him down . . . that is, after the big alpha from the North Country went down first. I'da called in my marker—you, to fill the void, and we coulda had this thing all sewn up. His sister is crazy as a bedbug, and nobody likes her . . . only a matter of time before her own demon-possessed mama rips her face off. That other bitch, Miss Sasha-thinks-she-so-much-Trudeau, probably gonna catch what her boyfriend got and will have to be shot soon any-hoo. We'da had us an empire, Daddy. I hate being second and I'm tired of being poor! For once, why didn't you just stay out of it?"

"Now, don't you worry your purty little head none," Buchanan said, leaning on the door frame. "Both of those boys are going down at midnight, anyway. They clans ain't got no evidence. They both got the contagion. And the way I see it, you're still gonna wind up the North American prom queen, but without the messy business of having to bed one of them foreign fellas." He opened up his arms and gave her a sly smile the moment the corner of her mouth gave way to one of her own.

"See, your daddy knows what he's doing—now come on over here and gimme some sugah, like fam-ily is supposed ta do."

"Why?" Ethan said in an angry whisper, holding a coffee cup so tightly in his hands that it shook.

Dugan leaned forward and looked over his shoulder nervously. "I didn't do anything. The gossip and speculation about me—"

"Stop it," Ethan hissed, sitting forward angrily. "The Witch networks have the story, the Fairies are abuzz, the wolves all know . . . I have a wife and children—"

"Like no one else has anythin' at stake, laddie?" Dugan slammed his cup down hard, but kept his voice a low murmur in the back of his establishment. "How long do you think it'll be, man, before the Vampires come back to you for testifying against them at the UCE? Did you ever think of that before you opened your big yap?" Dugan nodded when Ethan blanched. "Aye. Now it's all sinking in slowly."

"We have protection, guaranteed by—"

"Who, the wolves?" Dugan cocked his head to the side and pulled a small flask of brandy out of his breast pocket, adding some of the dark, aromatic liquor to his coffee. "You were out in the bayou. You saw the state of their affairs. Those sworn to protect you have serious problems of their own, laddie . . . and what's more, the local wolves . . ."

Dugan shook his head as he capped his flask and then took a deep swig from his spiked coffee, triumphant. "Have you seen the leadership that will step in once the two superpowers fall?" He waited a beat as Ethan's nervous gaze sought a window.

"Ethan McGregor, my boy, it's a new day after the flood. Casinos are being rebuilt by the cartel . . . New Orleans has to be rebuilt by those with power, money, and vision, and it will be. Out with the old, in with the new. The little people and poor could be swept away; Katrina showed us just how easy that would be. Only a few houses, in the grand scheme, will be built from charitable concerns—but the primo real estate and the real lasting power will be with you know who. So, while I admit to nothing, a thinking man must be realistic about his options. If you haven't considered that, then take a look around and after you do so, you can ask me that very naive question again, old friend."

"The minute we clear the drawbridge and path," Sir Rodney warned, "and reenter the bayou, we've got to run like the wind." He cast a worried gaze toward Doc. "I'll have archers in the trees covering us until we reach the edge of the wooded area, and from there one of our men will have a vehicle—but the darkness of the boggy areas . . ."

"I understand," Sasha said, clasping Doc's hand. "I'll flank him. I won't leave him. Just give me back my confiscated weapons."

Tension had kept Clarissa's body ramrod-straight all night as she and Winters sat hunched over computer systems. Bradley had set every conceivable supernatural barrier, while Woods, Fisher, Bear, and Crow provided constant guard duty. The general paced into the small work cell every few hours, asking on a status update that couldn't be given. The blown truck with invaluable equipment right after a firefight at Tulane had bases on lockdown and Homeland Security alerts at red levels. The only good thing was, Bear and Crow didn't have to be explained—they simply were a part of the shadow force the general didn't need to know about.

The moment her feet hit the spongy ground cover beyond the cobbled Fae path, she smelled it. Demon-wolf was on the move in the underbrush. A full-moon cycle had opened the door; the creature could never shift back to human anyway. But it could maim and kill in the darkness of the bayou depths.

Sasha clasped Doc's hand tightly, and their eyes met. Instinct propelled him forward. The Fae captain of the guards moved between trees in a blur of motion like the very wind itself.

Breaking branches and deep, feral growls followed them; Sasha's heart was pounding as Sir Rodney turned. Instant reflex brought her body down to cover Doc's in a hard fall as her hand gripped the silver dagger and released it. A savage howl echoed. Momentum carried a massive form over her head. A glint of silver caught sunlight dappling through the thick canopy. Arrows rained a curtain of protection as she and Sir Rodney quickly helped Doc up.

God help them, Doc was limping. That and his age were now life-threatening liabilities.

"Go!" Sir Rodney shouted, turning to meet the charging beast.

"No!" Sasha said, yanking her nine-millimeter out of her back waistband with one hand, pushing Doc off center with the other. She found that still place, aimed, and fired.

A last-second pivot sent a silver slug into the beast's shoulder rather than its heart, making it rear on hind legs with a roar before it disappeared again into the underbrush. Where it was, only her strained senses could detect, but she was sure that she'd slowed it enough for her to grab Doc under his armpit with Rodney on the other side of him, and haul ass.

But try as they might to keep moving with the injured beast circling, Doc was going slower and slower. Sasha stopped, her gaze hard on Sir Rodney.

"Go take to the trees with the other Fae and get off the ground. I'll meet you at the vehicle, you've gotta trust me."

"No, you'll be—"

"Go, man!" Sasha yelled, and pointed up to the other archers safe above. "He's part Shadow—my father . . . I'll take him through the shadow lands and we'll exit at the vehicle meeting place."

Snarls made Sasha start pulling Doc, despite his resistance.

"No, Sasha," Doc said his eyes and voice frantic, "if she follows—"

There was no time to explain or argue. A thunderous crash sent Sir Rodney into the trees with fellow archers; Sasha was pure motion, her hand a tight grasp on Doc's weathered palm, her amulet blazing. Shadow land, shadow time, the scent was wrong; something old and evil had followed them in just as Doc had warned.

Sasha spun, protectively circling Doc, trying to get a bead on the danger in the mist. A lunging form came out of nowhere. She fired, but only the empty sound of dead clicks echoed. Doc's horrified gaze was the last thing she saw as he fell back swallowed by the mist and the beast kept coming. Her wolf broke free, smaller, outmatched in weight and size, but not by insanity. Then just as suddenly a larger black wolf met the predator midair. She knew the phantom couldn't hurt the real, live threat, but it could disorient it, give it the panicked illusion of being attacked by one of its own, and buy them escape time. She took it.

Doc rolled away. Her human self returned and immediately swept up her clothes in a single deft move, running, amulet swinging, pushing Doc forward as scores of fallen Shadow Wolf spirits descended on the creature.

Sunlight smacked her face. Sir Rodney caught Doc as they came out of the shadows where his silver SUV sat on the emergency shoulder. He looked them both over for signs of demon contagion and then smiled at Sasha, appraising her naked body.

"I do so love how you do that, lassie," he crooned, opening the car door for her and Doc. "I just wish you weren't always under such duress when your lady-self comes back."

She was driving and dressed; Doc was still breathing hard and nursing a sprained ankle when they got to the base. Sir Rodney was long gone. An armed escort in to meet up with her human squad at NAS felt real comfortable, given where they'd just been.

General Westford was waiting in a pure huff when they got to the administration building. He gave her a disapproving glare as he studied her silk-and-leather outfit. The base was tense, seeming prepared for a foreign war to hit American soil at any moment—she could see it in the eyes of every armed soldier who stood at the ready near the general.

Nonplussed, Sasha saluted the brass and helped Doc out of the vehicle. She didn't have time for this crap.

"Blending in with friendlies, sir," she said to address his unspoken question while trying not to sound annoyed. "We've got a man injured," she added in a matter-of-fact tone. "Only a sprained ankle while on the run, no cause for alarm. We tracked a target as far as we could to be sure none of our samples got taken, sir. We need to get what we did acquire back to the labs at NORAD, ASAP, for security and eval."

"Well, I damned sure don't want that creature hazmat crap here," the general bellowed. "Take it to the boys up north in Colorado."

She never in her wildest dreams would have thought that going underground beneath two thousand feet of pure granite and being locked behind twenty-five-ton steel doors while surrounded by very nervous men carrying very big guns would be comforting . . . but it was. After what they'd all experienced, she didn't care that they had to do retina scans, match fingerprints, give code words, or say *Mother may I,* as long as she got Doc and her team into a safe place.

"How's the ankle?" Sasha finally said, bringing Doc a cup of coffee.

"All right," he said, clearly peeved at himself. "I coulda gotten you killed back there." His gaze softened. "But seeing you in action was . . . maybe the proudest moment in my very frightened life."

She didn't care if the walls had ears and eyes. A simple hug conveyed all she'd wanted to say. Doc took up his pen and scribbled a quick, cryptic note: *Thank you for allowing me to see my father.* Their eyes met for a moment, and she knew that Wolf Shadow had been there with the others, as had Shogun's and Hunter's father, attacking the demon and giving them time to escape. Sasha nodded and Doc slid the paper into his white lab coat.

"Clarissa," he said, taking command of his domain. "Let's go to work."

Hours passed, but you couldn't rush science. To her it was like watching a pot of water boil; maddening. Winters and Bradley, on the other hand, gave her something constructive to wrap her mind around—setting traps and collecting evidence.

Winters held out his hand, drawing Sasha, Bradley, Woods, and Fisher near. "You know how they use gold solder on most microchips?" he said with a wide smile. "How about if we silver-solder this sucker . . . then maybe the Vamps won't be able to so easily go in and wipe evidence off your flash drive."

"Yeah, but if we stick it in a laptop or a handheld DVD player or any electronic device to show the video of what happened that night over at Tulane, those guys can distort the image that goes to the screen, can't they?"

Winters wagged a finger at Sasha. "My kung fu is

strong, Captain. They can only distort the screen of its plain old liquid crystal, but I'm gonna add a little colloidal silver in there—basically dust the inside of the whole damned unit. Then old Bradley here is gonna say some prayers over it, give it proper anointing, and it oughta hold up in court."

"Good man," Sasha said, shaking her head. "Have you been able to break down the electronic voice phenomena from those screaming Fairies yet, Woods?"

"Got it lovely," Woods said, copying digital sound and video files over to NORAD systems, then burning disks, flash drives, and Winters's hard drive before uploading it to NORAD's secure servers. "EVPs coming through loud and clear, Captain. Like the man said, can't have too many copies in backup."

"I like the idea of sewing wolfsbane right into the lining of uniforms, along with silver threading, then adding a sprinkle of brick dust into the soles of your shoes—this way, where you step a demon couldn't, maybe? At the very least, you need a pocketful of that to draw a quick circle around yourself while in a camouflage blind," Bradley said with a droll smile. "But then, that would only work if Trudeau could manage to keep her gear on long enough."

"Ha, ha, ha," she said flatly, walking by Bradley to punch his shoulder and grin.

The team kept the banter up, but within coded limits to make sure nothing they said alerted the hierarchy to what they really knew, any more than was necessary. But she still needed a trap, a foolproof way to lure the demon out in full view of UCE witnesses—either that or some pretty compelling evidence to get the Vampires' asses caught in a sling. That solution would come, she hoped, once her mind relaxed. Improvised explosive devices were always a last-minute eureka for her.

"Sasha," Doc said, straining to quickly hop toward her on a crutch from the other end of the lab. Clarissa was on his heels trying to help him, but in his excitement he pressed forward, causing everyone to look up as Sasha ran to him. "Come see something I never saw before!"

The excitement that shone in his eyes seemed to make his hands shake. Aware of the cameras and surveillance, he spoke to her and Clarissa in code.

"The sample you gave me has the same taint to it as Lou Zang Chen's blood," he said breathlessly. "It's *different* from the taint in *yours,* or in *my* normal human blood."

Sasha held her breath, so did Clarissa. Doc was talking for the cameras, but they understood him completely. Shogun and Lou Zang Chen both had uninfected Werewolf blood prior to their attacks. Obviously, for all these years, without a comparison sample, Doc hadn't been able to tell the difference between normal Shadow Wolf blood and normal, uninfected Werewolf blood, because they were such close cousins.

"The last male subject we lost," Doc said after a beat, giving them time to process what he said while eyeing them hard, "was *a relative* of an earlier test subject."

Sasha rifled her fingers through her hair. The decoding was getting confusing, but she was pretty

sure that she got that: Shogun was the most recent
loss and was a half brother to Hunter. She nodded as
clarity came. Doc and Clarissa nodded. Although
communication under brass scrutiny was tough, no
one had yet broken the code. It was all in the eyes.

They'd said what they needed to, but if the brass
was listening, as they probably were, it would sound
as though they were all referring back to the tragic
loss of Captain Rod Butler. Fine. She'd still never
forgive the brass for playing God with that man's
life.

"Okay," Doc said, barely suppressing his enthusiasm, "just like it took you a brief recovery period to
build immunity once scraped, Dr. Chen's blood
seems to also hold a key to immunity—like *yours*."

Doc had avoided referring to his own blood for
obvious reasons, but with the hard emphasis he'd put
on the words, she knew he also meant like Hunter's
blood . . . which was half Shadow, half Werewolf.

"The others had been poisoned," Doc said, excitement making him seem like might burst if he
didn't say what was on his mind in plain English.

Sasha nodded emphatically. Yeah, Hunter had
been poisoned by nearly ODing on toxin, not anti-
toxin, thanks to a money-grubbing Elf, that fat-ass
Dugan, and a couple of sinister Vampires carrying a
grudge. "So what do you propose?"

"I want to make anti-toxin with a combo of agents
from Chen and a new subject that shares lineage."
Doc smoothed a palm over his scalp. "I want to turn
on that imprinted gene in a newly infected subject . . .
try to get whatever switched it off in a test subject's

system to turn it back on. If it worked for Chen, who knows?"

"Sasha," Clarissa said, biting her lip. "What we're going to do is lift some of the research that is already happening at some of the top national civilian labs."

"Synthetic DNA," Doc breathed out in an ecstatic rush.

"What?" Sasha looked from one doctor to another. Clarissa was hugging herself and Doc was grasping his crutch so tightly she feared his palm might bleed.

"Scientists in Maryland have already created the world's first entirely handcrafted chromosome. DuPont has made a microbe that replicates itself—a bacterium that creates a fabric polymer as its by-product. In San Carlos, California, the lab is already using *E. coli* bacteria that have been synthetically reprogrammed to produce alternative fuel from a diet of corn syrup and sugarcane."

"It works like this, Captain," Clarissa said, squeezing Sasha's arm for a moment, before remembering about the camera. "We composure a DNA sequence, right at the computer, that carries the cellular instructions for making a desired product—"

"In this case, untainted blood," Doc said, cutting her off. "Then we run it through an SNA synthesizer that creates a digital code in a long strand of actual DNA."

"Whoa, wait a minute," Sasha said, raking her hair. "You can actually—"

"Play God," Clarissa said, nodding.

"That's some scary shit." Sasha looked at them both.

"But in this case, Captain, very necessary." Doc gave her a look that she picked up on right away.

"You have a synthesizer here?" Sasha glanced at both Doc and Clarissa.

"That was classified, until the tragic loss of General Wilkerson." Doc's look intensified. "We have clearance to continue his vaccine goals in the lab."

Bingo. She got it. The Vamps were worried that if human technology made the breakthrough of creating synthetic DNA, who knew what vaccines or bioweapons could be created to make feeding on humans off-limits?

"You *understand*?" Doc asked. "Fully?"

"Oh, yeah," Sasha said. "I get it."

"Good," Doc said with a curt nod. "Until I had a complete DNA string that I understood, I couldn't replicate clean blood. I needed a full chromosome sequence to plagiarize. Up to this point I could only cobble together individual cells, a single gene or two, and loop them back into the strand, hoping to ward off the contagion . . . I was following the same process that the food industry uses to add one or two extra genes in the genetic spiral of corn DNA to make that living, edible plant impervious to certain insects, or improve its tolerance to drought. But I never had the *entire string*." Doc briefly closed his eyes as though he'd been summoned to Nirvana.

"Now that I do," he went on, his intense, intelligent gaze riveted to hers, "once the new, synthetic string is created, what we do is insert it into a bacterial cell—where it displaces older flawed DNA and spontaneously boots up its own genetic program within the host."

"Once it's in the host," Clarissa said, clearly unable to contain herself any longer, "the new cells follow the newly encoded instructions of the synthetic DNA. The cells and their offspring essentially begin cranking out the new product—which in this case is untainted blood."

"It's been used in medicines, such as those for malaria, Sasha," Doc said, beaming. "We've used it in the United States for new fuels that might eventually replace environmentally hazardous petrochemicals, and we're using it in applications as novel as textile manufacturing. All these years and all I needed was a comparison sample—I could kiss you, Captain!"

She smiled, unsure, but hating to crush their scientific enthusiasm. "And the downside is?"

"It could backfire." Doc let out a hard sigh and rubbed his jaw, suddenly deflated.

They both knew that that was as much as Doc could or would say. But at this juncture, trying a biosyn cure was Shogun's only chance.

"All right," Sasha said, slowly processing the information they'd hit her between the eyes with. "So you make this string of new synthetic DNA, using the blood sample I got for you as a template . . . you then inject or, essentially, reprogram a germ—something that grows fast, spreads in a body like wildfire—and hope like hell it reboots the host's body systems and then reprograms the host's autoimmune system as a by-product. Did I get this right? And if that doesn't work, the host succumbs to the contagion or dies, or maybe both."

"Correct," Doc said, he and Clarissa looking like Sasha had just popped their shiny new red balloon. "But the way I've seen your system fend off infection, if I add these additional elements to the antitoxin—but this time within a holy water base so it can't be tampered with . . ."

Sasha nodded. "You make it; I'll bake it, Doc. Load me up with tranquilizer darts, and I'm out."

CHAPTER 17

"That's it. No arguments," Sasha said, walking away from Woods and Fisher. "If you'd been back there with me and Doc, you'd know why I'm asking everybody to spend the night at NORAD." She kept packing her gear to avoid looking at their eyes. "You can't go the way I got out of the bayou with Doc. It's too dangerous now."

She looked up at Woods and Fisher, their eyes sharing a vision the way only a pack she-Shadow and her familiars could.

Woods stepped away and quietly punched the wall. "Like that makes me feel better, Trudeau?" He looked at Fisher, whose jaw had slowly gone slack as the vision entered his head.

Clarissa simply closed her eyes. Doc nodded. Winters and Bradley looked confused, but conceded that it had to be bad if even Doc was agreeing to this plan.

"You look alive and stay alive, Captain," Doc said with a worried gaze. His eyes said everything that his mouth simply couldn't at NORAD.

* * *

Hunter sat across from Silver Hawk and Sir Rodney, listening to the Fae captain describe what had happened. He stood as Rodney detailed each near miss, pacing as though caged.

"You got her to base, to the human military encampment?"

Rodney nodded. "She said she would return before sunset—my men are hidden in the trees, waiting to assist."

"Although appreciated, what she needs is an able-bodied hunter to track down and exterminate the demon that's waiting for her out there." Hunter stood. "Me, a full pack—"

"No," Silver Hawk said. "More death, more men at risk—your blood tainted, possibly, right before the tribunal where they are already predisposed to execute you. Unadvisable. Sasha is brave and smart and will—"

"She'll come alone," Hunter snarled. "She won't risk her people to what's out there!" he suddenly shouted, pointing toward the window in a hard snap. "She won't even call my men, Bear and Crow; I know how Sasha thinks."

A hard knock at the door temporarily stopped the dispute. Sir Rodney stood with Hunter and bid his men to open the door.

Hunter stared, his gaze narrowing with distrust as Lei strutted through the door flanked by a heavy retinue of armed guards.

"I'm requesting diplomatic courtesy," she said

coolly, glancing around Hunter's quarters. "Since it does appear that we are linked by blood and by an alliance, and the leadership of both wolf Federations is at risk, I request a private meeting—which is my due before tonight's tribunal."

Gear hitched high on her shoulder and armed to the teeth, Sasha's biggest issue was getting the brass to get off her back long enough for her to clear the base, lose their GPS surveillance, and head into the first shadow she saw. By now she knew how to listen for the high-pitched whine of microtransistors in her clothing that no human could hear—Hunter had shown her that when they'd first met. Those got stripped out of her clothes, first and foremost, on the sly.

All she had to do was pull her vehicle to a blind of trees or find a tunnel, and what could they do? It didn't matter that they could see her on satellite down to four inches on the ground or read her license plate from an orbiting big eye in the sky. What they'd never fathom was her going into a tunnel or a cave or a dense stand of trees and not coming out. She loved it!

If she hadn't been worried about traveling with her human squad, a stop at NAS in New Orleans wouldn't have been necessary. She and Doc could have exited right outside NORAD and saved hours of transportation delays. But that hadn't been possible.

Still, the return was gonna be tricky. First off, there was the not-so-small problem of a demon-wolf in the shadow lands. She understood how Dexter and his crew could travel through those pathways—after all, they had been Shadow Wolves that caught the contagion. But how in the hell did a Werewolf get to barrel through the shadow lands? Unheard of.

Even Hunter and Shogun's father wasn't allowed in until he was actually dead, a spirit, and only then because his spirit was honorable, he'd had a link to the North American Clan, and he'd had a pure heart . . . but he couldn't breach the divide as a living, breathing Werewolf. This was a conundrum to take to Silver Hawk at some later date and time. For now, she had to cover her own ass as she ran through the mist.

The second problem—which was quickly approaching—was how she might find Sir Rodney's men in order to get on the safe, cobbled Fae path. The bayou was a bitch right now. Plus, with all her evidence and techno-gear in a black gym bag, going wolf was out of the question. Her human would have to kick ass and take names.

Sasha kept running, the hazy, half-gray tones of the shadow lands disorienting. She clutched her amulet, feeling its warmth and comfort, praying for safe passage, a safe exit, and that what she carried with her was a cure.

Hunter watched the others leave and shut the door behind them from a very remote place in his mind. So much of him wanted to rip Lei's lungs out of her chest, he had to stand by the window on the other side of the room.

Exotic beauty or not, she was sick and extremely dangerous. She cocked her head as though posing a question. Hunter stared at her, not caring that his canines were beginning to show.

"For your safety," he said in a near growl, answering her nonverbal question about his stance so far away.

"I'm flattered," she said, going to the edge of his bed and sitting.

"Don't be." He walked to the table, then flung a chair in her direction for her to sit there instead. "What do you want?"

"A truce," she said calmly, standing and going to the rudely offered chair. Her voice was mellow and casual, as though they were longtime friends.

"How convenient," Hunter said with a snarl.

"No," she said pointedly, raising her forefinger. "*Prudent* is the word."

He didn't answer her, just stared at her.

"Have you been to see my brother?" Her hypnotic gaze raked Hunter from head to toe.

"Stop playing games. You know I have."

"You fed him what he needed to stop some of the suffering."

"You know that, too," Hunter said, beginning to circle her as his agitation escalated.

"That was honorable."

"What would you know about that word?"

Lei smiled. "That's fair, given some of the circumstances in the past . . . but now we must move forward."

Hunter stopped moving and folded his arms over his chest. "You're ready to form an alliance after trying to have me assassinated?" He looked at her, incredulous, and then laughed.

"And you returned the favor by infecting my dying brother," she said, her voice losing some of its casual charm. "Therefore, we're even. Fair exchange is no robbery."

"Who taught you that, the Vampires?"

Lei smiled, but her eyes narrowed. "In politics, many alliances must be made over the years . . . many cultures must be studied. One must also know one's enemy." She gave him a slight bow from where she sat.

A hard half smile graced his face. *"The Art of War."*

She seemed shocked but pleased.

"I do know my enemies very well," he said, looking at her with an unblinking gaze.

"As do I," she said, no smile on her face now. "But you and I both know that within hours, our collective threat—the Vampires—will call for an open wolf hunt against both federations on North American soil, trying to pin circumstantial evidence of two human deaths on our leadership. My dear brother is—"

"Innocent," Hunter said flatly. *"Our* brother." He walked deeper into the chamber to avoid snatching her by her throat. "Shogun hasn't even been found guilty yet, hasn't taken a bullet or been made cold in his grave, and you're already in my quarters trying to strike a deal for your continued rule?"

"The inevitable is upon us," she said in a falsely sad tone. "We must look out for the greater good of the—"

"Then confess, bitch!" Hunter yelled, losing patience and turning over the table between them. "Even if Shogun goes full blow tonight, I'll stand at the tribunal and recount all that I know to exonerate his name. Our father didn't become a flesh-eater, and neither did Shogun—I was down in the dungeons, and human remains had been nowhere near Shogun. I would have smelled that in what he upchucked, would have smelled it in his sweat! I don't care that he wanted Sasha—the two issues are mutually exclusive! You can't use that as leverage, and you most certainly can't use your body to lure me. Get out! The only way I'll ever concede to an alliance with you if Shogun dies is if you confess that you've been feeding a demon—your mother!"

Lei stood and smoothed her flowing red-and-gold silk robes. She calmly lifted her chin, eyes glittering with defiance and unspent rage. "I'm so sorry you feel that way."

Sasha cut a zigzag path, a Glock in one hand, her precious gym bag in the other. Speed pressed down on her lungs, sweat stung her eyes, while fatigue clawed at her abdomen and limbs. But she had to keep moving. The second she broke the plane between the shadow lands and the bayou, she could feel herself being hunted.

Demon scent lingered in the air. The underbrush had eyes—she couldn't see them, but she could feel them. Something moved, and lightning reflexes made her squeeze off rounds.

"Hold your fire!" a strong voice bellowed from the treetops. "You'll kill a guard!"

Her body slumped from sheer relief. Sir Rodney gave her a scowl, and then his expression brightened as he jumped down from a high limb.

"Good God, woman . . . how does the big alpha ever stand you?"

"These meds never leave my sight or my hand," Sasha said, her gaze flicking between Hunter and Silver Hawk. "You gentlemen hold the other evidence while I'm gone, but I'm going down there solo."

She'd already explained to them what Doc and Clarissa had concocted, as well as the other slim bits of evidence she had. Right now she was in no mood for any macho dramatics. She was going to see Shogun before the sun set whether they liked it or not.

Hunter blocked the door. "He doesn't want—"

"Do you know that for a fact?" she said, crossing her arms and challenging Hunter. "Did he specifically say, *Don't send Sasha Trudeau down here,* huh?"

"No, but—"

"You can't be the one to shoot him up with syn-DNA, Hunter!" Sasha yelled, her nerves raw. "You're already a suspect for trying to infect him in the first place! They might not even allow me down there with this stuff, but I stand a better chance as a woman going with a gun in my waistband than you do, brother."

She still wanted to snarl when the guards came to escort her to the dungeons. Her nerves weren't just rubbed raw, they were threadbare. The process of getting down into the main cell area where Shogun was being held was almost as daunting as what her senses ultimately had to process.

The acrid scent of demon infestation made her eyes water; finally she used her forearm to cover her face as they walked. She breathed into her fatigue jacket sleeve in shallow sips and watched the guards pull out kerchiefs to wrap their faces without even breaking their stride. By the time she reached the small area where guards played cards and drank ale wearing kerchiefs, she wanted to vomit. But that urge gave way: what her eyes took in broke her heart.

Shogun was lying on the floor, curled in a tight, shivering ball. He'd upchucked huge chunks of raw deer, which lay in nasty puddles of bile and mucus. A cold sweat covered his now deathly pale skin. Matted hair covered his face, and his spine was so twisted and knotted that she wondered if he could still stand. Sunken ribs jutted out as though he'd been starved to death, and his feet were elongated half paws, the bottoms callused where the pads would soon fill in.

"Oh . . . Shogun," she whispered and rushed over to the bars.

"Careful, little lady," the lead guard said, issuing a muffled warning from beneath his tight kerchief. "This one's been a monster all night. Can't tell when he'll wake up or the sun will set down here. No windows, for obvious reasons. But you don't want to be in limb-ripping range. He'll take an arm—been hankering and begging for human flesh since the deer came back up on him."

Sasha backed up as Shogun stirred, and the guard who had spoken motioned to several of the men that they could run down the long corridor for a moment to get some fresh air.

"I'll be careful," she said. "I just wanted to say good-bye to my friend."

"That one, love, you can't kiss through the bars, mind you—he'll rip off your face." The guard motioned to the deer, wiping nausea sweat from his brow.

"I know," Sasha said, allowing real tears to well in her eyes. "But still, can we have a minute if I promise not to get near the bars?" She motioned to the heavy locks. "What can I do at this point—and why the hell would I want to do it? Letting him out would be my death sentence."

The guards eyed their superior, pleading without words for a breath of fresh air. After a moment he nodded.

"Five minutes—but you stay back."

"I promise I will." She had barely finished her sentence when the room cleared.

She watched Shogun drag himself up to a half-sitting position. From behind a tangled curtain of matted hair, sunken, glowing eyes appeared. He smiled a sinister smile, his once beautiful mouth a mangle of twisted, yellow teeth.

"You came to say good-bye," he said in a frightening, demonic growl. "How touching."

"I came to save your life," she said, quickly extracting a small dart gun from the front groin section of her fatigues, and then frantically hiking up her

T-shirt to pull duct tape off two darts hidden beneath her breasts. "Rush the bars."

He laughed as she loaded the tranquilizer gun with meds and slowly stood. "Come closer . . . I can barely get up, much less rush the bars."

Pain seized her heart as she watched him jonesing for flesh, but as she heard the guards slow, meandering footfalls beginning to return, she stepped in close enough for Shogun to reach her.

In a lightning-swift move he crashed against the silver with a sizzling howl. She screamed for dramatic effect, stepped back with Shadow Wolf speed, and hit him once in the jugular and once in the chest with a med dart, then stashed her gun. He released an angry howl and snatched the darts out, flinging them deep within the cell in the pile of carnage behind him. If she'd been full human or any other slow-moving entity, she wouldn't have had a face.

"I'm sorry," she whispered as he growled and cursed her. Two big tears rolled down her cheeks. She glimpsed his cell floor, glad that his rage had buried the evidence in a place that she was sure no guard would go snooping. The two darts had rolled away to God knew where.

Thankfully, the guard returned in a running huff late enough to see her on the other side of the room hugging herself. No one frisked her; they smelled the silver sizzle and saw the burns on Shogun's hands and face, and incorrectly made their own assessment. So much for due diligence.

She gave them her most pitiful expression—it

was no act—and allowed the tears to fall. "I just wanted to say good-bye. He was my friend."

The return to her room felt like the longest walk in her life. She wished for a moment that the shadows within Sir Rodney's enchanted world were real so she could duck into one of them and have a really good cry. But if it were that easy, she and Hunter and Silver Hawk would have been long gone.

Melting down beyond theatrical effects to hide that she was packing a dart weapon wasn't an option. As it was, they'd taken her other weapons from her as she left the bayou for the cobbled path, allowing her to protect herself on the way back, but giving her no opportunity to dispute the tribunal's verdict, if it wasn't to her liking. She'd known that this would be the case going in, and had made provisions. Still, without her gear she felt naked.

Right now she needed a moment alone. The trial would begin at eleven PM. Judging from the pitch of the setting sun, she had several hours—ten minutes to breathe was in order.

Sasha quietly slipped into her room and closed the door behind her, hoping that Hunter and Silver Hawk hadn't heard her return yet. She leaned against the door and closed her eyes. So much had gone wrong in such a short time . . . if just one thing could go right.

After a moment she opened her eyes and pushed her body off the door, annoyed when the miasma of shimmering lights danced over the dining table in her room. A small domed silver tea tray sat next to a larger covered dinner tray waiting for her. Sasha shook her head.

"Go away, guys—I'm not hungry . . . and you really shouldn't spy on people. It's not polite."

Much to her dismay they followed her as she tried to get some peace by the window. She shooed them away from her hair like the annoying little gnats they'd become.

Disgruntled, high-pitched fussing battered her wolf hearing as they tumbled and dodged her hand waves. The entire thing was absurd. The more she waved them away, the more they flew at her like confetti hornets until she finally closed her eyes, allowed her hands to fall to her sides, and slumped against the windowsill.

"What do you *want* from my life?" she groaned, letting out a long, impatient sigh.

Soon she could begin to string together their squeaky chatter once they'd settled down long enough to stop trying to individually talk to her all at the same time. Frustration gripped her as she waited for them to communicate in short bursts in unison.

"The silver platter," Sasha said flatly. "Fine." She pushed away from the window ledge, seriously battling the desire to jump out of it. Even as a wolf, however, the forty-story drop would have been unkind. It amazed her, the enchanted world. On the outside the castle seemed much smaller than it did from within.

Folding her arms over her chest, she glanced down at the table. "More enchanted grapes—or are you going to spike my veggies with love-jones to make up for everything? Oh, like that'll work—not."

Sparkles rained down on the table, making her grow peevish. "Oh, yeah," she said, grabbing the knob of the small dome, "and that was so very, very rude showing up in Hunter's room last night—*that* I never want to discuss with you again!"

She snatched off the cover and just stared down for a moment. Sealed evidence bags from NOPD? What the . . .

Carefully studying them without touching what she saw, she set down the platter lid beside the platter. In thick Sharpie print along with the date and a detective's initials in the notes section, the first bag read: UNIDENTIFIED ANIMAL HAIR SAMPLES FROM BATHROOM WINDOW AT CHAYA TEAHOUSE—JANE DOE MAULING MURDER #2. Suddenly the silver platters made sense. It was a peace offering, as well as protective covering in case someone wanted to steal what the Fairies had stolen.

"I could kiss you guys, little voyeurs that you are . . . ," Sasha said, now picking up the bag by the corner with a linen napkin to study it better under a light.

Thick, amber strands caught in the light through the clear plastic. Sasha looked up when she clearly heard the sparkling cloud squeal, "Dana." She quickly set that bag down and read the next one: UNIDENTIFIED ANIMAL HAIR SAMPLES FROM ALLEY DUMPSTER—THE FAIR LADY ESTABLISHMENT—ERIC FRANKLIN MAULING MURDER #1.

"Oh, shit . . ." Sasha sniffed the bag, and the distinctive odor of demon-wolf stung her nose. "This is pay dirt." She set the bag down carefully. "I know, I know, but we're hardly even, despite the fact that basic DNA analysis will show who this came from, or at the very least that it came from a female—not Hunter or Shogun."

Sasha smiled. "All right," she murmured when they started turning gray and angry. "It is golden, I'll give you that . . . and, yeah, if we run the mitochondrial DNA testing, we can prove the boy's murderer was Lei's and Shogun's mother—not me or Hunter, or even Shogun. But what's with the Dana hairs? She was at Chaya helping feed the beast . . . is that what you're telling me?"

Again, angry sparkles plumed around the room and then danced in an agitated flurry over the larger platter. Without hesitation, Sasha lifted the lid. Initially she didn't understand. There was a plastic bag with no markings on it that seemed to contain some sort of fabric . . . and then slowly the scent of a healthy, aroused Shogun entered her nose.

She stood up quickly, slammed the lid back over the pants, and backed away from the table. Words pelted her in Fairy bursts. "Bathroom." "Dana." "Vampires." "Bayou."

Sasha paced away from the table, rubbing her neck and studying the floor. She remembered when she'd handed Shogun a change of pants—the sweats she'd purchased from the gift shop. He drew the blood sample in the men's room and came back without his incriminating khakis. Sasha stopped walking and looked at the cloud of color swirling around the room.

"Dana went into the trash after we left and got the pants, gave them to Vampires that night, and Vampires left them in the bayou for Hunter to trip over so he'd go after Shogun?" She turned in a circle hardly believing, but the evidence spoke for itself.

The response was a gleeful shower of bursting, shimmering Fairy lights.

CHAPTER 18

The waiting was the worst part, always. Court was court, a trial was a trial—although she'd prefer a human court-martial to a supernatural tribunal any night. Then there was the not-so-small issue of transportation through a bayou where the enraged demon could do serious witness tampering. It had already been enough that the more mild-mannered supernaturals had declined to attend the proceeding, opting to hear about it on the gossip grapevine rather than risk being savaged in the swamps. Who could blame them?

It meant, in all likelihood, that the only participants would be the Fae peacekeeping forces due to their forest agility; Vampires—who feared nothing; members of The Order of the Dragon, for much the same reason; and Wolf Clan members, who were always ready for a brawl and on trial anyway.

Therefore, unlike the very egalitarian and democratic process of the UCE Conference, this affair had the markings of a medieval town hanging. Even with a demon-infected Werewolf snuffling through the underbrush, there was an insanely festive mood rippling through the crowd as supernaturals headed toward the deep swamp.

Dragons lit the way with flame-thrown bursts; Phantoms slipped between the trees, their haunting presence sending chilled breezes through the otherwise humid night. Fleet-footed Fae archers performed breathtaking aerial acrobatics as they advanced through the dense overhead canopy. It was like watching Cirque du Soleil without the benefit of an arena or tickets.

Burly Werewolf Clan members at least two hundred strong—adding in Shogun's people—crashed through the underbrush wielding shotguns, baseball bats, tire irons, and pretty much anything else that could do damage. They surrounded their formidable female pack members with possessive warning snarls—as though anybody else wanted them.

No weapons were confiscated or going to be checked at the door. That was clear by the way everybody brandished what they had. If it was going to be all that, she wouldn't have tried to tone it down by only having a Glock and a few grenades. Hell, she would have gone all-out with an assault rifle and bazooka. Why not? Once in the bayou, apparently, anything went. Maybe it was the loosed demon-Werewolf; maybe it was just the wild west reality of it all. Who knew? At least all the Shadows had pump shotguns and silver shells . . . though an Uzi or two in her company sure woulda been nice. Had she only known.

Sasha rolled her eyes and kept walking as she spotted Dana and Lei flanked by Fae protective custody marshals. Until now it hadn't truly sunk in just how pitifully thinned out the Shadow ranks were from all the wars and the internal struggle with Dexter's infected wolves.

With Hunter, Silver Hawk, Bear Shadow, Crow Shadow, and her, there were only about fifty healthy members remaining in the North American Clan. Instinctively she knew that could not be a good thing.

Tornado clouds of bats blotted out the moonlight in a fluttering patchwork of agile bodies—leave it to the Vampires to come in by private flights.

But this time there were no Phoenixes with their gorgeous silken plumes in high colors to light up the night. There were no Fairy sparklers delightedly playing among the trees. The smaller Elves and Brownies were conspicuously absent, as were the slower-moving ground forces of Gnomes and Trolls. With a ravaging Werewolf on the loose, that was perfectly reasonable. The Mythics seemed to take the same tack—what peace-loving Yeti in his or her right mind would go up against a demon-infected wolf?

It wasn't until she saw Dugan walking beside Sir Rodney in merry discourse that she began to worry. Hunter and Silver Hawk saw it, too. The threesome shared a look. No doubt this was going to be a particularly long and deadly night.

A lonely howl sent shivers up her spine. She'd know Shogun's baleful call anywhere. Immediately two-hundred-plus howls answered him, sending a thunderous warning throughout the bayou; strength in numbers, intimidation by force.

Sasha looked at the silver trays she and Silver Hawk carried, and the gym bag Hunter had hitched up on his shoulder. What was the point if the entire process came down to firepower? If it was gonna be all that, she'd call in an F-18 air strike and show them some real fucking shock and awe.

"Easy, girl," Hunter said with a lopsided grin, needling her to make her relax. "The hair on your neck is standing up."

She didn't answer him as the crowd came to a stop at the deep water's edge. Everyone assembled glanced up at the moon. It was as though they all had just looked at the Big Ben clock tower in London, rather than the full moon. No self-respecting supernatural required a timepiece, and the Vampires apparently only wore ridiculously expensive brands to show off. Internal reckoning said the huge black marble edifice would rise out of the swamp in a few moments. Then court would be in session.

No matter how many times she'd seen it—and granted, she'd only seen it once before—watching the mist gather as glistening clean, sculpted columns rose up out of nothingness to appear like something out of the Greek Pantheon was nothing short of spectacular. Clearly she wasn't the only one who delighted in the process of the UCE being called to order. Applause thundered through the glen, and after the building settled in place, hardening the ground around it and spreading out to offer guests out-of-

place courtyards and gardens, individuals began fil-
ing up the massive stone stairs.

In keeping with protocol, she and other entities sat
with their group in predetermined orchestra seating
that had been assigned, no doubt, eons before her
time.

But oddly, this time the layout was slightly different. There were still aerial posts and catwalks for the
Fae, and huge chandeliers with delicate, miniature
seating for the Fairies, but rather than the thick wall
mounts for heavy Dragons and Phoenixes to loop
themselves around, the boxes had silver barriers
between them with burly Dragon guards pacing
back and forth. Gone were the comfortable, high-
backed upholstered chairs. Marble benches arranged
coliseum-style prevailed. The Mythics' boxes weren't
even shielded from view with privacy screens, and
slowly but surely she came to realize that the council's chamber had a dangerous arena feel to it.

Oh, yeah . . . this was definitely court, even if they
wanted to be politically correct and call it a tribunal.
Sasha glimpsed Hunter from the corner of her eye.
The large black marble U-shaped front bench was
empty, no seats taken. Then the dormant gavel sat up,
rose swiftly, and banged itself with a crack, yelling,
"All rise!"

Everyone stood, muttering and grumbling.

Gone was the beautiful Siren stenographer,
whose mermaid fantail provided modesty for her Ti-
tan carrier. An old crone with a big black book hob-
bled in and opened the dusty tomb, peering over

Ben Franklin glasses. Then she set it in the air where it floated of its own volition. She cackled a screeching laugh that stilled the crowd, pulled out a small wand from behind her pointed ear, and flung it at the book, causing a small explosion that made her have to adjust her lopsided black hat.

"Truth will print, lies will burn," she warned, gazing around the group with a crooked eye. "All proceedings are written in blood. This court has come to order."

Then just as abruptly as she'd come in, she walked out of a side door and vanished. Three black hooded figures filed in right behind the crone's exit; one very tall and lean, one extremely robust, and one short and round. It wasn't hard to guess who they were even before Baron Geoff Montague, Buchanan Broussard, and Elf Dugan climbed up to the bench, removed their hoods, and then sat.

"There are very serious charges being presented tonight," the baron said, his steely Vampire gaze roving the crowd and setting off murmurs of accord and dissent. "Two humans have been savaged— eaten, bringing human authorities dangerously close to our secret way of life." He nodded to Buchanan as though the entire proceeding had been scripted.

"In addition," Buchanan said, rearing back and allowing his hefty frame to add size and dimension to his commanding voice. "We have an eyewitness account of contagion being used in a wolf fight as a weapon."

Gasps rang out and the crowd began to grumble louder until the gavel jumped up and began shrieking for order.

"That's right," Buchanan said. "Shocking as that may be, we have an infected man now Turning while in custody. We might unfortunately have to publicly execute him tonight."

Sasha's gaze narrowed as she watched the blood-lust ripple through the crowd. Not on her watch. She was glad that Hunter and Silver Hawk gave her a sub-tle nod.

"We also have," Dugan said with an unsteady voice, "evidence of willful toxin usage . . . man-ufactured demon infection from the human experi-ments being injected by the same wolf who went rogue and savaged an uninfected man. The death of the one now Turning is truly an act of violence, be-cause the one who willfully infected himself and then passed on the contagion has a natural immunity to it once it runs its course—because he's a Shadow Wolf."

The crowd erupted. Everyone was on their feet, and it took repeated gavel whacks and shrieks to re-gain order.

"Yes," Baron Montague said in a silky tone, his expression smug. "It appears from all the gathered evidence that the sleeper cell within the same Shadow Pack that caused all the chaos during the last full moon is none other than the North American Clan leadership." He pointed at Hunter and Sasha as the crowd broke into angry growls, barks, and jeers.

After what seemed an eternity, order was once again restored. Baron Montague crooked his finger toward the floating book, and as it moved to him through the air, silence echoed in the great hall. He peered down and materialized a pair of reading glasses on the bridge of his aristocratic nose.

"For the felony crime of human murders that could destabilize our supernatural havens, we hereby charge Maximus Hunter, North American Clan leader of the Shadow Wolf Federation. Note in the margin: The Southeast Asian Clan Leader of the Werewolf Federation is exonerated of this act, given that his contagion was willfully thrust upon him in a dastardly act of felonious infection spreading. In addition, for biohazardous toxin smuggling and usage, again, Maximus Hunter is charged, along with his life-mate and accomplice, Sasha Trudeau. Given the serious nature of these multiple charges and offenses, these and all charges carry the weight of the sentence, death by silver bullet firing squad."

Shadow Wolves were on their feet, with Werewolves in the adjacent booths yelling back across the Dragon divides. Pandemonium took several minutes to quell, and even then shouts of discontent rang out.

"This sentencing, should we find the defendants guilty, is based upon the fact that more than human collateral damage occurred. We do have the loss of a valuable member of supernatural society—no matter what, Shogun is Turnin', ladies and gentlemen," Buchanan said, glancing around the court. "I was there and saw that part myself. And who knows what else is out there in the bayou—y'all heard it, y'all smelled it . . . who knows who else that boy bit while he was druggin' and thuggin'?"

Dugan nodded. "I have evidence of what he was

shooting up in me own establishment. Those who know me know that for years I've run a clean B and B. There's never been an incident that leaked to the human world." He leaned forward and glanced down the bench. "Aye, this is a dark time, if we small businessmen cannot safely run an enterprise. Worse yet, our community cannot have sleepless days worryin' ta death that some new infection drug may cause violent chaos to reign."

The baron made a tent before his mouth with his fingers for a moment, and sent a withering gaze throughout the crowd. "It is bad for business," he said succinctly. "It is bad for secrecy." He sat back and let out a long, impatient sigh. "It is bad for the UCE and every group represented here tonight. We cannot have this rogue behavior on our streets."

Vampires sneered and hissed as Shadow Wolves growled low warnings.

"We must stamp out this scourge where we find it," the baron said, slowly standing. His eloquence enraptured the group, as did his charismatic style. Sasha and Hunter watched, snarling, as he manipulated the crowd until it was practically eating out of his hand.

"Clearly, these two are guilty from the preponderance of evidence of credible eyewitnesses," the baron pressed on, gloating. "Unfortunately, by midnight, when the moon reaches its zenith, an innocent young man will have to lose his life—as there is no known cure for the contagion. In addition, there appears to still be a feeding monster on the loose in our fair bayou, which we will have to hunt down. My suggestion is that those who cannot catch the moonlight madness should take on this hunt—Vampires, Dragons, and Fae—in support of our wolf citizenry who are vulnerable to the disease. Shadows, given that this is probably another rogue Shadow Wolf, would necessarily be exempt from this hunt as well. But know that I propose this with no less humility and deference than if this were a daylight matter, whereby I'm sure our Werewolf brethren and sisters would respond to a call to arms for our needs. It is about cooperation and mutual respect."

"Put your evidence on the table, Baron!" Sasha shouted, causing another crowd uproar.

"Gladly," the baron said evenly through his teeth once the noise had died down. "But young lady, we will follow due process in this courtroom." He sat back and sniffed. "You have heard eyewitness testimony from two tribunal members. In addition we have spent needle casings, vials, and drug paraphernalia that were confiscated from Dugan's B and B. Let that be entered into the record."

Sasha watched in horror as the Elf held his wrist over the book and the wand made a quick slash at it, splattering blood onto the pages.

"I did not plant these items on the accused," Dugan said with his chin lifted, gazing at the crowd confidently, "and they were collected by my Pixie staff from the suite of the accused."

It seemed as though the entire room held its collective breath. Then a low murmur rippled through the crowd as the wand wrote and the page it wrote on didn't burn.

"You may be seated," the baron said with a sly smile, nodding to Buchanan Broussard.

The burly redheaded Werewolf stood, sauntered over to the center podium, and held out his wrist. He waited for the strike and smiled like a heavyweight wrestler about to go into the ring.

"I seen him clear as day, the accused, in a wolf tussle in the bayou—bit the hell out of that po' dying boy. When they came out of the brawl, Shogun was tore up bad."

Again the wand wrote and nothing burned. Sasha's nails dug into her fists as she watched a miscarriage of justice in the making.

"I would like to call Dana Broussard," the baron crooned, causing an audible ripple in the crowd. "Come, my lovely, tell us what you saw."

Dana stood, preened, and finally sashayed forward, making every male in the room crane his neck to watch her stand before the book. She licked her wrist vein first, and several audible whistles sounded in low appreciation.

"Right there, honey," she said to the wand. "Don't leave too bad of a mark, wouldya, sugah?" She closed her eyes as the blood splattered the page and the wand waited for her testimony. "Don't get me wrong," she said in a sensual murmur, staring at Hunter. "I think the man is a beast . . . and I was attracted to his dark danger . . . but he was really upset by that po' student human boy—the waiter who died. Why, that chile came up behind him while he was feeding and I could tell he was high on something . . . I can't say, but

Ethan had to change staff, Hunter was so bristled. Then he turned on my date, his enforcer, they had words out of my earshot a bit, and finally Hunter saw his lady friend and they went into the same alley where they found that human in a Dumpster—behind Ethan's restaurant."

"That's not how it happened," Hunter snarled beneath his breath in Sasha's ear.

"Yeah, buddy, but if you haven't noticed, those were the facts—out of context or not. The pages didn't burn," Sasha replied beneath her breath. "This shit happens every day in human courts, so get over it. Save it for the defense."

The Shadow Clans watched with burning gazes but dejected spirits as yet another testimony held. Dana gave Sasha a smug glance as she slipped by the Shadow section to return to her wolf pack.

But when they called Bear Shadow, all hell broke loose.

"No!" Bear Shadow shouted, on the verge of a shape-shift. "I will not be a party to this charade! My alpha is clean; he is honorable—as is his mate!"

"Then testify to what you know happened that night," Baron Montague said. "We want a balance of testimony from all entities represented here tonight, so that it can never be said that Maximus Hunter and Sasha Trudeau were railroaded. There must be Shadow testimony. We are endeavoring for fairness."

"You were there that night, darlin'," Dana called out from her box. "You saw your alpha go into the alley and you know it. In fact, if he won't tell it, I'd be more than happy to come back up there and tell the court where he was standing and what he wanted from me when the big guy sulked off."

All eyes turned to Bear Shadow. The book swiftly flew toward him, the wand hovering dangerously near.

"Did. You. See. The accused. Leave by way of the alley?" Baron Montague sat back and tented his fingers before his mouth, retracting fangs as Bear Shadow clenched his jaw and lifted his chin, refusing to speak. "Add this in the notes in the record— Shadow Clan member refuses to testify. Let it never be said that we didn't ask, but to me this seems more incriminating than a simple yes or no."

Rolling his shoulders, the baron gazed around the room. "In lieu of Bear Shadow, I would like to call Silver Hawk, then."

The entire Shadow Clan was on their feet. Silver Hawk held up his hand. The baron smiled, showing a slight hint of fangs.

"Excellent," Geoff cooed as the elderly shaman made his way to the podium.

Silver Hawk held out his wrist and waited. The wand struck him, and then the Vampire turned to gaze as him with glittering hatred in his eyes.

"Tell me, *mon ami* . . . did your grandson Maximus Hunter ever experience infected Werewolf contagion?"

"Yes, but—"

"That is all!" the baron shouted, cutting Silver Hawk off. "Let the record show that even the accused relatives knew that he was a carrier, but allowed him to freely mingle in our taverns, frequent our establishments, and roam the streets of New Orleans! By rights, any and all who were aware and did not, by wolf pack law, take him out of circulation are also guilty of aiding and abetting his disease spreading! These are not our UCE laws," he said, now standing and pointing at the Shadow Wolf section that had erupted in jeers and growls. "These are your own laws that you've violated."

"Yeah, that's right!" a disgruntled Werewolf yelled across the divide. "We take our own down, that's the way of the wolf, man!"

This time it took several minutes to restore order. Geoff remained standing, pulling down his black robe sleeves and shaking his head.

"We of the Vampire Cartel hate to see this lack of civility among entities," he said quietly, causing the crowd to listen, rapt. "Ours is a long-standing community that has lived in symbiotic harmony with our human environment. We also solve issues within our ranks—quietly, discreetly, efficiently. This conduct is deplorable . . ." He clucked his tongue and again began to shake his head. "How you can sleep in the morning is beyond me. To bring a disease carrier amid all these healthy wolves and allow him to use toxin in our best Fae establishments—even to compromise his mate to the point that she's jonesing for Werewolf blood, willing to prostitute herself to get it at a teahouse."

"What?" Sasha was on her feet. "I did no such thing! It wasn't like that at all, and you know it!"

"Save it for the defense, right," Hunter muttered under his breath.

"I would like to call Takiyama," the baron said

coolly. "A delicate Phoenix hostess who was also kind enough to bring me this." He materialized the blood-drawing needle between his graceful fingers. "We could have this tested, but I think my Vampire colleagues and I are all above reproach when it comes to our ability to positively identify blood sources. This is Shogun's blood, which he drew at the request of one Sasha Trudeau. I will ask that this court be mindful that the Phoenix nervous system is extremely sensitive. This poor woman burned to ash once already and she's just coming back—that happened the morning she came to work to open up and found a dead server in the teahouse gardens. Our Dragon brothers brought her to our lairs that same evening to help restore her. Therefore, we kept her in protective custody, assuring her safety, until now . . . so if you'd be so kind, no outbursts, although her testimony is extremely shocking."

He sat calmly with a placid expression, allowing lumbering Dragons to walk between the wolf boxes breathing fire until everyone else also sat and fell silent. Then a timid dark-haired beauty stepped out from the misty doorway as though a fawn testing her first dawn. She took two steps and covered her shy face with an elaborate fan of feathers. Brightly hued streams of silk ribbons and scarves floated away from her fragile, birdlike body as she advanced to the podium, eyes lowered. She held out a porcelain wrist, trembling, and released a shocked chirp when she was struck till she bled.

"My dear, just in your own words . . . what did you see?" Baron Montague cooed.

"They must have loved each other dearly," she said quietly. "I thought . . . they were so passionate that the girls blushed at the shadows on the privacy screen and I shooed them away."

Sasha closed her eyes. She'd take the silver bullet in the skull now please.

"Then, when it was all over . . . she brought him a new pair of pants to hide his shame. It was a kind gesture of discretion. But when I was cleaning the stalls and saw the needle . . . I was shocked." The Phoenix lifted her dark eyes and revealed irises engulfed in flames.

"Go on, *ma petite,* then what happened?" Geoff leered.

The other Vampires sat forward, hanging on every lascivious word. Sasha glimpsed Hunter's jaw, watching the muscle in it throb. Shadow Wolves stared at the floor, their once outraged spirits crushed. Even Werewolves hung their heads in shame; their leader, Shogun, had obviously given his blood to a female toxin junkie and screwed her. You could have heard a pin drop in the hall.

"He kissed her," Takiyama said. "And handed her the vial. We could see their shadows through the screen . . . and the Fairies are so nosy, they didn't want to miss any of the romance—I couldn't hear but they said that Shogun said, 'I know, Sasha, this never happened.' "

"Oh, *my* God! In a regular court that would be hearsay!" Sasha shouted through cresting canines, unable to contain herself. "*The Fairies said that he said*—what kind of bullshit is that?"

"Ooooohhhh . . . You said there would be no violence or anger directed toward me personally,
Baron," Takiyama wailed, gathering her silk skirts
around her and dashing back and forth like a chicken
with her head cut off. "I wasn't involved; I was just
there at the teahouse! A girl was murdered. I don't
want to be murdered!"

"She's gonna blow," Dugan said, getting up and
taking cover with Buchanan as suddenly a burst of
flames and spiraling colors swirled across the
podium. The baron never moved. He just sat calmly
as ash rained down on his robe, and then he casually
brushed it off.

"Add another *petite morte* to your portfolio of
charges, Ms. Trudeau," he said flatly, gaining laughter from the Vampire box as Dragons frantically
tried to scoop up Takiyama's burning remains. "Do
note, however," he added with a droll smile. "She
burned, but the book didn't. Fascinating, isn't it."

"Do we get a turn at bat or is this entire travesty
only about you guys saying what you heard and saw
and we don't get a chance?" Sasha strode forward,
unable to stand next to Hunter at the moment. She
held out her wrist. "Strike me," she said. "Let the
goddamned games begin."

CHAPTER 19

Sasha made a fist as the wand viciously slashed her wrist. She glared at it, noting that it had taken more blood from her arm than from any of the previous witnesses.

"I'm gonna chalk that up to the fact that I have more to say than the others," Sasha said in a low growl, making the wand and the book back farther away from her. She looked at the bench and held up a hand as the baron took a breath to begin another line of insidious questioning. "Under oath, I have reason to suspect foul play on the bench, and I hereby call Sir Rodney to ask for my testimony."

"No, overruled," the baron said, hotly standing.

Fae archers positioned as Vampires hissed and Wolves sat back, new awareness slowly dawning in their eyes.

"It is *the law,* Baron," Sir Rodney said with a wry smile. "Any witness can call a neutral interrogator. We, the Fae, have been that for years. We were the jailers—to both Werewolves and Shadow Wolves this

time around. I see no harm, as long as no one has anything to hide." He flashed the baron a dashing Gaelic
smile and then shrugged.

The Fae captain strode to the front of the room
with a cheerful expression and held out his wrist.
Once struck, he bowed politely to the book, as only
the Fae can do, and spoke to it respectfully. "So help
me, I swear to tell the whole truth and nothing but
the whole truth no matter who is involved."

The pages took and Sasha relaxed. She watched
Sir Rodney pace before the front of the courtroom
with his hands behind his back. Then, as though the
mood simply struck him, he laughed and threw up
his hands.

"I have no further questions," he said cheerfully.

Vampires snickered as wolf packs sent nervous
glances between them. Sasha closed her eyes and
groaned. She'd picked a madman to represent her—
or maybe one who was in cahoots with Dugan.

"Really, I don't, for a thousand questions 'ave
crossed my mind, but I think the whole truth requires
Captain Trudeau to tell us wot 'appened in that teahouse from her own sweet words." Sir Rodney stood
before the crowd, charisma oozing from every pore.
"But I do know the woman is no junkie . . . truth is, if
she was, I would have most assuredly been the first
in line to supply her."

She was going to kill herself.

Laughter rang out from the Fae archers from
overhead. Werewolves smirked despite themselves.
Only Vampires and Shadow Clan members seemed
offended.

"You *must* ask a *specific* question or her testimony is void," the baron said through full fangs, leaning forward.

"All right, all right, due process, yes, of course," Sir Rodney said, waving off the offense with merriment in his eyes. "But do note for the record that, when I said she was no junkie, the book didn't even smolder, laddie."

Sasha opened her eyes. Sir Rodney's disarming charm was all a front. The man was sly as a fox. She watched him hold the courtroom spellbound as he turned to her, his smile belying the new intensity that burned in his piercing blue gaze.

"Ah," he said, rocking back on his heels and clasping his hands behind his back. "Here's a specific question, Captain Trudeau. Can you tell the court, in your own words, the purpose of your meeting the Southeast Asian Clan leader at the teahouse that fateful day? I think we should get through the juicy part of the testimony first, since we just lost a Phoenix behind it."

"Of course she *can* tell us, but—"

"Well, that's wot I want her to do, man," Sir Rodney said, cutting off the Baron's objection and seeming shocked.

"I went to the teahouse to meet with Shogun because I wanted a blood sample for medical reasons," Sasha said carefully. "I wanted to see if there was any way we could find a cure for the contagion that plagues wolves."

"Good, then—"

"And why was that a necessary thing?" the baron

said in a sinister tone, cutting off Sir Rodney's line of questioning.

"Are we to follow due process of your witnesses testifying, and then mine, and then we each have time to cross-examine? Or have Robert's Rules of Order changed here, sir?"

The baron sat back as the Vampire section fell eerily quiet. "Forgive me . . . do continue."

Sir Rodney nodded and turned back to Sasha, seeming to choose his words very carefully. "Did you need this blood to inject yourself, or was it to study?"

"To study," Sasha said.

Sir Rodney's gaze bore into hers for a moment. "Did you kill anyone at the teahouse or otherwise eat a human or feed a human to your Shadow Wolf mate?"

"No!" Sasha said, appalled.

"Under the duress of making an exchange with the Southeast Asian Clan leader, did a quasisexual act occur?"

Sasha lowered her gaze. "Yes."

"But do you have evidence that shows a Fairy enchantment was involved?"

Sasha nodded as the room erupted into murmurs.

"I call forward evidence captured on digital video with sound enhanced so it can be presented in court." Sir Rodney motioned to a Dragon guard to pass up the black gym bag Hunter had been holding. He smiled when the baron's eyes narrowed and he began rubbing his temples as though vexed by a sudden migraine. "I should warn our Vampire friends in the room to be wary of trying to penetrate this particular bit of evidence, as it had been anointed and silver-protected." He chuckled and passed the handheld DVD player to Sasha. "Would you be so kind? I haven't a clue as to how human technology works."

She set up the digital image and turned to the crowd. "This is just after an incident at Tulane Hospital, where Fairies sought my human dark arts expert to reverse an enchantment spell they'd performed at the behest of Lei—and in return, they thought their gardens would be safe from demon incursion. But Lei double-crossed them, so they came looking for me to tell on her, as well as for someone who could help them reverse a love spell."

"Play the tape, Captain!" Sir Rodney said like a mad hatter. He pointed to the tape as the Fairies' complaint rang out in the courtroom. "You see, this woman is no junkie. There was foul play that obviously contributed to the intimate events, which may well have never happened under normal circumstances . . . and, what's more, if the Fairies had believed that the accused ate a human in their gardens, they most assuredly would not have come to her or her familiars!"

Grumbles rippled through the room. Wolves on both sides began hot debate, but Lei remained extremely silent as Dana Broussard and her father stared her down. But Sasha's gaze sought Hunter and then her Shadow Clan. One day she would seriously repay Sir Rodney for the not-so-small gift of restoring her honor in her clan's eyes . . . in her mate's eyes.

"Then that is all I would like to ask about the subject of allegedly what happened at the teahouse—that Captain Trudeau is not a toxin user or a murderess is

the only fact of relevance here, and any further innu-
endo is simply in poor taste." Sir Rodney lifted his
chin and walked about as though flustered; he then put
a graceful finger to his lips for a moment. "Let's talk
about who was at the teahouse following her, though."

Using two forefingers, Sir Rodney waved toward
the silver platters that had been held in the Shadow
Wolf section. Murmurs broke out, but even the gavel
was so curious as it pirouetted to see that it failed to
bring the courtroom to order.

"Can you tell the court what this is, Captain?" Sir
Rodney said, whipping off the silver domes and pur-
posely setting the silver dangerously close to the
baron and Buchanan.

"It's human evidence gathered by an impartial and
supernaturally ignorant party," Sasha said, her gaze
scanning the entire room. "NOPD has no idea what
species these hairs come from. They think it's a dog
or a wolf. But I think it's rather ironic that basic human forensics could show that the hair in bag one—
which came from the Dumpster where they found
that young male college student—belongs to an infected Werewolf *female* in the Southeast Asian Clan."

Sasha waited for the barks and growls to die
down. "Isn't that right, Lei? We could easily take a
strand of your hair, run it next to this one, and find a
genetic match because this belongs to your mother."

"My mother has been dead for decades," Lei said
coolly. "We all know that she was slaughtered at the
hands of the North American Shadow Wolf Clan,
which contributed to the tensions between our Federations."

"Call her to the stand and make her say that crap in front of the book," Sasha growled.

"In a moment," Sir Rodney said calmly. "But first, can you describe the other evidence?"

"Yeah, gladly," Sasha said, whirling on the platters. "In bag two, the human authorities took a hair sample from a window—it's from an auburn female wolf, who was in the window of the teahouse men's room. That's the way she exited, they believe. I'd lay bets that if we took a hair sample from Dana, it would match up."

Buchanan was on his feet with his daughter. "Now just you hold on," he bellowed. "My daughter ain't no infected flesh-eater!"

"No, she's not," Sasha said coolly, making the spectators' heads pivot between her and Buchanan. "But she is a wolf traitor."

Dana instantly shape-shifted. Only the Fae archers perilously pointing silver arrows in her direction stemmed an attack.

"You'd better watch your mouth so close to a full moon with four-to-one clan odds bucking up against you," Buchanan warned. "Them's some serious odds, since you're a betting woman by your own admission."

"If you match the hair sample found in the window of the teahouse," Sasha said as calmly as possible, ignoring Buchanan and addressing the crowd now, "you'll see the same hair on that as the pants that were left in the bathroom . . . after the enchantment spell. Takiyama found the needle that Shogun used to draw blood, but she didn't find the pants. Why?" Sasha waited a moment and looked at the bench. "He went in a stall to do that blood draw, and he probably tossed the needle in the john where it floated back up—Vampires could still smell that blood to ridiculous parts per billion. But the pair of khaki pants . . . he put those in the larger bin on the way out the door after he'd changed."

"What has any of this got to do with my Dana?" Buchanan threw up his hands. "I fail to see the relevance of—"

"She went after the pants." Sasha pointed at Dana then whirled on the baron. "Then she gave them to the Vampire Geoff Montague, who put them in Hunter's path to start a wolf war—all so he could have an open wolf hunt against both Werewolves and Shadows in order to gain back cartel control of the UCE!"

Again the courtroom erupted. Dragons blasted aisles with treacherous plumes of flames and archers released warning shots until a strained peace settled among the boxes again.

"You'd better have damned good proof for these allegations," Baron said in a hissing threat.

Sir Rodney offered another casual Gaelic shrug. "The proof is easy enough. Human DNA testing can match up hair strands and tell if somethin' came from Lei's ma."

"But you are missing a very crucial point," the baron remarked coolly with a smirk. "These proceedings wrap up tonight—the time to bring forward such evidence has elapsed."

"It takes weeks, sometimes, to get that kind of accurate forensic data," Sasha argued as Vampires sat back in their booth and smiled. "The truth demands time!"

"You have run *out of time*," the baron repeated with emphasis.

"But we have not run out of testimony," Sir Rodney said appearing unfazed. "I'm sure we could call Dana up to ask her if she went to the teahouse and stole the pants, or if she actually gave them to you trying to cut a side deal for herself around Lei." He sighed and began walking while raking his hair. "But the lady could just plead the Fifth, as Bear Shadow just did, as could you, Baron . . . and we most certainly won't be able to get Lei to testify against herself or her brother. Hmmm. I don't suppose a father would go against his daughter, so Mr. Broussard is out."

"Therefore, I guess that wraps up the case," Baron Montague said with a smirk.

The boxes went wild, but following Sir Rodney's calls and the gavel's shriek, entities gradually sat down again, straining to hear what would happen next.

"I have to ask the man who is going to the gallows—that's only right. We heard from the lady . . ." Sir Rodney glanced up at Hunter.

Hunter stood and held out his wrist, eyes rimmed in amber, furious and unafraid.

"Tell us, sir, answer yes or no," Sir Rodney said as the book positioned to take the harsh scribbling of the wand. "Have you now or ever in your life eaten or savaged a human?"

Silence echoed; no one breathed. "No," Hunter rumbled.

All eyes turned to the book, which didn't burn. The courtroom was again out of control.

Sir Rodney raced down the aisle. "Do you know who did?"

"Yes," Hunter said flatly. "Lei's mother. She's not dead and she's still in the bayou, infected. That's not hearsay; I saw her."

"Strike the testimony!" the baron yelled above the din. "Speculation—he never saw her!"

"How would you know, unless you were there?" Hunter shouted. "Like you were when you lured me and my blood brother, Shogun, into mortal combat!"

"Order, order!" Buchanan shouted, grabbing the screaming gavel and pounding on the bench. "These are some serious charges that can't be substantiated, because some of these people have an agenda and shouldn't be allowed to take the stand!"

Dana had transformed back and was dressing amid ogling spectators, but Sir Rodney was striding up the aisle to where Dugan sat.

"I, as the captain of the Fae guards, can call martial law among my people," Sir Rodney said with an angry smile. The courtroom went dead silent. "You're right; there are many that I cannot call, despite what we are beginning to see as a pattern of lies and backroom deals. But I can call a Fae tribunal member and under our enchantment oath of truth—which he unwittingly took from me while walking to court during a leisurely stroll—he has to tell me and this court what happened. Don'tcha, Dugan? I want ta know about the deal you cut with the baron, and how you delivered Vampire-doctored meds to Hunter at your B and B without him knowing . . . how you know the Vampires are playing both ends against the middle to get the wolves to war—and you know Lei's demon mother is eating humans in teahouse gardens and leaving young boys in Dumpsters! Ya even gave Lei a spell that she could pass on to 'er demon ma to breach the shadow lands, did ye not? That way she could ambush Shadows. No more lies, you 'ave shamed our Parliament. The spell-casters gave you up—tell me, man, outta ye own mouth before I shoot you meself for such treason!"

A black bolt from the Vampire boxes hit Dugan in the chest, splintering it to burn his heart and cook it before the rotund Elf could even open his mouth. Werewolves were over the divide with Shadow Wolves. Fae archers were no longer neutral as they targeted fast-moving Vampires. Dragons kicked over seating sections, snapping at Vampire vapor mist. The gavel ran away screaming as the book slammed shut and the wand spiraled like a missile to find the old crone and tell.

The battle raged in the great hall, then spilled down the marble front steps and into the swamp. Bloodshed splattered on the trees and ground cover as fierce hurling bodies in a blur of chaos broke branches. It was all-out, full-scale war—Vampires against wolf packs with irate Dragons caught in the crossfire and vexed Fae lending aerial support from treetops.

Shotgun shells flew, claws and teeth slashed. Plumes of bats took to the air only to be scorched by Dragon fire blasts. Transforming Vampire bodies were caught by silver arrows as they came out of the vapors. Phantoms fled the scene. But Sasha was looking for Lei. This was personal.

She found Lei locked in mortal wolf combat with Dana, savaging the weaker wolf while Buchanan fought through an ambush of Vampires yelling *no*. Sasha dropped her right hand into the palm of her left to get dead aim to blow Lei's head off. Then a whiff of demon-wolf made her turn.

A huge claw swipe missed Sasha by mere inches. She tumbled backward just as Lei dropped Dana's limp body on the ground and hurtled forward. In the frenzy, the demon-infected Were reared back and swiped again, her goal to gore Sasha, but she caught Lei in the gut. Entrails splattered the swamp floor. The demonic female hesitated a second. Shock, pain, remorse flitted through her twisted expression, and then fury replaced it. A second was all Sasha needed to find the bull's-eye that should have been found years ago. The demon's head snapped back, then oddly a second shell blew open her chest. Sasha scrambled up to see Silver Hawk standing ten feet behind her and slowly lowering a shotgun.

"Just to be on the safe side," Silver Hawk said.

Sasha nodded and looked down at the glassy-eyed Lei, and then put three more silver bullets in her skull. "Just to be on the safe side—before there's more hell to pay."

CHAPTER 20

The injuries were severe and the fatalities many, but as the unified wolf Federations walked side by side with the Fae and The Order of the Dragon to the safety of Sir Rodney's enchanted camp, everyone felt a sense of quiet victory—the Vampires had been defeated in this battle.

Currently, there was enough evidence to convict Baron Geoff Montague and sentence him to death by daylight, if they ever caught the rat bastard. However, the Vampire estates in the region would be seriously taxed to make restitution to every family that had suffered a loss. There was also enough evidence of foul play to keep the Vampire Cartel from a leadership position at the UCE Conferences for many, many moons to come.

But despite the short-term victory, Sasha's mind was on the long-term view as she studied Hunter's solemn profile. The Shadow pack for the North Country was followed on the march to Sir Rodney's castle by members of the Southeast Asian Werewolf

Clan, and after them all other regional Werewolf clans. Hunter was the only living relative of alpha status who was related by blood to Shogun. It was the way of the wolf—to die by honor as a warrior, if the contagion hit.

She grieved for Hunter as they all quietly processed to the place where Sir Rodney made the damp earth a cobbled path. They would walk through the town gaining curious stares, and this battle at UCE court would go down in infamy. Yet at this very pressing, intimate moment, a man who cast a large shadow—not just from his spirit, but also from his very huge heart—had to take the life of the brother he'd just found, just battled, just infected, and now would invariably lose.

The drawbridge lowered. She watched a bloodied, muddied Hunter walk across it, back straight, eyes forward. The military couldn't have asked for a better soldier, if they'd ever been aware such existed. Pedestrians and town entities stepped aside, watching the blended army file toward the castle. Gnomes sounded the alarm until they realized that Sir Rodney wasn't being held hostage, but was walking in complete lockstep with the front line.

Castle doors swung open, and guards seemed to sense where everyone was going. An echoing howl filtered out of the dungeon the moment the doors were unbolted.

"I'll go alone," Hunter said, stopping the group.

Silver Hawk shook his head. "Protocol is to be observed whenever possible. Tonight we saw how the absence of that can make men monsters. One witness from the Werewolf Clan—the clan that will lose a man. One witness from the Fae—to be sure all is done in decency and order. One other than the blood relative to be the shooter, so that this pain is not bonded to the relative's soul forever. Two more from the heartbroken one's clan to hold that relative up and help carry the body home. And if you have the good fortune to have a mate, your shadow should be there. This is how it has been done since the beginning of the Great Spirit's time, since the dawn of wolf time on earth . . . and since the contagion has been our plague."

They watched a member of Shogun's family step forward, his eyes glassy but his chin lifted with pride. "I am a cousin. I will step up."

Hunter nodded and looked at Sir Rodney.

"It is my honor," Sir Rodney said, accepting a crossbow from one of his rear guards.

"Let me be your shooter," Silver Hawk whispered, placing a hand on Hunter's shoulder.

Hunter simply nodded as Bear Shadow and Crow Shadow stepped forward.

"Until we are one with the shadow lands in spirit, my pack brother, I will always stand with you," Bear Shadow said in a low rumble.

"And I," Crow Shadow said, crossing his chest with his forearm.

Sasha didn't need to be asked. She came near, her gaze holding Hunter's for a moment in silent understanding.

No one spoke; they all just waited for Hunter to begin walking. Wall torches sputtered as bodies went by, but the group didn't flinch away. Bone-weariness, post-battle fatigue, and heavy spirits just made them trudge forward through the labyrinth. Guards stood as they approached the central area and saluted Sir Rodney. Execution—and remorse that it had to be done—was in everyone's eyes.

"Sir, is it time to move the prisoner to court?" the lead guard asked, seeming confused. "The holding spells and chains can be activated and . . ." His voice trailed off as he looked into the eyes of those standing around him. "Just here, not with Vampire witnesses then, sir?"

"Never with Vampires gloating witness to a wolf death," Sir Rodney said, his voice angry and tight.

The guards who had stood up and abandoned their cards when the execution team entered backed away.

Sasha's gaze tore around their faces. "When did you take off your kerchiefs?"

"Milady?" a guard asked, confused.

"Wait, wait," she said, circling the group. "When were you able to breathe in here? It was wretched before."

"No disrespect to the heartbroken family," another guard admitted, "But aye, it was terrible."

"It's not now."

"Sasha," Hunter said quietly. "I don't want to do this, either, but he knows why we're here, he can smell the silver and is hiding in the blind of destroyed furniture."

The lead guard nodded. "Maybe milady should go up to the great hall?" He peered around. "The poor bastard has been begging for raw meat for the last two hours and might have finally passed out. The only thing I'd know to do, short of opening the cage, is to move him with the vines and pull him to the bars—then do it."

"Hold it—you said he was begging for food?" Sasha said, moving toward the cell. "Since when do full-moon-insane demon-infected Werewolves have a conversation about what they want for dinner?"

Nervous glances passed among Fae and wolves alike. Sasha ran to the bars and began yelling Shogun's name.

"Send in the vines and knock that debris away—everybody hold your fire."

Her fingers wrapped around the silver-coated bars. A vine pushed aside a fallen table and privacy screen to reveal a naked man curled in a ball with a spill of silky onyx hair tangled about his dark bronze shoulders. The figure was dirty but very, very human-looking. The horrible demon scent was gone, albeit the stench of dead deer and a body's rejection of it remained—but by comparison that was manageable. Sasha watched Shogun draw in stuttering breaths with tears in her eyes. "Nobody shoot," she said repeatedly, quietly, reverently as Hunter's arm slid across her shoulders. "Just nobody shoot . . ."

EPILOGUE . . .

With the Fae as hosts, the party in the castle could last a week, a month, or longer. There'd be funerals, to be sure—that was part of the process adding to the bard's songs tales of triumph and tragedy, wailing tears and raucous laughter. Time to love, and cry, and recall, and retell the story until it was burned into the collective memories of all the groups that had fought side by side.

The fallen were reverently remembered, the living cheered. Food was ridiculously plentiful, and somehow rooms continued to annex themselves or contract in the castle to accommodate whoever stayed or left. There was no judgment, just a sort of free-for-all of experience. The Vampires had missed the party of the century—all at their expense, of course. And maybe it was a foolish thing to do, but Sasha thought it only fitting that those who'd wondered at the stars and had heard myths and legends and fairy tales as children should just for once get to see what all the hoopla was about. Maybe meet some real Fairies, who actually did tell the best tales.

Of all the new friends she'd met along the way, she owed Sir Rodney an incalculable debt for having her back and for allowing her father and human squad to hang out while on leave to take it all in. It was a pure delight to see their faces, to see Doc and Clarissa nearly swoon when they'd discovered their synthetic DNA had worked. The hospitality was amazing.

Yet with all that, watching death in the bayou had a way of making one throw caution to the wind and not want to wait to give people peace of mind. She saw how important it was to help people laugh when they could, let them love when they could, and pay them homage when you could.

Besides, there was a long hard talk she had to have with her brother, once Doc told him some family secrets man-to-man . . . just like Hunter needed time to talk to his sibling, who still had to cope with the loss of his mother and sister, no matter how twisted they were.

Lines of demarcation had finally blurred, family customs, cultures, histories had to get shared across what had once been a great wolf divide. So Sir Rodney was wise in allowing the party to rage on into a fortnight. She'd think of something to tell the general so he wouldn't get pissed off—and would bring him some more glowing evidence that might earn him another star. Truthfully, if it was quiet and nothing was going bump in the night, the man really didn't wanna know.

All of that was fine by her. Her family was around her safe and happy, the Fae made fantastic ale, plus she'd learned to dance a Pixie jig, and . . . Max Hunter was to die for.

Anyway, folks were partying hard because, although nobody said it, everybody knew that once the music stopped they'd have to pay the band. Sir Rodney seemed to know it more than anyone. He kept milling through the throng and checking like a local mayor at a county fair to be sure every entity was having a good time—and *he* sure was, two different ladies on each arm at all times. They said the wolves were bad, but the man was quite literally an animal.

Notwithstanding, it was an unspoken fact that you just didn't screw Vampires out of a power position and kick their butts and then figure they'd make nice. Oh . . . nooooo. Instinctively everyone seemed to know that they'd better get their party on now, hard and fast. Give it a day, a week, a year, or a coupla centuries—the old boys would be back, undead on arrival, and there'd be hell to pay.

Don't miss the Vampire Huntress Legend™ Novels from
New York Times Bestselling Author

L. A. BANKS

THE SHADOWS
ISBN-10: 0-312-94915-4
ISBN-13: 978-0-312-94915-0

THE FORBIDDEN
ISBN-10: 0-312-94002-5
ISBN-13: 978-0-312-94002-7

THE DARKNESS
ISBN-10: 0-312-94914-6
ISBN-13: 978-0-312-94914-3

THE BITTEN
ISBN-10: 0-312-99509-1
ISBN-13: 978-0-312-99509-6

THE CURSED
ISBN-10: 0-312-94772-0
ISBN-13: 978-0-312-94772-9

THE HUNTED
ISBN-10: 0-312-93772-5
ISBN-13: 978-0-312-93772-0

THE WICKED
ISBN-10: 0-312-94606-6
ISBN-13: 978-0-312-94606-7

THE AWAKENING
ISBN-10: 0-312-98702-1
ISBN-13: 978-0-312-98702-2

THE FORSAKEN
ISBN-10: 0-312-94860-3
ISBN-13: 978-0-312-94860-3

MINION
ISBN-10: 0-312-98701-3
ISBN-13: 978-0-312-98701-5

THE DAMNED
ISBN-10: 0-312-93443-2
ISBN-13: 978-0-312-93443-9

Available from St. Martin's Paperbacks